MILITARY BRAT

MILITARY BRAT

PETE MASALIN

RIVERS TURN PRESS

RIVERS TURN
P R E S S

Rivers Turn Press
617 Rivers Turn Road
Orangeburg, SC 29115

This book is a work of fiction. Names, characters, places, and incidents either are products of the author's imagination or are used fictiously. Any resemblance to actual events or locales or persons, living or dead is entirely coincidental.

Copyright © 2024 by Pete Masalin
All rights reserved, including the right to reproduce this book or portions thereof in any form whatsoever. No part of this book may be reproduced or transmitted in any form or by any means, except by a reviewer who may quote brief passages in a review, without permission in writing. For information address Rivers Turn Press, 617 Rivers Turn Road, Orangeburg, SC 29115

First edition, first printing September 2024
Cover Photo by Suvajit Das, Architect of Design
Author Photo/Drawing by Larry Perdue
Printing by Major Graphics, LLC

Manufactured in the United States of America

Trade Paperback edition ISBN 978-0-9985755-9-9

Dedication

For Katie

Without you, this never gets finished. Every day with you brings sunshine into my life no matter the weather or strife. My love for you is without limit. Alone, I am ordinary. With you, I am made special. Thank you for saying yes!
"We're still smiling."

MILITARY BRAT

Preface

Chapter 1: And So It Begins

Chapter 2: Chocolate and Tollhouse Cookies

Chapter 3: Aloha

Chapter 4: Summer, Menehunes, Ono!

Chapter 5: Farewell to Paradise

Chapter 6: It's a Small World

Chapter 7: Wild Horses and Stall Surfing

Chapter 8: Snapper Blues

Chapter 9: Monkey Business

Chapter 10: Casualty in the Ranks

Chapter 11: Close Quarters

Chapter 12: An Entrepreneur in the Making

Chapter 13: Mountain Men

Chapter 14: End of the Dynamic Duo

Chapter 15: License to Drive

Chapter 16: Hello Ladies

Chapter 17: A Time of Testing

Chapter 18: Dam Summer

Chapter 19: Cap and Gown

MILITARY BRAT

Chapter 20: Hello Low Country

Chapter 21: "Get Your Hand Off My Desk!"

Chapter 22: I'm Not Dreaming

Chapter 23: The Fourth-Class System is Now in Effect

Chapter 24: Liberty

Chapter 25: A Semester Ends

Chapter 26: Regimen Returns

Chapter 27: Recovery

Chapter 28: Upperclassmen Return

Chapter 29: Halfway Home

Chapter 30: Lightning Strikes

Chapter 31: Gorilla in the Room

Chapter 32: The Stage is Set

Preface

"I got this," Finn replied as he lowered himself, gripping the steel rod for dear life. He hesitated for a moment, looking beyond his tennis shoes to the dark, red clay 180 feet below. Any mistake and the fall would be unsurvivable. He completed one pull up, and in a single motion, quickly secured a resting spot next to Sam.

Approaching blue lights soon pierced the calm, dark sky and illuminated the acrobats' positions while the accompanying sirens signaled their detection. Stopping at the base of the tower, two police officers stepped out from their vehicle, ceased the siren, and pointed a spotlight towards two thrill seekers perched atop a crane.

Over a police car PA system, a law officer commanded, "You there! Get your asses down here! Now!"

Finn held tight but winced at the thought of being caught. How did he entangle himself in such a situation? It wasn't normal behavior for someone of his age. It wasn't normal behavior for anyone of any age.

Northern Virginia was blossoming as an area of expansion outside of Washington, DC. Development was occurring at a rapid pace. Tyson's Corner, with its shopping mall and high rises, was a short distance from Finn Makinen's home. On this summer evening, Finn and his friend, Sam Trenton, were bored and decided to seek adventure at one of the construction sites. With reckless forethought, they drove to a building being erected, which included a rooftop mounted crane for moving materials on high. On impulse, they challenged each other to a ludicrous dare: Climb a crane 17 stories high, reach its end, and do a pull up.

Sam and Finn were teammates of a state champion high school gymnastics team. Climbing and pull ups were easy for both. The apparatus they practiced on required a strong upper body and a sure grip. Every day during the season, all team members were required to finish practices with numerous repetitions of muscle building exercises. For Finn, the physical challenge of climbing the metal tower and performing one chin up at its end didn't give him pause. He knew he had the capability and endurance for such a feat. But confidence of having the physical attributes alone often is not enough. He stood upon the foundation of the crane and assessed its enormity. From a distance, it seemed manageable.

MILITARY BRAT   Pete Masalin

Standing next to it, feeling the cold steel, and eyeing the climb in the darkness brought anxiety to the forefront and his confidence wavered. Had Sam not been there, and he was alone in the attempt, he probably would have surrendered.

Neither one of the two gymnasts was built to back down. At the base, they looked up, smiled at one another, and began to climb. Certain that Sam's emotion matched Finn's, they climbed higher into the night air. There was fear, but both laughed, masking their shared apprehension.

Finally, reaching the top and before traversing across the horizontal arm of the crane, Sam asked, "You still want to do this?"

Finn paused for a moment, looked down and reflected on the height before responding, "Of course. You're not wimping out on me, are you?"

This only solidified Sam's decision, and so as not to appear weak, he stated, "I'm not backing out."

They crawled to the end and stopped. Finn questioned what his body would look like if, in one careless misstep, he fell to the ground. Surely, the body would be unrecognizable to those who knew him. Before he could finish his thought, Sam was on his way, hanging from the last cross bar and executing a perfect pull up. Afterwards, he hoisted himself upon the crane and secured a sitting position.

"Your turn, Finn," was all Sam said, and Finn immediately dangled from deathly heights.

"I said for you two knuckleheads to join me down here on the ground. Now! Let's move it!" Again, the police officer encouraged Finn and Sam with a harsh tone.

"Let's go," Finn offered, and they started their return to earth.

Both climbers were silent as they descended. Neither looked at the other, instead concentrating on securing their footing. There was a soft wind that sang as it whistled through the crane's framework. Finn focused on the silence as the wind's whisper taunted him for his idiocy. He was more fearful in the descent than the ascension. He visualized his achievement only to be overshadowed by thoughts of failure in mishap and his plummet to the ground.

MILITARY BRAT   Pete Masalin

Finn and Sam dismounted the crane together and simultaneously cheered as they relished the victory, relieved of their trepidation.

"Hey! What the hell are you two celebrating? Do you know how much trouble you are in?" a second police officer questioned.

Both stood in silence, unable to respond. In that moment, Finn thought of the mayhem, boldness and adventure of the event, and reflected on the Viking heritage that was storied by his family as he grew up. Surely, he thought it was in his gene pool. It wasn't. It was careless, but it was demonstrative of his activities as he traveled and navigated his youth.

"Guys! I am talking to you. Do you understand the danger you put each other in? That was not smart," the officer reminded them.

Finn and Sam remained silent. "Hey! Say something," the second officer demanded.

"I'm sorry," Finn responded. "We didn't mean any harm."

"Yeah," was all Sam could add.

The police held and lectured them for half an hour. The two boys were polite and quietly listened to their rebuke. Eventually, the police released Finn and Sam on their own recognizance with a promise from them that they would never attempt such foolishness again.

Finn could make such a promise; however, he couldn't keep it. Often, he was incapable of resisting stupid acts of courage. As in this incident, he was delivered from potential incarceration; and after conquering the crane, he felt confident and triumphant. This one occurrence was emblematic of the story of Finn Makinen. Born into a family of steadiness and reason, one could never envision an offspring of theirs being a brat, a Military Brat of such unruliness, risk, and adventuresome exploits while navigating his journey of growth. He was the opposite by almost all measures. From his birth, Finn knew little restraint yet thrived in the challenge of finding his own path and defying certain failure. The future was never dull for Finn. This is his story.

Chapter 1
And So It Begins

He was the son of a Maine fisherman and grandson to Finnish immigrants who farmed the rocky slopes of the Central Maine coast. The oldest of four siblings, although one would pass in his youth, John Makinen demonstrated a steadiness and determination early in his childhood that offered stability and pride to his family in the Depression years and beyond. He worked odd jobs, cutting the town's expansive library lawn with a manual, non-powered push mower, picking up lobsters at low tide and selling them for a penny a piece, and any other small task to secure income for himself and family. A gifted athlete, John particularly excelled in baseball and later played on a semi-pro team while still in high school.

His grandfather's farm, in the hills not far from his coastal home, was a place of enjoyment for John. He loved his grandfather Timo Makinen dearly and he greatly enjoyed his time toiling on the family's homestead. At five years old, he savored a cup of coffee in the morning with Timo. In the evening after dinner, in the months when wild blueberries were in season, his grandmother would serve him fresh pie made from berries raked from the fields that morning. Nothing ever remained on the dessert plate as John consumed every morsel of golden pie crust and licked the plate until it was clear of the sweet purple syrup that previously had stained the plate.

John's father Ero Makinen was a sturdy, quiet and capable fisherman. John would accompany him to the depths of the cold, deep indigo waters off the rocky shores that are unique to Maine. It was hard work and often times treacherous. Many fishermen lost their lives providing fresh seafood to those whom they referred to as landlubbers. It was during this time with his father that John developed love, appreciation, and respect for the sea.

What is astonishing is that it was uncommon for any of the fisherman in this day to know how to swim. John Makinen was no exception to this tradition. It is equally astonishing that the son of a fisherman and the grandson of a farmer would escape these humble but memorable beginnings and attend the Naval Academy. It is humorous to think that the son of a fisherman, who had been on the sea most of his life, did not learn to swim until he went to the Naval Academy. John enjoyed a storied

MILITARY BRAT   Pete Masalin

career in the Navy and later returned to his homestead developing it into a thriving Christmas tree and wild blueberry farm. John's life personifies the American dream.

She was the daughter of Norwegian immigrants who had descended upon Massachusetts as their home. Like John, Susan Ofstad led the hierarchy of children with a younger sister and brother. Her father, Welding Ofstad came to this country and relished the opportunity of America. As a young man in the golden age of sports, he was an accomplished professional wrestler. His accent resulted in him being assigned the wrestling name of Canadian Panther. Apparently, whoever assigned this moniker obviously had no idea of geography.

Susan's mother, Thyra, was one of 12 children and came to this country without any knowledge of how to speak, read, or write English. Even so, she accepted her surroundings, overcame them and thrived, eventually meeting and marrying Welding. The Ofstad's life was a happy life. Thyra raised Susan and her siblings while Welding was comfortably employed providing for his family. Susan's father relished his times hunting and fishing. Fish was a mainstay in the diet of any Scandinavian, and he was a skilled fisherman who easily provided his family with ocean provisions - cod, flounder, mackerel, and bluefish. The Ofstads enjoyed the variety. Often, he would take Susan fishing and while she enjoyed the ocean and fishing, she more enjoyed the quiet times with her father.

The Ofstads were of rugged stock, and the children grew up in a loving but disciplined family. As is often with eldest children, Susan set the tenor for the younger ones. She was steady, and her sister Inga and brother Johan were steered by her temperament. In many ways, she mirrored their mother which was looked upon favorably by her parents. She was sure of herself and dependable. Yet, unlike her parents, she went to college, attended Simmons and earned a nursing degree. Upon graduation, she became a skilled practitioner, assisting emergency room doctors as a nurse at Massachusetts General Hospital in Boston.

Love stories rarely can be planned or foreordained. Such was the case with John Makinen and Susan Ofstad. It was, by chance, failed execution of a plan and plain dumb luck that they met. One spring night, Susan's

MILITARY BRAT   Pete Masalin

friends had arranged a blind date for her, and as circumstances unfolded, her date was unable to meet his planned rendezvous with Susan. Not to be discouraged, her friends quickly rallied to fill her evening's dance card with a substitute suitor. Susan was tall and attractive, and a suitable date of equal stature was sought out to ensure that there was balance among the group of close friends. Each young lady required a gentleman to accompany them for the evening events.

Enter Lieutenant JG John Makinen; six foot three inches tall, athletic and sure of himself. His ship had just returned to its home port harbored in Portsmouth, New Hampshire. After six months at sea, John had a much-deserved weekend pass in his possession. While contemplating his options for liberty, his bunkmate, Lieutenant JG Skip Samson, spoke of his planned weekend trip to Boston. Skip was the longtime beau of a friend of Susan. A quick call from his girlfriend and Skip was on the hunt for a Navy Officer to fill the party's vacancy. John was really unmoved, but he accommodated as he had no plans for the weekend. He could have gone home to Maine, but he preferred to take leave for a more extended visit at a later date. Early afternoon on Friday, John hopped into Skip's red '48 Ford Coupe and headed south to Boston. As they travelled, John never envisioned that this trip, mundane compared to his worldly excursions in the Navy, would change his life's direction more than any trip before or since.

Arriving in Boston, the two vibrant Navy Officers met their equally vibrant nurses and the larger party at a harbor side restaurant for clam rolls and beer. The allure between Susan and John was immediate – both the oldest children of Norse bloodlines, their similar upbringing created a connection and silent draw towards one another that was both immediate and sustaining. The night passed quickly as the two spoke to each other. At night's end, both John and Susan were sure of their destiny together; not the future path together, but the certainty of their bond as they traveled along a shared path.

John left Boston knowing that he had met the woman to whom he would marry. Susan waved goodbye and watched him leave knowing that he would return asking for her hand in marriage. It was a certainty. A short time later, John returned to Boston and presented Susan with a

MILITARY BRAT   Pete Masalin

miniature Naval Academy class ring representing his commitment and engagement to his beautiful bride-to-be. She accepted, and in November, they were wed.

    Born Finn Charles Makinen, I was the second son of this union; a loved and blessed child to have been born of these two standards of strength, forthrightness, and devotion. Better parents are not to be found. It is hard to fathom that these two pillars, who exuded steadiness and regularity, begot this brat of irregularity and mischievousness. Yet in all my flaws and shortcomings, the character of my parents tempered me as the reigns of a thoroughbred control the steed as he pursues victory.

Chapter 2
Chocolate and Tollhouse Cookies

    The first recollection of my youth is a bitter winter in New Hampshire when my father was again stationed at Portsmouth Naval Shipyard. Memories of cold gray days, where hastened breaths are revealed in clouds of frozen vapor, remain fresh in my mind. It was a joyful time in my life. The Makinens, a family of five, arrived at Brackett Road in a 1964 Chevy Impala station wagon with a moving van in tow. The youngest, an infant daughter named Leigh was little more than a nuisance to the brother team of Finn and Levi, as she had just graduated from crawling annoyance to unsteadied bipedal of disaster. First born Levi was two years my senior, and as the first born, shared the legacy of both our parents. Levi also shared their focus and uprightness.

    For adults, moving is often a time of increased stress. For two young explorers such as Levi and me, it was a great adventure. However, I must admit that often my antics in my adventures with my brother created unexpected disruption to his *fixed design*. On this particular occasion, as our new home was filled with our possessions, a welcomed byproduct was provided in the accumulation of a mountain of empty boxes in the front yard. Imagine our excitement as we built castles and reinforced citadels to defend our home against our envisioned monster neighbors. Imagine Levi's disappointment when remodeling our fortress, one of the corner buttresses wilted from liquid absorption. It hadn't rained all day, yet our stronghold had been compromised. Levi never discovered the cause of this breach. Me – I was four years old and a trip to the bathroom was beyond my capability at nature's calling.

    Levi and I maintained a misperception that we enjoyed free reign of the neighborhood. It was a time when parents never worried about the safety of their children. Brackett Road was a neighborhood of modest homes predominately occupied by military families. In this era, mothers stayed at home with their families. Truth be told, it was the mothers of the neighborhood who were the law. They each quietly wore the badge of Sherriff; a security detachment was always on patrol. The authority in every mother was the fear of every child. There was a uniting agreement among the mothers that they would rule the neighborhood with an iron fist. They were a cohesive team in their effort to deny the neighborhood

MILITARY BRAT   Pete Masalin

children's union our full entitlement to frivolity and nonsense in the guise of safety. Fortunately, there were gaps in their perimeter. I quickly learned that a bright smile and cheerful greeting to anyone in the posse of mothers garnered modest protection from their suspicious eye. It was a valuable lesson and one that served me well throughout my life. I never did anything terribly wrong, but I secured a measure of liberty greater than most other children of the neighborhood.

At the conclusion of one heavy snowfall, Levi and I were eager to join other neighborhood kids playing outside amidst the two feet of new crystal powder. Mom readied us for the elements of winter. She covered our feet with plastic bread bags to prevent our socks from getting wet when the snow breached the top of our boots. Our grandmother, Thyra Ofstad, was known to us as Mor Mor. Mor Mor was the Norwegian nomenclature for "Mother's Mother and She loved knitting mittens for us to wear in the patterns of her heritage. They included a long tether between the two mittens, enabling my mother to strand the mittens from one winter coat sleeve to the other. A matching knit cap was also provided by my grandmother. Underneath our jeans and sweaters, we adorned long johns. A scarf wrapped around our necks. A narrow slit allowing for vision was created by the muffler resting on the bridge of our noses and the knit cap pulled down upon our brow. She yanked the coat hoods atop our knit caps, drew the hood strings tight, tying them in a double knot, zipped our jackets to our chin, and sent us off to the winter wilderness of our front yard.

Quickly the children of the neighborhood joined us – Vinnie DeVito, twins Marty and Manny O'Malley, Steven Ketchins, Bobby Silver and Samantha Johnson. Samantha Johnson: nobody wanted her in our seasonal adventure. A girl would only ruin our limited time together and cause dissention in the ranks. After all she donned a pink jacket decorated with white and red flowers. What kind of soldier wears pink when building a fort and in my front yard. As soon as she arrived, Bobby did his best to dissuade her from joining us.

"Samantha! Why don't you leave us alone? I hate you and you stink," Bobby shouted.

MILITARY BRAT   Pete Masalin

She stood in silence not knowing how to respond. Bobby only disliked Samantha because he liked her. The previous summer he was caught trying to kiss her at a neighborhood cookout, thinking no one was witness to his attempt. The ensuing torment he received from the boys was relentless and Bobby thought it best to be demonstrably hard on Samantha.

I was the youngest in the group. All the others were classmates in Levi's second grade class. None of them liked Samantha either, but the Sheriffs of the neighborhood demanded that she be included in the installation of the Brackett Road bastion being constructed in my front yard. Like it or not, she would have a presence, but it didn't mean that she would have an active role. The older boys isolated her as she stood silently watching them build their stronghold. They didn't much appreciate me either, but they liked Levi and reluctantly included me in the build. Mostly, I served as a go-fer, grabbing shovels and pails when they needed them. Still, Samantha maintained her position, watching a flurry of activity, never indicating whether she really wanted to be in the cold with us or not. She hardly spoke. At one point, I sat staring at Samantha. Her brown hair was wet and disheveled, partially obscuring her eyes. The frigid temperature caused her nose to run, and the dry air created modest incrusted patches around her nostrils. For a moment, I thought she was going to speak to me when out of nowhere a missile exploded upon her face. One of the soldiers launched a snowball, and it hit its intended target. Samantha left in tears. The infiltrator had been vanquished and order had been restored.

Finally, construction was complete. We were all proud of the structure that had been erected that day. We marveled at the engineering of six- and seven-year-old contractors. There was a front and rear passageway revealing an interior large enough to house our small squad of defenders. Within the walls was a small compartment holed in the snow. Certainly, if we had a stash of goods to conceal, they would go unnoticed by any of the sheriffs or their husbands if they entered our domain. There was, however, a design flaw in the vault. The entry was too small for the older boys to enter. Finally, I was the most important among us. I was small enough in stature to navigate through the hand excavated aperture.

MILITARY BRAT   Pete Masalin

Vinnie directed "Finn! Crawl in and see if you can fit."

Cheerfully, I approached the vault not knowing that it soon would nearly become my tomb. I crawled into the opening on my hands and knees, headfirst. As my shoulders passed through the passageway, light became inaccessible to the cavity and my surroundings became dim. The twins, Marty and Manny, thought it wise at this time to test the structural integrity of the roof above me. It collapsed, sealing my body within the snow. With my feet protruding from the encasement, the boys pulled them to secure my release. Together, they did not possess the strength to free me. My breathing was labored, and I was unable to move. I could hear Levi's muffled voice shouting "Finn! Finn!" followed by an extended "Mom!"

Surrounded in silence, my stillness was instantly disrupted by a violent expulsion from my entrapment. Levi's calls had summoned the sheriffs within earshot of his cries. First to the scene was my mother, seven months pregnant with her fourth child. Standing by her side were Mrs. Johnson, who lived directly across the street, and Mrs. DeVito, who resided two doors to the left of our home. They quickly assessed the situation as well as my condition and determined that I was unharmed. Relieved, the women turned their attention to the surviving soldiers. The fun was over. For the occupiers of the snow fort, spankings followed and then they were banished to their respective bedrooms. Mrs. Johnson's ire was easily visible standing next to her daughter, Samantha, who had been dispatched from our activities earlier in the day in the most inhospitable manner. Reluctantly, I approached our front door expecting to pay the price for awakening a small contingency of the mothers' alliance. Levi was admonished and found guilty of crimes against good order and discipline; while it was determined that I was the victim; tormented by the older neighborhood boys. I was sent to the kitchen as my consequence for the day's events. I felt bad for Levi, but what was I to say? I was in no position to question my mother's judgment. I was only four, the tollhouse cookies I rapidly devoured were delicious and the hot chocolate warmed my chilled body.

Months later, Ashton "Ash" Carl Makinen was born. The youngest of us all, he became the curse against my privacy until many years later

MILITARY BRAT   Pete Masalin

when Levi moved from our home. Leigh, the lone daughter, was assured her own room. As the middle boy among three sons, I was destined to always share a room with one of my brothers. At first, Levi and I shared a room, but once Levi became a teenager, my parents decided that he deserved the privacy of his own room. I was demoted to a room shared with Ash who was four years my junior. At ten years old, I was forced to live with a child.

The arrival of Ash in conjunction with orders for my father's change of duty station prompted more frequent visits with close family members in New England. Most notably, the grandmothers made visits with their grandchildren a priority. Our next assignment would be Hawaii, and the distance between the coastal shores of Maine or Massachusetts and Pearl Harbor would restrict visits for years to come. We received four months' notice in advance of my father's report date to his new duty station, and the displacement of the Makinen family from Portsmouth New Hampshire. Visits remained relaxed and not forced.

Grandmother visits were not without excitement and comedy. In the summer, Mor Mor, a widow of five years, would make the weekend trip to provide her daughter with relief from daily trials of caring for four children, ages seven to a newborn. On one weekend, Mor Mor packed Levi, Finn, and Leigh into her Ford Falcon for a day on the beach. Ash, being an infant, remained in the care of our mother. It was a beautiful day and Thyra Ofstad stood proud as she escorted her grandchildren to the sandy shores of Jenness State Beach. All of us personified the traits of our heritage: blonde hair and blue eyes. There was no doubt of our "Norwegianess" and inwardly she smiled at the contribution she had provided to our bloodline. Mor Mor was proud of her lineage and rightfully so. Her brother fought the Nazis as a member of King Haakon's Hans Majestet Kongens Garde.

As we progressed from the street side parking to the beach, we passed an ice cream truck. Ice cream vendors understand the appeal of their treats upon the most innocent and uncontrollable members of society. We, the Makinen children, demanded the coolness of a treat on a hot summer's day. Mor Mor was as stern as any descendant of Viking stock but as soft as any grandmother who loved the children in her

MILITARY BRAT Pete Masalin

charge. She was powerless against our cuteness. This was her undoing on this day. So, she compromised and promised that she would buy us an ice cream on our way back to the car. The ocean was grand, but the draw of an ice cream to a recently turned five-year-old was too strong to resist.

Mor Mor basked in the sun while we splashed in the tidal pools of low tide. The receding waters revealed a beach of great expanse. We were safe within her sight as she read a book, periodically dipping its top edge to observe her grandchildren. Levi was measured and Leigh was too young to be distracted. I, on the other hand, had ADHD before anyone ever proclaimed such an ailment existed. I was the second born. A carefree soul who knew that ice cream awaited me on the return to that Ford Falcon. Details eluded me. I had no concept of purchasing. I only knew that a frozen delight awaited me. I made my move, separating myself from the siblings who remained content to pause for the escort of their grandmother in attaining the promised reward of an icy treat.

At the next gaze of her grandchildren, I had disappeared; vacated the tidal pool ascribed by my grandmother. Horror set in as Mor Mor imagined the worst of outcomes. An inquiry of Levi and Leigh delivered no relief of her fears. They were content with their folly on the shore and never noticed my vacancy. Horror turned to panic, and Thyra Ofstad ran along the shoreline calling my name in her heavy Norwegian accent; "Finn. Finn, Fiiiin!" Within minutes, a teenager approached with the false promise of finding her "Finn." He held out a swim fin and innocently asked, "Is this what you are looking for?" His friends laughed, but she was not amused. She was fearful that her grandson had drowned, pulled out to sea. What was she to tell her daughter Susan? After an hour of searching and numerous conversations with other beach goers, she was convinced that her next conversation with her daughter would be a revelation of the tragic loss of Finn; lost at sea and never to be recovered. This was a day long before easily accessible pay phones. Communication was direct and in person.

She had endured a similar loss before. As a child in Norway, her younger sister wandered from the house. The absence went unnoticed long enough for tragedy to darken the memory of her youth. Her mother found her sister, face down in the farm pond and pulled her lifeless body

MILITARY BRAT   Pete Masalin

from the water with a rake. This memory haunted her as she gathered Levi and Leigh, slowly progressing to her car, dreading her next conversation with Susan. As she reached the pavement of the beachfront road, she saw ahead of her a shirtless towhead lad sitting on the curb in front of the ice cream truck. Her pace quickened as she advanced to confirm the youth's identity. "Finn!" she yelled. I looked up and smiled. She smiled back. It was hot chocolate and tollhouse cookies all over again. Never mind that I had caused her the worst strife imaginable. She was happy that I was alive. I enjoyed my ice cream, and she had her grandson. I was oblivious to her torment, but I enjoyed my vanilla cone as we returned home. She should have beaten my ass.

At five, I was incapable of comprehending parameters. Levi was solid and dependable. He grasped the direction conveyed by our parents. I, conversely, was drawn to the promise of things unknown. It is only by God's providence that I survived. As a child, for the most part we have no understanding of evil. Those who surrounded me were good, so I assumed everyone was good. Fortunately, in my case, this was true to my life. I took risks unaware of the dangers to which I exposed myself.

On our trips north to Camden, Maine, we visited my father's parents Ero and Olive Makinen. This was a wonderful town – a town of true American character. The mailman walked the streets with a mail pouch and an arsenal of lifesavers to provide to children he encountered along his route. Fresh milk and butter were delivered daily to the back stoops of every home. My father's sister, Aunt Sarah, is still the sweetest person I have ever met. My grandmother Olive Makinen, "Grammy" as we called her, was a cheerful and loving soul who doted on us all when we visited. She never learned to drive a car. She would walk to the market each day and purchase food to prepare delicious dinner meals for her family. Camden was a magnificent town, unpolluted by the distraction of selfishness. When we visited the small house of my grandparents, bedtime resulted in a mass accumulation of children in sleeping bags cramped into the front foyer of their home. It was a memorable time and repeated often, without complaint, while we resided in the neighboring state of New Hampshire.

MILITARY BRAT   Pete Masalin

On one particular visit, my penchant for ignoring limitations was again stirred within me at the promise of sweet indulgences offered by a grandmother. Grammy, her sister Mary, and a few of the town ladies planned to bake doughnuts midmorning on the day of our visit. Sitting at the breakfast table, my mother and Grammy were chatting over coffee regarding topics of little import. Who cared if Levi lost a tooth, Leigh liked to dance to music or that Ash could finally roll over? I had lost interest in their conversation as early as when it had started. I was ready to leave the table to find Levi when details of interest seized my attention and halted my actions. Doughnuts? Grammy shared her mid-morning plans of walking to a neighbor's house to produce these fine delicacies with her friends. Noticing my excitement, Grammy looked at me and pledged to provide me with warm, sweet, mouthwatering goodness. I watched her as she arose from the table, hugged my mother and me, and shouted goodbye to her remaining grandchildren in another room. She grabbed a large cotton bag filled with flour, sugar and whatever else one needs to bake doughnuts, exited the house, and walked in route to the ladies' makeshift bakery.

I was elated by the news but disheartened by the delay. It had been more than an hour since my grandmother's promise to me. It might as well have been two days. I stared towards the direction Grammy had travelled up Mill Street, waiting for her return. For a short time, I spoke to my grandmother's parakeet but bored quickly of its inability to talk. Couldn't all birds talk as in the cartoons I watched? What a stupid bird. Finally, I acted. I wanted my doughnuts, and any more delay was unacceptable and intolerable. Leigh was taking a nap while Levi worked to complete a puzzle of the United States. It was at the moment my mother left for the privacy of a bedroom to feed Ash that I made my move. Silently I exited the house, telling no one of my plan to hunt down the mysterious bakery up the inclined road where I spied my grandmother until she disappeared at its crest. There were no sidewalks, and the road was fairly less traveled by motorists at the time of day. My PF Fliers carried me along its path.

Not knowing what the house of baking looked like, nor its distance from my point of origin, I had to rely on my two best senses for such a task – my nose and ears. Reaching the crest of Mill Street, I began to smell the aroma

MILITARY BRAT
Pete Masalin

of fresh baked goods. The summer air in coastal Maine is quite pleasant, and the windows of every home were open to their fullest. As a hound dog tracks its quarry, I continued my search. My nose led me in the direction of a more prominent scent. Finally, my ears took over. I could hear my grandmother and her sister. Olive and Mary found much joy in everyday life, and they greatly enjoyed each other's company, laughing often. The laughter became my focus of attention and beacon of direction. Soon, I was standing on the back step, looking into the kitchen of a house I had never visited before.

Startled, my grandmother looked at me and asked, "Finn, where is your mother?"

I just pointed in the direction from which I came, and she peeked around the now open screen door to witness an empty road. "Did you walk here by yourself?" she inquired.

I just nodded and told her that I was here for my doughnut. Her response was a tepid rebuke and a warm hug.

The bakery ladies sat me down at the kitchen table, provided me with a glass of milk and rewarded me with a fresh hot doughnut. They giggled and whispered. I paid them little attention as I sloppily consumed what had been presented to me. As I finished, Grammy provided me with a bag of doughnuts, took me by the hand, leading me out of the house and down Mill Street to return to my rightful place of duty among my siblings. As we approached her house, I could see my mom frantically looking for me in the yard and yelling my name. Once in view, my mother ran to us, meeting us in the street. She asked my grandmother where she found me, and Grammy explained how I had just appeared at her friend's doorstep. She was angry and voiced her displeasure of my antics in a stern manner. I suspect that I was only pardoned from a well-deserved spanking because we stood in plain view of the neighbors, and they may not have understood my requirement for a more physical rebuke. Her anger was quickly replaced by relief, and again, I received a hug. In the end, my thoughtless venture was rewarded by another doughnut and the appreciation of my siblings, Levi, and Leigh, as they enjoyed the fruits of my labor.

MILITARY BRAT — Pete Masalin

For Levi and me, life on Brackett Road presented a venue of unsupervised exploits, affording our mother relief from the mayhem of spirited young boys trapped inside a house. Mom was always eager for us to spend the majority of our days outside. The mothers' collective sheriff patrol, always on duty, assured her of our safety. Television offerings in the 1960s were limited to only a few stations and in the evening that meant national news. Levi and I had no interest in watching middle aged men, dressed in suit and tie, peering at us from inside the glowing tube. No matter the commentator, his report was inconsequential to the important adventures that lay in wait the next day for the duo of Levi and Finn. However, on a summer night, urgent news of a meteor grasped our attention. A fireball was to illuminate the night skies above our home while we slept.

In the morning, we could hardly contain ourselves as we rushed to the kitchen table. Mom prepared us Cream of Wheat and asked, "So, what do you two boys have planned for this morning?"

Levi responded, "Did you see the meteor?"

"Your father and I saw it as it passed over the house headed to the woods."

"Wow," I said. "Was it on fire?"

She knew she had our attention and manipulated us for her entertainment and relief. Certain that the energy we exerted in our search would tame our enthusiasm, she encouraged us to establish a salvage party and retrieve the asteroid. "Why don't you boys get your wagon and search for the meteor? It's certain to be somewhere in the woods at the end of the road."

"Can we? Really mom?" Levi responded as my father sipped his coffee and smiled.

"Sure, I'll fix you some peanut butter and jelly sandwiches and fill a thermos with grape Kool Aid and you can head right out."

Dad added, "I'll bet you kids will be on tonight's news. Can you imagine what the other kids will say when you bring home a glowing space rock? You'll be heroes."

MILITARY BRAT   Pete Masalin

We ran to our rooms, got dressed and raced to the garage to grab our wagon and venture to sites unknown. My socks didn't match, and my shoes were untied, but no matter, we were going to be the envy of the neighborhood; heroes when we returned. My mother and father came to the garage to see their two explorers off before certain fame would limit their access to us. Mom bent down and tied my shoes, handed us both lunch pails, and kissed us both goodbye.

Hours later we returned home embarrassed by failure. We had found no grounded fireball. During our journey, we quickly discovered that a wagon was not the appropriate expedition vehicle. Still, we trekked through seemingly endless miles of vegetation in hope of fame and treasure from space. We arrived at our home station covered in dirt and sweat, exuding the pungent odor of skunk cabbage through which we encountered on most of our trail. Mom was happy to see her two explorers arrive home; however, she never told us what she knew from the onset of our undertaking - the meteor had landed in western Canada.

Until our family moved from New Hampshire, Levi and I would continue to explore worlds and things unknown. As was usual, Levi was the leader and I, the younger, his loyal companion. It was not unlike a show we enjoyed in our youth, Mutual of Omaha's Wild Kingdom. He was Marlin Perkins, and I was Jim Fowler. Mr. Perkins would narrate as Jim did the heavy lifting. "Watch as Jim wrestles the Black Cayman Crocodile into submission. See Jim as he scales the sheer cliffs of the Andes to feed baby condors from his mouth."

"Finn, grab the garter snake as I use this fallen limb and lift this big rock." The stick would break, and the small boulder would crash upon my head causing me to nearly sever my tongue with my teeth.

"Finn, go see if that's a beehive." Moments later I would be swarmed by stinging assassins sending me into anaphylactic shock followed by a year of immunotherapy. The joy of weekly bee venom injections ensuring a greater tolerance and resistance to future stings was my reward for being Levi's dependable associate. My brother loved me and always looked after my welfare. Obviously.

Chapter 3
Aloha

At the end of the summer in 1966, the Makinens left the coastal regions of New England. Theirs was a destination of dreams for most Americans – Hawaii. It was my first memory of plane travel, and it was in an era when plane travel was much more glamorous than today. Our family of six boarded the plane together; however, our seats were dispersed about the plane. Traveling with children allowed us to be assembled in the front section of passenger seating; for although this was an era of luxurious travel, smoking was permitted in the rear section of the aircraft. Susan preferred that her children not be exposed to the toxins as we traversed the Pacific Ocean at an altitude above 30,000 feet for so many hours. My seat assignment was a middle seat next to my mother with Ash asleep in her lap. I am certain that she felt it best to sit next to one whose inclination for self-control could be described as impetuous and unpredictable at best. Not to mention the chatter.

"How long is the plane ride? Look at that fat lady? Where's Levi?"

"He's right there – two rows up."

"Oh. Where's dad?"

"Finn, you need to speak with your quiet voice. He's right back there with your sister Leigh," she said then pointed.

We settled in for a long flight, seat belts fastened. Once at altitude Levi was being escorted by a stewardess headed to the lavatory. "Where you goin' Levi?" I asked.

The stewardess smiled at me and addressed my mother; "Your son needs to use the restroom. You sit right there, and I'll have him back to his seat in a jiffy."

Mom smiled back to her and said, "Thank you."

"Oh, that's alright. You seem to have your hands full," the flight attendant responded with a wink, causing both my mother and her to giggle.

I couldn't comprehend Levi's good fortune to walk around the plane. "Hey, Levi!" I shouted.

"Keep it down, Finn – Shhhh," Mom directed towards me as she

MILITARY BRAT   Pete Masalin

grasped the top of my head and pointed it back towards the front of the airplane.

"I gotta go. I gotta go, Mom."

"Shhh," Mom said as she placed her finger in front of her lips.

A short time later Levi returned from the aft section of the plane and was re-buckled into his seat by the stewardess. My mom silently whispered "thank you" to the woman as she glanced back at her. Complimentary lunch service had started soon after Levi sat down, and I was excited to see what it was. This was a day when airlines provided their travelers with delicious meals, not like today's meager rations of peanuts or pretzels. When the tray arrived, we were offered a shrimp cocktail – a delightful lunch indeed, one that I had never tasted before. I tried a couple when placed upon my tray table, and I was thrilled! It reminded me of lobster.

I had enjoyed lobster only a few times in my life. It was a meal that my extended family prepared on celebratory clam bakes with aunts, uncles, and cousins gathered for family visits at Mor Mor's summer home in Scituate, Massachusetts. And even then, it was only the scraps of the crustaceans that we were allowed to consume – the eight tiny legs of the lobster ripped from the underside of its carcass. Still, the taste of the morsels was desirable for all of the cousins, and we stood in wait as our parents evenly divided them among us. It was a treat worth waiting for and it came at the end of the meal. As they picked lobster meat and peeled the necks off steamers, preparing them in a bath of melted butter before feasting on the succulent flesh, the youngsters ate grilled hotdogs. When the adults had finished their meal, they gathered us all at the picnic table and rationed the remaining limbs for each of us. We would hold each leg at its tip; place it in our mouths, teeth to the fingers. As a squirrel gnaws a nut, we would quickly chomp our front teeth together while simultaneously pulling out the leg slowly forcing the trapped meat towards the open tear of the leg and onto our awaiting tongues. Lobster tasted good!

After sampling just a few of the shrimp before me, I nodded off in my seat. It wasn't long before I awoke to a bowl empty of shrimp and a lone

MILITARY BRAT   Pete Masalin

piece of cake on my tray. Where had it gone? I wanted my shrimp. When asked about its disappearance, my mother could only utter, "Isn't that a nice piece of cake? Eat your cake."

I didn't want cake. I wanted my shrimp and demanded its return. Mom had to admit her larceny. "I'm sorry, Finn. I thought you didn't like it."

"Where is it?" I demanded.

"I'm sorry. I ate it. I really didn't think you liked it," she consoled.

It was of little comfort, and I remained wounded and saddened that my mother would steal my food. The cake went uneaten and was later discarded from my tray table by the stewardesses as I sat silently pouting. It left an impression so lasting that to this day it is more than an irritant if anyone removes food from my plate uninvited.

We arrived in Honolulu and deplaned to the presentation of leis. The Ross family, friends of ours, were there to greet us. Mom and Dad received draped floral adornments around their necks while Levi, Leigh, and I happily bowed as we received a ring of candies upon our shoulders.

The differences between New Hampshire and Hawaii presented me with accommodation of new and endless adventures, unhampered by cumbersome winter clothes. I scarcely wore shoes, and long pants rarely restrained my legs. At first, our new ranch house offered me nearly as many venues for exploration as my past neighborhood on Brackett Road. Just the trees alone offered reward. I climbed them all, and privately enjoyed my prize as I sat among the branches eating sweet fruits I had never experienced: guava, lychee, mango, star fruit, papaya, lemons as big as grapefruits and of course bananas. In the sun, my skin became richly tanned and my hair platinum. The next three years, kindergarten through second grade, were carefree and memorable.

From the perspective of a five-year-old, Hawaii was a dreamland, rich with new discoveries. My mother loved Hawaii. When I was an infant, too early for me to recall, we had been stationed here. It was her second tour on the volcanic chain dotting the Pacific Ocean, but

MILITARY BRAT   Pete Masalin

this time presented hardships for my mother not experienced in her last tour. Dad's deployment schedule obliged her to serve as sole parent for durations lasting many months. Our country was at the height of the Viet Nam War and dad was a naval officer. Our ages - Ash one, Leigh three, me five, and Levi seven - demanded constant supervision. In my father's absence, mom expended much of her energy during the day ensuring for our comfort and safety. It was a responsibility she enjoyed; but each night, bedtime for her children provided welcome relief.

Dad was a submariner and while Viet Nam did not have much requirement for involvement of his vessel, in the dark cold waters of the world another war loomed quietly. Two powers – the Soviet Union and the United States jockeyed for global influence. My father would disappear for months to participate in a dangerous and clandestine game of cat and mouse with Soviet submersibles. It wasn't until decades later that anyone knew the nature of his and fellow sailors' mission. In his time away from his family, John Makinen and his shipmates quietly entered enemy waters, violating territorial boundaries as they trailed adversarial vessels gathering intelligence and information. Had they been discovered and destroyed, we would have never known the cause of their demise. So secret were their missions that my mother would have simply been informed that "he had been lost at sea." No other details would have been revealed.

In the weeks before school started, our family had the opportunity to become acclimated to our new surroundings. Living on an island surrounded by warm, turquoise tropical waters was a delight for my mother who relished the idea of visiting the beach year-round. The dilemma faced by my parents was easily identified: Four children and only Levi could swim. Leigh and Ash were young enough for mom to manage on her beach outings, but there was understandable concern that I was a risk on family beach visits. A recent family trip to the Officer's Club pool provided my parents with incentive for my immediate aquatic training. As I casually walked around the pool deck, the appeal of laughter from those swimming and the cool blue water drew me to action. I jumped in and sank. The lifeguard quickly sprang from his stand and hauled me from the depths in an instant.

MILITARY BRAT   Pete Masalin

"Finn! What are you doing? Why did you jump in?" my mom asked.

"It said "5" mommy. I'm 5!"

I had mistaken the marker on the pool's deck indicating depth to represent age. I was five years old and that seemed logical to me at the time. This simple mistake moved my parents to enlist the greatest swimming instructor of all time. A man who had been around and on the water his entire adolescent life, spent countless days of his youth in harsh conditions upon the ocean, yet he didn't learn to swim until he was 18. Who was this great master of coaching? My dad, John Makinen.

The next weekend, our family visited Bellows Beach, a Navy installation providing recreation of service members. We arrived at our cabin on Friday night and the next morning, after breakfast, we all headed to the beach. Mom established a beachhead for our landing party while my father attended to logistical matters. No sooner had my mother settled our position did my father show up with a surfboard under his arm.

"Levi, Finn. Let's go."

Levi and I raced to get up and follow my father into the surf. This was great! We arrived at the shore and Dad said, "Climb on board, boys." Orders to which we eagerly complied. Dad walked us beyond the breakers at a depth equaling his shoulders. Levi knew the basics of swimming and could tread water fairly well. Me, I was the rock that sank at the five-foot mark of the Officer's Club pool. Levi went first as dad assisted him from the surfboard to the freedom of the open water. He floated easily next to dad's improvised swimming platform. It was my turn to dismount the float, and seeing Levi's enjoyment, I released my grip easily, promptly sinking to the sandy bottom beneath us. Fear quickly left me as my feet hit bottom and I propelled myself upward, taking in a deep breath each time I breached the surface. Each time I arose, I could see my father's smiling face and hear his words of encouragement, "Good, Finn! Kick, Finn!" I learned to swim that day, later becoming a strong swimmer and have not feared the water since.

My mom's trip to the beach became less worrisome. I could at least keep my head above water. On weekdays, while dad was at work, she

MILITARY BRAT   Pete Masalin

would pack the Impala station wagon with beach toys, towels, foldable chairs, and snacks. Upon closing the tailgate, she would align her four children in the back seat, seat belts not required, and off we went to Bellows Beach. Ours was an enjoyable summer in our tropical home before the start of school.

Hawaii was also a strange land which challenged me with exotic words to add to my vocabulary. The Hawaiian alphabet is smaller than the traditional alphabet I had only grasped last year. It consisted of 18 letters: 5 normal vowels: A, E, I, O, U; 5 vowels with macrons: Ā, Ē, Ī, Ō, Ū; 8 consonants: H, K, L, M, N, P, W, and ʻokina (a small "6"-shaped mark above the baseline). Comprehending an alternate assemblage of letters was difficult enough for a newly arrived "haole," but for one who had yet to enter kindergarten, it was formidable.

We resided on Uluhala Street in Kailua on the island of Oahu. In a few short weeks, I would attend Maunawili Elementary School underneath the watchful tower that was Olamana Mountain. There was no Main, Elm or Maple Street. This was a very different place, indeed.

It was an easy walk to Maunawili Elementary School, and once our mother was assured Levi and I knew the route, we walked together each school day morning, rain or shine. School was great. From my perspective, school served as an assembly of friends, gathered together to enjoy the company of equally minded thrill seekers every day. Education was the requirement of our gathering, but the most relevant fact remained that two dozen children met together each day for the purpose of play, not enlightenment. This was the challenge of our stern teachers: How do we focus the attention of our pupils on elementary instruction when every day excitement embodied in 5-year-olds assembled in a classroom seek only playtime with their classmates? Our teachers were rigid, daughters of a culture demanding regulation. As a student for three years at Maunawilli, all of my teachers were of Japanese descent. Mrs. Yamamoto was my kindergarten teacher and had little tolerance for amusement. The same could be said of Mrs. Ono my first-grade teacher, or Mrs. Nakamura who led my second-grade class. They were mirror images of each other, firm and disciplined.

MILITARY BRAT
Pete Masalin

Yet, Hawaii was an environment that beckoned looseness. The slotted glass windows were opened every morning to allow sweet smelling breezes that wafted above and among tropical fruit trees and flowers to pass into the classroom. Children came to school barefooted, which didn't go unnoticed by me. Each day, my mother laced my shoes upon my feet, and each day, I ditched them in the bushes of Mrs. Brown's house as I walked to school. Being barefoot was liberating, and I can say that I was never able to enjoy the experience again throughout my schooling after leaving Hawaii. Of course, my return home was delayed by my requirement to pause at the Brown's residence and restore my shoes to their proper place, avoiding confrontation with my mom.

The Browns were wonderful neighbors: affable, caring and British. They had an accent noticeably different than anything I had heard before, and they introduced us to a culture and foods I had never tasted. I never appreciated "afternoon tea," but my mom and Mrs. Brown shared this tradition often. Mrs. Brown acquainted me with lime marmalade, a delicious jam that I still enjoy when I come upon it. Mr. Brown was an accomplished numismatist whose collection offered pieces dating back to the Roman Empire. Levi would spend hours evaluating Mr. Brown's assemblage of coins inspiring Levi to become a capable collector of his own. All this was wonderful, but to a youngster with a sweet tooth, the most valuable attribute of our British allies was their affinity for confections. Our mother was careful not to load us with sugar, especially one as energetic as me; however, I had a covert supplier in Mrs. Brown. Through the knotholes of our adjoining fence, our agent would secretly distribute candies to the Makinen children.

"Psst. Here you go. Don't tell your mum." Mrs. Brown would plead as she handed us candies through a secret hole behind the lychee nut tree. We never did.

Chapter 4
Summer, Menehunes, Ono!

My first year of school in Hawaii was one of acclimation and assimilation. It was an easy transition, and I effortlessly made friends with my classmates. My year in kindergarten was a little more than an extended summer camp. We played games, sang songs, finger painted, and had story time. Our day was split in half as we laid down in our denim sleeping bags for a post lunchtime nap. Life was good, and so was I. I would help clean blackboards and erasers. My teacher enjoyed her towheaded helper. First Grade would be less serene.

With our first year of school behind us and with the family fully adapted to our surroundings, my mom mapped out summer events for her children. Ash remained a detached appendage to my mother. Although he was now walking, he was still entirely dependent upon her. For Leigh, it was dance and more dance. My father was deployed to depths uncertain, and my mother rather enjoyed Levi and I being away at school during the day. Summer had thrown her daily interval from us back upon her. The solution was simple. Nearly every mother in the neighborhood suffered from similar circumstances and sought a summer long diversion for their energetic school age offspring. Most families had station wagons capable of transporting at least ten tots at a time. The neighborhood mothers' affiliation devised a plan to revive their daily liberation of children that had been provided by the public school system – summer camp! In one evening, they counselled together. Camps were selected and a carpool schedule was quickly agreed upon over Mai Tai's and Whiskey Sours.

As much as the mothers congratulated themselves upon the genius of their plan, we were the beneficiaries. The camps we attended were loose assemblies of children governed by teenagers who were more interested in surfing and a paycheck than mentoring their charges. Not to worry, there were more activities and games than we could possibly attend to on our daily visits. On occasion, we would leave the premises and visit a store across the street to purchase five cent chocolate bars. For all its chaos, we still lived in a time where children were safe.

Levi, a couple of other boys, and I discreetly voyaged to a natural pool not far from our camp. In an effort to deter our wandering, one of the camp counselors spoke of a natural pond in the island forest, adjacent

MILITARY BRAT   Pete Masalin

to the property. His was a story of Menehunes that guarded the pond to protect it from trespassers. During the day the Menehune took the form of lava rock, while at night they came alive to devour any previous interlopers. Naturally, our curiosity drove us beyond his intended warning, and we secreted away to find the enchanted body of water. It wasn't long before myth met reality. We found the pond.

"Here it is!" Levi, point man of our patrol, shouted as he raced to the pond.

"Wow!" exclaimed one of our companions.

We all soon followed. Kemo, who was part of our carpool, hesitated as we all rushed down the hill. We all looked up at him and encouraged him to join us. Reluctantly, he finally arrived as we inspected the small boulders of pitted lava rock that lined the translucent pool. We expected the stones to burst into Menehunes at any moment, but our attentions were quickly averted as we chased guppies and swordtails in the shallow waters. We would splash in the water with cups to catch the minnows.

"Got one."

"Me too!"

In a makeshift holding pond on the bank, we would collect our catch.

Levi would count, "One two...27, 28. We got 28!"

It was a trek we would embark on many days, and every time our absence would remain undiscovered. Each day, we would try to break the previous record. As the summer progressed, the population of pond fish diminished. We didn't understand the food chain at the time and arriving to our shoreline retaining pool, our previous day's catch had disappeared. We surmised that, in the evening, the Menehune awoke and devoured our catch. We weren't the only interested party in the fish. They were a mainstay of the creatures of the island, but to us, we knew it was the Menehune. From then on, we kept a watchful eye on the lava stones when visiting our private oasis.

These visits helped foment my innocent recklessness. Caution became absent in my judgment. I took risks not knowing they were risks. I just did what I did, never calculating peril. We lived in paradise. At six years

MILITARY BRAT   Pete Masalin

old, I didn't understand that danger existed. It was never apparent in my cocooned world of Hawaii. We were safe and I had only encountered good people. Like any other child of my age, you trust. Distrust is something you are taught, or it is learned. I had done neither. Levi, on the other hand, being older had received lessons: Don't talk to strangers; stay away from people you don't know. At the end of camp one day, Mrs. Feng could not retrieve us as was her assigned duty per the carpool schedule. She had arranged for a mechanic and family friend to carry us home. When he arrived, Laura and Lilly Feng, Mrs. Feng's daughters, quickly jumped in the van to be *limousined* home. I followed immediately behind them.

Levi protested, "No, Finn. We don't know him."

I just stared at him, and my brother implored, "Get out, Finn! Run!"

"C'mon," I replied.

"No," Levi said. "He's going to kill you."

The poor driver, acting in good faith, looked at me and said, "Maybe you should just go join your brother."

I jumped out of the van, disappointed that I had to remain behind and not knowing how I would get home. We headed back to our summer camp and alerted the camp counselors. Within the hour, my mom arrived to take us home, furious that Mrs. Feng had not alerted everyone to the change but satisfied that Levi knew how to respond to strangers. At the time, I didn't understand the conflict. The mechanic seemed like a nice man, and Laura and Lilly knew him.

That summer taught me lessons that did not serve me well for my following school year. I learned that rules were only established as suggestions, and that fun was paramount in the execution of one's day. After all, the entire summer ingrained in me that there was little consequence in not following instruction. It was a flawed tutorial that required correction and my correcting authority had no patience for my cavalier penchant for foolishness. In the end, she would win the war, but there would be small battles along the way where I was the victor.

One day I was penalized for an infraction that I had not been guilty of committing. Just prior to lunch, a violation of order had occurred. While

MILITARY BRAT   Pete Masalin

Mrs. Ono had her attention turned towards the blackboard, an eruption of conversation ensued. To demand order, she quickly turned, causing a hush to fall upon the classroom. This was a breach of her classroom decorum. Determined to punish the guilty party, she embarked upon an inquisition to discover those at fault. Her efforts were in vain, as the offending parties, fearful for their lives, refused to incriminate themselves. Although innocent of the charges before me, Mrs. Ono surmised that, based upon my previous violations, I was likely the voice of encroachment upon her demand for silence. Pleading my case, I was ignored by Mrs. Ono. She decided that as punishment, I would not be allowed to join my classmates as she escorted them to the cafeteria. I was denied any lunch at all and was instructed to remain behind with the students who had brought their lunches from home. It was a decision that Mrs. Ono would soon regret.

    I was furious. The two most anticipated events of my school day were lunch and recess, and Mrs. Ono had just denied me one of them. I didn't cry or mope as I designed my retribution. I wanted revenge and revenge I would receive. It came swiftly. Many of the children asked me what I was going to do. I stood up and announced to my friends in the classroom, "I'm walking home."

    "Finn, you can't. You're going to get in more trouble!" a boy in my class responded.

    I remained silent. Determined in my plan, I exited the classroom door and headed to my home on Uluhala Street. My classmates watched with their eyes wide and mouths agape. Their reaction was minor compared to Mrs. Ono when she discovered my absence. It wasn't long before she returned with the balance of the students, lunch trays in hand. Once Mrs. Ono and my classmates sat at their desks to dine, my empty chair was blatantly obvious. Mrs. Ono stood up and asked, "Where is Finn? Does anyone know where Finn is?"

    "He walked home," was her unwelcomed answer.

    Her face went pale. She ran to the door with the hope that I was still visible so that she might retrieve me. It was too late. I was nearing my house where my mother would be shocked to see me. She returned to her

MILITARY BRAT   Pete Masalin

desk and pushed her lunch tray aside. She was fearful and worried, and her fears were about to be justified as I arrived at my home, opened the front door and shouted, "Mom!"

Of course, my mother was inquisitive as to why I was home early. I quickly retold the reasoning for my premature self-dismissal, and as I did, she became noticeably angrier with each sentence. She asked if I was talking in class, and I told her, "Not this time." It was always better to tell mom the truth than face the wrath of her wooden spoon across our bottoms. It was rare to see my mother become enraged, but on this day, one of her children had been wrongfully denied sustenance. My plight had stirred the protective wild beast mother within her. She quickly collected Leigh and Ash and she took me back to school. I had no expectation of what was about to unfold but when it did it was swift, powerful, and unrelenting.

We darkened the doorway of Mrs. Ono's classroom. I was standing in front of my mother while she carried Ash upon her left hip and held Leigh's hand on her right.

"Good afternoon, Mrs. Makinen. I'm glad to see that you brought Finn back. He shouldn't have left school on his own." Mrs. Ono addressed my mother as polite as she could, hopeful that it would diffuse her obvious and deserved rebuke soon to be delivered by my mother.

My mother said nothing and walked slowly to confront my teacher at her desk. "Did you deny my son lunch today?"

"Yes, but he was being punished for talking in class."

"He told me he wasn't, but that's not the point. Even if he was talking, you will *never* deny my son food. Do I make myself clear?"

Mrs. Ono tried to defend her methods, but she was cut off mid-sentence as my mother, a tall statuesque woman, towered over her as she leaned in and stated again firmly, "Never. Do you understand? Never."

Standing in the front of the class as my teacher and mother conferenced, I observed my classmates' faces showing disbelief as my mother counselled our teacher in front of them. I thought of myself as a great hero who, in the form of my mother, had brought justice for all

MILITARY BRAT Pete Masalin

of us against the tyranny of Mrs. Ono. It was a small victory, and I was vindicated. A wrong had been righted.

"Finn. Go take your seat," my mother directed, loud enough for the entire class to hear. "And you make sure you pay attention to your teacher and don't act up in class."

What? I was the wounded party here. Didn't my mother remember that I was the one who had been denied lunch? My mother was smart and wise enough to realize that she had sufficiently corrected Mrs. Ono. Rightly offering corrective counsel for her misjudgment and satisfied that it would not be repeated, my mother rescued Mrs. Ono from any embarrassment in front of her class. Her short directive to me was a clear statement that while she would ensure my protection when wronged, she would not serve as a vehicle to undermine a teacher's authority in the classroom. After my mom's short visit, there were still many times when I was chastised by Mrs. Ono.

One such occasion involved Mary Tanaka while on the playground. Mary was a mean-spirited and selfish little girl. She thought herself better than everyone else and was quick to monopolize as many playground activities as she could, sometimes just to deny others using them. On this day, Mary sat atop the playground jungle gym with a jump rope in hand. We boys enjoyed using the jump ropes as well. They were necessary for our makeshift games of tug-o-war.

"Mary – can I have the jump rope?" I asked.

"No."

"Give me the jump rope!" I demanded.

"Go away, Finn. It's mine," Mary insisted.

"Give me it!"

"No!"

We were allotted only so much time on the playground, and I had exhausted all reasonable efforts of diplomacy. I grabbed the dangling rope and pulled it with all my might. Mary tried not to relinquish her grasp and pulled back. A short battle ensued. I had the secure footing of

MILITARY BRAT   Pete Masalin

the ground below me, while she struggled to maintain both her balance and control of the rope. She could do neither as the rope snapped from her hand towards my direction. The momentum of my final yank caused Miss Tanaka to lose her perch, and she fell. I remember watching her tumble from the very top; and as she plummeted, it seemed her head hit every crossbar until she landed on the pea gravel covering the playground's surface. Her head was reminiscent of a chip upon a Plinko board, bouncing from one rung to the next.

Mrs. Ono witnessed the whole affair and ran to us at its conclusion. The boys beside me were clapping, and Mary was crying. I was immediately disciplined for my misbehavior. Recess was over for me, as I was instructed to return to the classroom and sit in silence, but I did get to eat lunch that day.

My final year at Maunawilli Elementary School, Second Grade was much the same as my first two years. During the school year, we spent our days in the classroom. On most Saturdays, the expansive school's playground served as an improvised theme park for neighborhood adolescents. We flew kites, rode bikes, threw ball, and generally socialized all day. It was great to be a kid in these simple times. Rarely a day went by that wasn't as pleasant as the former one. There was, however, one day, a Saturday when our easy life was interrupted. I remember approaching the park with Levi and noticed the playground's population was significantly diminished. We wondered why but did not dwell on it. We unfurled our kites and sailed them into the sky, unrolling our kite string as the wind carried them to ever increasing heights. We happened to overhear some of the parents discussing current events of the previous day. Today was November 23, 1968, and yesterday was tragic for America. Robert Kennedy had been killed by an assailant.

Uncertain of the relevance of the calamity, Levi and I continued to watch our kite's soar. Neither of us knew who Mr. Kennedy was, but the mention of a gun and someone being shot piqued our interest. Levi and I had cap guns along with many other boys in our neighborhood. We all would divide ourselves into two groups, good guys and bad guys, cops and robbers and run house to house in fierce battles. Beyond these skirmishes I had no ability to understand the gravity of our nation's loss.

MILITARY BRAT   Pete Masalin

I remember returning home and discussing it with my father. He did his best to explain the event to me, but it was beyond my comprehension. Levi understood, I did not; however, it was the first time I was awakened to a world beyond the carefree realm that is childhood.

Quickly, my attention averted from the fate of Robert Kennedy, and I was back to the contented life of a seven-year-old. Thanksgiving was less than a week away and Christmas with its long break from school was soon to follow. Apart from an upcoming recital, there wasn't anything not to be excited about. Leigh was a dancer. Is there anything more boring than dancing? Perhaps, but watching my mother knit was not an option available to us since leaving New Hampshire. The tropical climate had forced her knitting needles into hibernation. The Friday evening before Christmas, Mom and Dad packed us into the family station wagon. On the way to the event, Levi and I protested.

"Do we have to go?" Levi complained.

"Dance. yuck!" I said in support of my brother.

"I hate dancing Dad. Why can't you take Finn and me to watch the Islanders play? Mom can take everyone else to the dance *retisel*," Levi pleaded, mispronouncing "recital."

It was a brilliant idea. Ash was too young to care where he went, and even though he didn't admit it, I am certain that the idea of watching the Islanders was a more appealing proposition for Dad. He had to say yes. Dad loved baseball and he loved sitting in the stadium with his boys, eating hotdogs. Levi had just hatched a foolproof plan to free us from the agony of watching a compulsory dance routine performance by our little sister. It was perfect, except that it was December and the offseason for our beloved Islander's. Levi and I (and Dad) were the beneficiaries of a well-choreographed show of five-year-old girls demonstrating hula and ballet; a combination of genres I have yet to see repeated.

Our time in Hawaii was soon to end. My father received orders for his new assignment at the Pentagon. Time is sometimes conceptual, and its restrictions were not fully grasped by Levi and me. We continued our adventures with the same zeal we had always maintained except that we were older and comfortable in our environment, and I more reckless. I lacked common sense and a natural fear of stupidity. Levi was reliable and sensible. We balanced each other well except on rare occasions when Levi suffered the wrath of my foolishness.

School ended its year, and we had the majority of the summer to enjoy before our transfer to the mainland. Maunawili Elementary School was often a destination of choice. We were free from the interruption and nuisance of parents. In my three years visiting this haven of youthful sovereignty, I don't ever remember being under the watchful eye of an adult. One afternoon, Levi and I ventured to join other children at the playground. We soon became embroiled in a confrontation with two older girls, resulting in a battlefield casualty that quickly ended our day and sent Levi to the infirmary. Ours was a turf battle for rights of the sandbox, which I correctly claimed by virtue of our first arrival. Matters quickly escalated by my insistence.

"Can we play?" one of the girls asked.

"No. We were here first," I said.

"It's not yours!" The remaining girl proclaimed.

The conversation ended as I threw sand in one of the girl's faces. As the other girl advanced, I grabbed a fistful of sand and covered her hair. Stalled by my actions, everyone backed away and reassessed the situation. One more time the girls asked, "Can we play?"

It happened so fast that Levi was never able to respond. My response was swift. I again filled my hands with sand and hurled it at the enemy. I was in front, obscuring Levi's view of the battleground. It was an unfortunate vantage point, as one of the opposing combatants picked up a stone and hurled it in my direction. I quickly ducked, avoiding the projectile completely; however, continuing its path, Levi's left eye met with trauma. The stone hit Levi with full force, sending him to the ground as his eye bled profusely. It had nearly been dislodged from its socket. I helped my beleaguered brother to his feet while he covered his eye with both hands, holding it in place. As quickly as our legs would allow, we rushed home to our mother for attention.

Immediately, my mother tended to Levi. Quickly, we all piled into the station wagon headed to the Pearl Harbor Naval Hospital. Soon, Levi was stabilized and joined us as we headed back home. He looked cool – like a pirate with a patch over his left eyeball.

"You look like pirate, Levi!" I exclaimed excitedly.

Levi's face quickly displayed a grin at the notion of being a swashbuckler, but mom was not amused. She had learned the full details of our confrontation and was very angry.

Uncharacteristically she said, "Shut up, Finn. That was intended for you. Your father will want to talk to you when he gets home."

I knew I was in trouble and didn't say anything for the rest of the ride. Later, I was thrown in the brig and the rest of my family treated Levi as if he was Blackbeard himself and they were his crew.

Chapter 5
Farewell to Paradise

Our final summer in Hawaii seemed to pass more rapidly than the previous two. We lazed many days at the beach, soaking in the tropical sun. My mother was particularly fond of Bellows Beach. Levi and I were competent swimmers and didn't require much of her attention, as the beach was wide and routinely had gentle surf conditions. Leigh and Ash were content to sit close by and play in the sand with beach toys.

My father was transitioning out of his duties as he prepared for his new assignment. His workload became less taxing as his departure date approached, allowing for him to spend more time with us during the day, sometimes accompanying us to Bellows Beach. His deployments ceased, enabling him to join us on family outings, resulting in fewer Levi and Finn adventures without the tether of surveillance. Still, we had a great time together.

As a final family summer joint R & R venture, our family vacationed at Barbers Point, a Navy installation offering service members beachfront cottages for leisure. My parents decided to enlist a babysitter to accompany us so that they could enjoy Oahu evenings sans their children in the final few weeks of our domicile. Shelley Trask was probably a nice girl, but she was a babysitter. What authority did she hold over me? Certainly, none that I recognized. The Makinens and Shelley journeyed to Barbers Point Beach for a weeklong vacation. Overall, it provided a restful atmosphere, but then there was Shelley. In my mind she was a witch, a person who had no right to correct or direct me. We had babysitters before, and I got my way more often than not with them. Shelley was different and not easily moved to my way of thinking. And worst of all, she never flushed the toilet in the morning. My memories of Shelley include me immediately following her first morning visit to the latrine. It was a cruel punishment she bestowed upon me; arriving to a porcelain bowl filled with amber colored water was unnatural. And the odor only added to my torment. The strong aroma reminded me of Special K, and I hated that cereal. Levi and I assigned a name to her that we only shared in private – Smelly Shelley.

One evening after supper, we all gathered around the fire rings on the beach for a bonfire and s'mores. Levi and I were dispatched by dad

MILITARY BRAT Pete Masalin

to collect driftwood along the shore. Leigh slowed our progress, as we were directed to bring her along while we foraged for fuel for the fire. Nevertheless, we stayed on mission, carrying our younger sister along the way. Our first return provided enough kindling for our father to start a blaze. We were sent out to gather more wood and Leigh prepared to continue along with us.

"Does Leigh have to come with us?' Levi protested.

"Yeah, she's a girl," I added.

My mom responded, "You boys take your sister."

"No!" I complained. "She only brought back a handful of sticks."

My dad interceded, "Leigh, why don't you stay here and help us get the s'mores ready?"

Levi and I didn't wait for a response from Leigh. No sooner had Dad finished his query did we run off into the twilight glow to gather more wood, never allowing Leigh an opportunity to answer. We laughed at each other celebrating our small victory. We made three more trips assembling ample wood to fuel our roasting pit for the entire night.

We sat patiently roasting marshmallows on sticks prepared by Dad. Quietly observing the glow of ambers, I noticed small creatures exiting the ring of fire as their home became untenable. Scorpions! Soon, everyone was alerted, and we backed away to assess the situation. No more than an inch long, they seemed inconsequential to our position. My father was unmoved and grabbed two small sticks. With chopstick like actions, Dad secured the scorpions as they scampered and threw them into the furnace before us. Taking his lead, Levi and I quickly supported his effort, and the nemeses were vanquished. Our family returned to task while Levi and I remained on patrol, picking off stragglers and throwing them into the fire.

Shelley abstained from assembling her own s'mores, and our parents required that we provide her with the delectable treats we carefully prepared at her asking. I found this was unfair and the request stirred resentment within me. Who was she not to assemble her own s'more? She had authority over us. As Levi perfected a s'more for his enjoyment, my mother handed him a plate and directed Levi to give it Shelley. At the same time, I noticed a small scorpion exiting the ring, and, in the darkness outside the glow of the fire, I grabbed the insect. As Levi placed the s'more on the plate, I quickly and secretly placed the scorpion next to it. Levi was too distracted by the plight of losing his desert that he did not notice my attachment of the assailant.

"Ahhhhh!" Shelley screamed as she lifted the plate to her face.

Casting her offering into the darkness, the collection of graham crackers, melted chocolate and golden roasted marshmallows scattered into the night air. The plate landing upon the campfire erupted in flames while remnants of s'mores dotted her hair and shoulders.

"What is it?" my mother yelled.

"Scorpions!" Shelley replied.

My father jumped to his feet and examined everyone's setting finding no indication of poison tailed intruders. Still, he thought it best to assemble his family, douse the fire, and return to the safety of our cabin. My actions undetected, I smiled and contemplated my victory. Although our evening ended abruptly, I was satisfied that I had achieved retribution for the cruel treatment delivered to me by our babysitter. I held no objection to our early termination of festivities. I slept well that evening while Shelley inspected every inch of her quarters to ensure for her safety.

Our family vacation concluded, we returned to our Kailua home and prepared for our Trans-Pacific, cross country trek to our new home. After three weeks of preparation, the movers arrived to pack up our belongings. Mom's greatest responsibility was to keep her four children from interfering with the packing crew as they disassembled furniture, carefully wrapped family delicates, and filled containers with Makinen household goods. This was no easy task, but she managed well, balancing our intrigue with the moving company's mission.

By the day's end, the house was vacant, and we headed to Aiea Heights, home of my father's coworker. It was here that we would await our day of embarkation on a cruise liner headed to mainland United States. It was

MILITARY BRAT   Pete Masalin

a one-week delay. During that time, the quarters were absent its tenants while we marshalled together. The only stipulation of our stay was that we tend to a small dachshund while the home's owners went on a vacation of their own.

In short order, Levi and I quickly introduced ourselves to the neighborhood children. We would join them in a garage across the street and listen to music. It was my first introduction to The Beatles. The lyrics were nonsensical to me as I incorrectly heard them as "Jojo was a man who thought he was a woman…Get back." No matter, the beat was pleasing, and we all fell under the spell of The Beatles, as did the rest of the world.

As it happened, this week included the Fourth of July. On the night of celebration, Leigh and Ash went to bed before the island lit up with explosions easily observed from our heightened position of Aiea. Never before or since, have I observed the magnitude of festivity among the locals. Power lines aligning the streets were strung with firecrackers such that the entire neighborhood would pop as a string of tiny explosions, cascading the avenue from one end to the other. It was a marvel. At the conclusion of the celebration, Levi and I wandered the neighborhood. Coming upon an intersection at the bottom of the hill, a car was parked alone.

"Do you want some firecrackers?" a passenger asked.

Immediately I said "yes," but Levi declined.

"Come here. You can have what we have left."

I advanced to the car and Levi pleaded with me not to go. I continued, but Levi persisted in his appeal. I stopped and looked at the car, desiring what they had. Sensing Levi's reservation, the occupants of the car simply threw their remaining fireworks to the pavement while driving off. I quickly ran to the stash of our good fortune and brought them back to Levi.

Neither of us had the experience with such an assembly power. I was eight, and Levi, ten. Before us was a pile of Black Cats and Lady Fingers. Our bounty included matches and punks; a wick of sorts that when lit,

MILITARY BRAT   Pete Masalin

burned for an extended period of time and allowed us to light the fuses of the firecrackers at will. Our inexperience was of no concern to me. It was just the two of us and we had the power! We would take turns. One held a pack of firecrackers while the other lit a fuse with a punk. It was thrilling and glorious – no supervision while we created our own display of demolitions in the street.

Everything went as planned, even though there was no plan. That was until Levi lit a short fuse resulting in an entire package exploding in my hand. I remember the numbness in my fingers and the ringing in my ears. We thought it best to end our free reign of destruction and head home, leaving the remaining cache in the street. With our ordinance depleted, we joined the family. Mom and Dad were unaware of the demolition team that Levi and I became in the neighborhood, or that the small burst of fury they had been hearing was created by their two sons. Had they known, we surely would have received a different welcome than we did when entering the house. We said good night and retired for the evening. By morning, my hearing had returned but my fingers remained numb for days.

The next day, we joined other children of the neighborhood. As had happened before, Levi and I got in an altercation with older girls. It was reminiscent of our previous schoolhouse battle in a sandbox. I am not certain of the cause, but Levi again became the fallen soldier of our conflict. I was on roller skates while Levi was afoot. Whatever the argument, one of the older girls drove the front fender of her bike into Levi creating a small gash mid shin. Blood ran down his leg hampering his retaliation. I kicked off my skates, hurling punches at the attacker. Quickly, a parent interceded, and we dispersed. Levi and I went home, not realizing the impact of his wound until we were passengers on a ship bound for San Francisco.

Our family climbed the gangplank of the ship and positioned ourselves on the rails as the SS Lurline left the port of Honolulu. Passengers waved to the dockside assembly of well-wishers as the ship slowly slipped from its mooring. We all shouted, "Bon Voyage!" and threw steamers of confetti. As the Lurline drifted from sight, we made our way to our staterooms and readied ourselves for the enjoyable journey.

MILITARY BRAT   Pete Masalin

    Levi was still suffering from his injury and Mom, the nurse, had been attending to him with a bath of Epsom Salt. Concern mounted as infection set in. A visit to the ship's hospital revealed little. Fortunately, on our second day at sea a small sliver of metal fell from the wound and Levi quickly healed. Levi's fever broke and all concern halted. Suffering abated, Levi's healing was nearly instantaneous, and our family immediately ventured among the other passengers to enjoy the offerings of our luxury liner.

    Surprisingly, Levi and I were afforded a liberty pass to travel about the ship and explored the Lurline freely. There was shuffleboard, a pool, and the fresh salt air of the open sea surrounded us as we roamed the upper decks of the vessel. We watched flying fish explode from the waves created by the bow as the ship cut through the Pacific and crash back into the deep blue ocean.

    The ship even had its own movie theater. Of particular interest to Levi was the movie *2001: A Space Odyssey*. Levi dragged me to the viewing so as not to be alone. The movie bored me as I sat quietly fidgeting and waiting for events to change. Then suddenly, excitement filled the screening room. A pack of wild apes projected upon the screen. I marveled at the scene of crazed simians jumping up and down, beating their chests, and crushing bones. I knew not the context of the scene, but to me it was the film's most captivating moment. Immediately, I jumped from my seat and mimicked their every move, running up and down the aisle I imitated their calls and actions.

    "Finn! Stop!" Levi whispered, not wanting to add to the disturbance. It was of no use. I continued throughout the entire sequence. Other movie goers were incensed by my antics and directed their ire towards me.

    "Shut up!"

    "Shhh!"

    "Sit down, young man!"

    It didn't matter. I paid no attention to my critics. I was amused and joyful at playing and I continued my antics and disruption, running to the

MILITARY BRAT   Pete Masalin

front of the theater casting a shadow image of myself upon the screen. As I interpreted my ape like rendition through the aisle, I was met by an usher who quickly intercepted me while trying to rejoin Levi at my seat.

"Come with me," he insisted.

"You too, young man," he instructed, pointing to my embarrassed brother while slumped down in his seat to avoid detection.

We were both escorted out of the theater and as the doors closed behind us the usher advised, "And don't come back."

We returned to our family's room where Levi quickly recounted my superior acting abilities. He was furious as he recounted my behavior. My mother was sympathetic to Levi's frustration and disbarment from the theater. Observing my father, I could see that he was trying to hold his reaction within. He could stand it no longer and left our stateroom. Once the door had closed, I could hear my father roar with laughter as he pictured his son, Finn the ape-man, hopping through the dimly lit cinema. I knew that there would be no serious ramification of my foolery this day.

My mother stared at me sternly and only stated, "Oh, Finn. Must you?" But behind her admonition, I could see a restrained smile so as not to encourage me on future ventures during our journey.

"Let's all get ready for dinner," was her final directive.

Dinners were a glorious feast. Never before were the Makinen children afforded such accommodations for dining. Each night, we ate at the same time and our server, Pedro, presented us offerings beyond our belief. We experienced delicacies previously unknown to us. Levi had rabbit his first night and liked it so much that he never deviated from it each evening meal at sea. I preferred the Mahi Mahi, and true to Levi's lead, I requested it every suppertime. Leigh was more adventurous and tried something new at each seating. As for Ash, he ate what babies eat and I paid no attention. Nor did I follow the menu of my parents. However, desserts were a subject of great interest to all of us children. The treats seemed endless and given our good fortune, we each chose more than one. Never completing one individually, but sampling at least three each night.

MILITARY BRAT   Pete Masalin

Our journey wasn't only provided for the children's enjoyment. The cruise staff planned and ensured that there were great events for my parents to enjoy. Lieutenant Commander Makinen escorted his wife to a formal ball. Dressed in the formal attire of a naval officer and accompanied by his lady, my parents enjoyed the company of the ship's captain for an evening of fine dining and dancing. Add a beehive hairdo to a statuesque 5'9" woman coupled with a daunting 6'3" officer in formal dress, my parents' commanded distinction. Any pretense of superiority and distance presented that evening was quickly mitigated the following night. My parents were approachable, regular Americans.

The night's event following the Lurline's formal ball was a relaxed fun filled gathering including participatory games for its passengers. There were minor competitions, but the one of particular intrigue was a beer chugging contest. Susan Makinen had remained a bystander throughout the evening until, with her husband's encouragement, she acquiesced and joined the final signature match of the night. Entrants took the stage, looking out towards the assembled guests. A line of 15 or so competitors gauged their challengers as beer mugs were filled to the brim before them. 10, 9, 8…the countdown commenced.

"Go!" Glasses raised; ale poured down the throats of the competitors. My mother, emptying her vessel, slammed its bottom upon the table. As she completed this action, a belch echoed throughout the chamber to cheers among the spectators. Victory was hers. My father stood tall and clapped enthusiastically in recognition of her achievement. Her trophy - a tote bag adorning the Lurline logo.

We had a most memorable time on our transit across the Pacific Ocean. As we approached the California coastline, a cool, dense fog engulfed our ship obscuring our view of the shore. Deep tone fog horns sounded as we passed under the Golden Gate Bridge. There would be no pomp and circumstance when we arrived similar to our send off in Honolulu. We disembarked and sought out our reconnection with our copper-colored Chevy Impala station wagon to carry us the rest of the way to our new assignment in Washington, DC.

Chapter 6
It's a Small World

Early in the morning, following our arrival to San Francisco, we headed south to the warmer and sunnier climate of Anaheim. It was our first detour of a lengthy, indirect cross-country trek that offered our family opportunity to see so many of our country's greatest wonders. Unfortunately, we started with the greatest wonder of all – Disneyland! Our remaining stops along our progression east, while thrilling on their own merit, could not compare to seeing Mickey Mouse in person. Tomorrowland, Adventureland, Fantasyland, Frontierland - so many new worlds to discover. We stood in wonderment of it all. We were in awe of the rides. In one day, I rode a safari boat down an African river and was splashed by wild hippos. I marveled in line as I saw those in front of me enter a passageway only to exit as insect-size thrill-seekers through a clear tube, exploring Disney's microscopic world. I saw snowflakes 5 times my size. I visited Robinson Crusoe's tree top home. I witnessed the drunkenness and debauchery of pirates in the Caribbean.

An early family ride, together we visited the globe by way of "It's a Small World," and, upon exiting the experience, we each discovered that Mr. Disney was a sophisticated evil man who had brainwashed us all. No matter what the next attraction, meal, ice cream or pause in the shade, his diabolical message pounded in our heads. It was unshakable – irremovable. That song… *"It's a small world after all. It's a small world after all."*

There were rides where Leigh and Ash did not have the composure or sophistication required to survive the trauma that might be cast upon them should they join us. I thought myself so mature; no longer recognized as a child. The reality of the separation between the four children was that Levi and I were taller than the outstretched hand of a Disney character placed in front of each attraction. "You must be this tall," the sign read. Leigh was most damaged by the circumstance of her "not tall enough" revelation. Wise in her resolution, mom provided consolation to the two "toddlers" in the form of gifts and candy at each attraction where Levi and I went, and they could not. These rewards were denied to Levi and me, but it was a just trade.

The Haunted House was the scene of hilarity and embarrassment. At

MILITARY BRAT   Pete Masalin

the commencement of the tour, Levi, I, and my father entered together with other guests through large French doors into a grand vestibule. In the dimly lit room, I noticed regal statues dressed in Victorian attire along the perimeter. The doors closed and the lights went dark. Flashes of lightning and the rupture of thunder reverberated in the assembly. When the lights returned, a body dangled from a noose hanging high above us at the center of the elevated ceiling. What happened next still amuses me today. Naturally, Levi and I stood in uneasy bewilderment, wide eyed and jaws ajar. As we assessed our surroundings, Levi thought it beneficial to use all the senses afforded him. Rather than rely solely on his eyes, he moved towards the outside wall where a sculpture of a woman clad in a long velvet dress stood. Reaching up to verify the prop, Levi filled his hand full of plush material. Startling the figure, she jumped back and slapped Levi's hand.

"Stop that!" she demanded.

Levi retreated in shock. My father gathered him back to our position, apologizing to the young lady. I witnessed the contact, and my already wide eyes grew wider. Along with the velvet, Levi had filled his hand with her breast. Understanding Levi's innocent intent, she smiled at my father, realigned her costume, giggled, and replied, "It's okay." Mindful of the incident, I continued to laugh as we continued the tour watching skeletons rise from graves and ghosts fly in front of us.

That night, each of us grabbed an ice cream cone and settled on the curb of Disney's Main Street, preparing for the Electric Light Parade and fireworks that signaled the end of the day's adventure for all theme park visitors. Ash was nearly asleep, and Leigh was close behind as she leaned on our mother with her veil trailing princess hat askew. Levi and I kept jabbering endlessly with dad about the day's events. Relief for my father came when the brilliantly lit parade approached our position. Ash and Leigh were alerted and regained their stamina as magical, musical floats drifted by. Fireworks exploded in the sky, casting beams of bright and colorful light, reflecting excitement upon our awestruck and smiling faces. As the last embers cascaded downward from high the midnight sky, the Makinens held hands and walked towards the exit. This night's slumber would include dreams that could not possibly match the day's events.

MILITARY BRAT   Pete Masalin

After breakfast we packed our suitcases, loaded the car, and advanced north to Yellowstone Park. Leigh demonstrated a pattern that benefitted her beyond equality with her brothers. From San Francisco to Disney, Leigh rode in her makeshift stateroom in our station wagon. In fairness, my father drew up a rotation schedule for his four children. There were four stations; right and left window seats, middle seat and the expansive back where one could lay prone and sleep comfortably. Obviously, the back was the most prized real estate. Leigh devised a plan, an ailment, that would solidify her position in family travel for the rest of our years traveling together – car sickness. How could someone not old enough to extend beyond Mickey Mouse's outstretched hand craft such a cunning plan to secure herself such prominence in our travel accommodations. Car sickness could not be diagnosed by any doctor. It was something she "felt." From the outset, Leigh sabotaged Dad's rotation plan. It wasn't ten minutes of her first assignment when the claims started.

"I feel sick," Leigh complained.

"Close your eyes, Flopsy Mopsy," my dad replied.

Two minutes later. "I'm going to get sick."

"Try to rest," my mom said.

Another two minutes. "I'm going to throw up."

"Finn, why don't you switch places with your sister?" Mom asked.

"No – why?" I responded.

"She's sick."

"No, she's not," I protested.

"Finn. Do as I say," Dad commanded.

"No."

"Now, Finn!"

Reluctantly, I climbed over the back seat, as Leigh and I switched places. At the next break, we rotated seat assignments. Levi was rewarded with the prized tail gunner position. Ten minutes went by and Déjà vu. "I feel sick." On long trips, our sister was never assigned anything but views from the rear window. Dad still had a rotation schedule, but the positions were reduced to three for his sons; left, middle and right.

Stopping for a restful night along our route, we arrived at Yellowstone National Park the following noontime to another parade. As we drove through the preserve, we came upon a row of parked cars greeted by the local residents, eager for handouts.

"A bear!" Ash shouted.

We all sprung from our slouched positions and pressed our faces against the windows.

"Look at all those bears, kids," my father exclaimed, parking the car among the others. Quickly, we were met with a woolly greeting from inhabitants hoping for a handout.

"Nobody open a window," my father cautioned.

"Can we feed 'em Dad?" I inquired.

"Certainly not," Mom directed.

"But *they* are!" I exclaimed, pointing to a neighboring car whose occupant was distributing sugar cubes through a slightly opened window.

"He's going to lose his fingers." My dad laughed as we all reeled back from the window.

We sat silently watching the bears roam around to provide us with an impromptu show. There were mother bears with their cubs and a massive male who all seemed as tame as a pet rabbit. Observing their calm demeanor, I felt as though we would be safe petting them from our car. Slowly, I began to roll down the window.

"Finn! Are you crazy? Get in the middle seat," Dad commanded.

"But..."

"Move it!"

We remained parked for another few minutes before Dad reversed the car and moved out.

"Where are we going?" Levi asked.

"You kids are going to see something really amazing, *Old Faithful*."

"What's Ol' Fayful?" Ash wondered.

"It's a geyser that shoots water way up in the air," Mom said.

I was excited. When we lived in Hawaii, my father would often place the sprinkler on the front lawn and turn the water on full force so that we could run through it. I envisioned running through the same awaited us when visiting Old Faithful. We drove for a short time before parking again in an open field.

"C'mon kids. Let's go." Levi and I rushed out, but Leigh was hesitant and refused to leave the car.

"What's wrong Leigh?" my mom asked.

"Bears. I don't want to be with bears," she stated.

"Oh, honey. There aren't any bears here."

Comforted by my mom's comment, Leigh left the car and joined us as we walked across the barren land surrounding Old Faithful. From a distance, I could see steam rising from the earth. I wondered where the water was. We waited for what seemed to be hours. Finally, I asked, "When are they turning on the water?"

"Patience, Finn," was my father's response. "It takes a little while, but it's coming."

At last, the ground rumbled, and an eruption soon followed, spewing a mass of water high into the air. I could hear the roar and feel the power emanating from the explosive force, ejecting a broad stream nearly 150 feet high into the air. I stood in awe as I witnessed the power presented before us. We all froze and quietly marveled at the site, and then stillness. After only just more than a minute, the rage of Old Faithful ended. I thought to myself how my dad said this would be amazing, and that was it? I had waited longer in line for attractions at Disneyland, but at least I was rewarded with a thrilling experience no matter how short the ride. That was it? This was the highlight of Yellowstone?

"Why did it stop dad?" I asked.

"That's all it does, son."

MILITARY BRAT   Pete Masalin

"Tell 'em to turn it back on. I want to run through it."

My dad laughed at me and said, "You can't turn it on. Mother Nature only does it when she wants to, and she's done for now. Besides Finn, that water is too hot. It would boil you alive."

"Well, let's go back to see the bears," I pleaded.

"Sorry, son. We must head out."

I felt cheated. For hours we travelled, crowded together in our car with hopes of exhilaration and marvel, and that was it, forty-five minutes with the bears and a shot of hot water in the air. Adding to my disappointment was the awareness that we were departing on another long leg of our venture to places unfamiliar, and I had to occupy the middle seat.

We stopped late that night at another roadside inn in the Black Hills of South Dakota. There was no moonlight when we arrived, and my ability to assess our surroundings was limited to the extension of neon sign illumination and an overhead floodlight mounted high above the parking lot. Our family of six occupied a tiny room to settle in for the night. It presented the typical accommodation of the day, two full-sized beds and a bathroom with a tub. With the day quickly closing, mom ran the water to fill the tub and readied her children for a bath. As she did this, my father exited the room to acquire provisions. Leigh and Ash would be the first to clear themselves of the day's accumulation of road dust. Mom placed them both in the tub and quickly washed their hair. She allowed little time to frolic and splash in the tub, quickly pulling them into a towel, drying them off and dressing them in their pajamas.

I would be next, but Levi and I were old enough to shower on our own. As the murky water holding the cast-off dirt of my siblings spiraled down the drain, my father returned with a six pack of beer. He pulled a cold can from a plastic ring, opened it and handed it to my mother. Immediately, he grabbed one for himself and toasted Mom.

"Finn. The shower's ready. Jump in and quickly wash yourself," my mom charged.

"Get behind your ears, sport," my dad added.

I did as they asked, finished my shower, and ran around the room

MILITARY BRAT — Pete Masalin

naked looking for my suitcase.

"Finn. Put on your towel!" Mom yelled. "Your pajamas are on the bed."

I acted as if I couldn't find my bedtime attire and ran around the room. Hawaii had bleached my hair nearly white and toned my skin to tobacco. Without clothes, my bottom, which had not been exposed to the sun, glowed as I pretended to search for my clothing. The Makinen children were laughing, but as amusing as we may have thought my display was, my parents were in no mood for my pranks. Dad reached down grabbing my pajamas, took a sip of his beer, and threw them in my direction, hitting me in the head. More laughter erupted.

"Get dressed Finn. It's bedtime. Levi, jump in the shower and let's go," Dad directed, defusing the situation.

Clean up complete, our parents readied us for sleep. Wearing her Disney royal adornment, Princess Leigh and baby Ash were tucked into one of the full-size beds. Levi and I were relegated to sleeping bags at the foot of their mattress. The remaining bed was reserved for our parents. Once settled, Susan and John grabbed another beer, and moved to the concrete slab outside our room to enjoy the night air and relax absent their children.

On the morrow, we embarked on our next leg of the trek. There would be no more points of interest to interrupt our deployment, as we followed the most direct route to our new home. As we travelled, the scenery from South Dakota towards the East was uninspiring and the conditions of our transportation were uncomfortable. Any car with air conditioning was a luxury. Additionally, 1960s technology limited us to the static interrupted music reverberating from a small AM radio mounted in the center of the dashboard. A heat wave stifled the bad lands of the Midwestern plains. It was thought that relief would be provided by the rolled down windows of the car. Heading down the open road, the thermometer fixed at 102 degrees, air rushed into our faces as if opening an oven door while retrieving evening supper.

"I'm hot," complained Ash.

MILITARY BRAT   Pete Masalin

"Me too," whimpered our sister from her position near the tailgate.

"Drink some water," my mother said as she passed a thermos back for us all to share.

Quickly, we all guzzled the container bare. Lunchtime was soon upon us, and we welcomed a stop as we piled into a roadside diner. I ran to the door, opened it and felt the cool breeze from the air-conditioned cafe brush over my overheated skin. In response, my skin filled with goosebumps and encouraged me to dash inside leaving the kiln-like atmosphere of Sioux Falls.

"Hold the door for everyone, Finn," my father said.

"But..."

Dad interrupted me. "Hold it, mister."

His command did not offend me as I stood in the cool gust enjoying my relief. We were all a little aggravated by our long drive through unfavorable conditions. And Dad was no exception to our shared displeasure. The normally comfortable station wagon transformed into a communal sauna. The road grime mixed with our own sweat added to our stress.

The small diner was an escape for all of us. Once inside, tension subsided. "Six," my father told the hostess, and we followed in line as she led us to a table. Ice cold glasses of water immediately arrived as we sat down. Without a word, I hoisted the clear glass to my mouth, and drained it before the waitress could say hello.

"More, please," I said.

"Yes! More please!" Levi panted.

"Your children sure are thirsty," the waitress said to Mom.

"How could you tell?" my mom asked as they both laughed.

Enjoying the welcomed the hospitable environment, everyone shed the tension of our suffering, and returned to our normal selves. The torture of our half day expedition passed, and we quickly resumed our typical dispositions. I chewed off a corner of a paper napkin and curled it into a ball with my tongue. I discreetly pulled the straw from my glass, loaded a wad at the end in my mouth, and with a mighty blow, shot in the

MILITARY BRAT   Pete Masalin

direction of Ash as he sipped from his cup of water. Splat! My spitball cracked upon his forehead causing him to lose his grip. The glass, half full of water crashed down on the table alerting everyone in the eatery. Startled, my mother turned her attention to my little brother. "Ash!" she shouted embarrassed by the attention. Observing a pea-sized mass mashed above his left eyebrow she quickly assessed the situation.

"Finn! You will go sit in the car and wait for your food if you do that again," Mom declared.

I retired my weapon as the waitress brought us our menus. Allowing ample time for us to decide on a selection, the waitress returned to take our orders. Mom ordered for everyone - Grilled cheese sandwiches with chips for her children, fried chicken, green beans, mashed potatoes and a roll for Mom and Dad. As the waitress walked away, a clap sounded as another projectile crashed upon the earlobe of Leigh. At first, she was startled by the suddenness of the assault. Realizing the attack, Leigh began to cry. By now the entire diner was aware of the Makinen family, and all eyes were upon us. It was a masterful attack, stealthy as to the assailant.

"Finn!" my father roared.

I had no defense. My nature and reputation indicted me.

"You go sit in the car until your food comes," commanded Dad.

"But it wasn't me." I protested.

"Go."

I left the table and headed outside to the car. The hot air filled my lungs as I exited the diner. Looking back, I witnessed Ash smiling at his deception and his ruse against me. He had been the culprit and relished my punishment. He looked at me and waved while savoring his treachery. The youngest of us all was considered to be incapable of such behavior. My family was against me in this act, and any attempt to prove my innocence would be futile. As I sat in the car, waiting for my call to join the family in the comfort of the diner, I contemplated a new dynamic in our family hierarchy. Until this day, Ash was not a factor to be measured. From this day forward, any action I calculated would require awareness

MILITARY BRAT   Pete Masalin

for Ash. Previously, he was not a consideration in my planning, but in his assault of Leigh, he had revealed that in any of my future schemes, I would be required to assess Ash's position and potential threat to my planning. I had a new enemy within the ranks. If not an enemy, he was at least relevant.

Finally, Levi ran to the car instructing me to join everyone at the table. As I entered, all the patrons looked in my direction, following me as I moved to our seating. At first, I was uneasy, but I soon surmised that I would never see these people again. It was an awakening for me. I realized that I cared little of their opinion. The old adage of "What will people think?" moved me not. From this day, I determined that the opinion of others unknown was not important to me. In most situations, it served me well as I grew older. It is liberating to be oneself and not apply any pretense of something or someone you are not. People will like you for who you are, or they won't. There are enough who will.

Our lunch was leisurely, as we slowly enjoyed the food presented, talking and relaxing before returning to our taxing journey. It would be the highlight of the day. Finishing our meal, we pressed on. Reprieve would not come until our evening stop at another roadside inn. In the meantime, we travelled for many more hours, Levi, Ash, and I rotating positions in the back seat. Leigh held her esteemed position in the reclined status of the station wagon's rear space. By the time we finally did stop, we were completely depleted. The road had drained us. I was suffering from heat exhaustion and vomiting in the toilet. We made it as far as Des Moines, but as we travelled easterly, so did the heat wave. Mom quickly threw me in a tub drawn of cool water to reduce my core temperature. While my health was restored, the motel we occupied had no air conditioning. Levi and I slept on top of our sleeping bags, and the remainder of our family attempted to rest atop mattresses absent of blankets.

We raced across the country for the remainder of our trip, eager to rid ourselves of unsubstantial accommodations and roadside eateries. Finally, we arrived at our Virginia home. It was a glorious site. On Paddock Lane, our new home was built per my father's direction. While in Hawaii, given a new assignment, the Navy provided him with transitional visits to prepare for his new role. On these visits, Dad was able to recon for a new

MILITARY BRAT   Pete Masalin

home. He chose Reston, a planned community that would set the country's standard for other towns across the country. I remember him bringing pictures to Hawaii of a house being built; unearthed red clay covered the site while provisions were provided for construction. When we arrived, the house was complete. Four white scalloped columns stood at the face of the muted yellow house. The entry presented French doors centered against double windows with white shutters. Mom took a deep breath as we pulled into the driveway. Coming to a final stop, we all poured out of the car and ran to the house. It was twice the size of our Hawaiian home and the expansive back yard with open fields beyond seemed endless. My mother and father held each other as the Makinen children ran through and about the house satisfied by the mansion provided for the family. Air conditioning filled the home with cool fresh air, as we camped in the house that evening, awaiting the arrival of our household effects. In the morning, we were awakened by the sound of a moving van arriving in front of our new home. We were now Virginians, and a new offering of adventures awaited me.

Chapter 7
Wild Horses and Stall Surfing

Our new home was spacious. The yard was at least three times the dimensions of the yard we left in Hawaii. So large was our house that it required one floor to be stacked upon the other. A two-story home, we had stairs! Previously, we always lived in simply designed, single story ranch homes. Our voices echoed throughout the residence as we called to each other while movers placed our belongings in rooms as directed by my mother. Still, the home required that two siblings to share a bedroom. The bunk bed that had belonged to Levi and me was assembled in the lone downstairs bedroom for us to occupy. Levi would maintain his holding of the bottom bunk, and I would ascend the attached ladder each night.

Within a year, birthing accommodations would alter according to Levi's advanced age. In 1970, Levi turned twelve; a pre-teen entering junior high school suddenly became too old to share a room with an immature grade schooler such as myself. The bunk bed was relocated to Ash's room, and Levi held the prestigious downstairs room for his own. The only advantage I perceived in the new order was that I would claim the bottom bed. No more would I climb rungs to sleep. In short order, I would surrender my status for the loft above me, as Ash met with tragedy one evening. While climbing to his perch, Ash fell to the ground and lacerated his forehead immediately above his right brow. Dad delivered him to the emergency room. Ash, stitched shut by a handful of sutures, caused a birthing realignment. I was relegated to the upper bunk. My parents thought that Ashton was too young to navigate the ladder to the upper bed. The irony was that I was too young to room with Levi, but I was too old to hold the esteemed position of the lower rack as long as Ash was my bunkmate.

Being closest in age, Levi and I still palled around in our free time. A common attraction was a horse stable across the pipeline immediately behind our home. Initially, we approached the paddocks with caution, as we had never seen horses except in western movies and TV series. They were magnificent and surprisingly docile creatures. The staff often let us feed and help groom them, allowing Levi and I to became comfortable around such noble beasts. All except for one.

MILITARY BRAT   Pete Masalin

    Pinky was an albino Shetland pony, who we both recognized as an evil equine possessed by demons. He was pure white, whose opaque, pink eyes bulged from sockets as the animal stared menacingly in our direction. His demeanor was as nasty as a cornered rat. At first, we tried to make friends with the miniature stallion; however, our overtures were met with snorts and raised hoofs. Persistent, we offered strands of straw, thinking they would be sufficient enough to win his affection. We were wrong.

    While attempting to encourage Pinky to the rail, Levi leaned over with a handful of fresh mown hay. Alerted, the midget horse immediately galloped towards Levi's outstretched hand, bypassed the gift, and bit his forearm. He pulled back to reveal impressions of Pinky's upper and lower teeth. No blood had been drawn, but a private war between Levi and his new nemesis had been declared. We decided that Pinky could never be tamed and only partially avoided passing his stall. Along our route to the stable, Levi made it a point to pass Pinky's paddock and spit in his direction. On rare occasions, Levi would pick up a small stone and pelt the Shetland, causing a great commotion within his stall. It gave Levi great satisfaction as he exacted his revenge. My laughter and approval only encouraged him more. As far as I was concerned, a horse that no one could ride was folly. Add that he was unfriendly and unapproachable, I never understood his purpose.

    Another attraction we enjoyed on our visits was the few stable dogs that resided and roamed the paddocks and pastures behind our home. Neither Levi nor I cared much for the feral cats that likewise wandered the grounds in search of mice and rats. Our reasoning was sound. As we approached, the dogs would eagerly run towards us with their tails wagging joyfully for our attention. We loved being with the dogs and wished one for our family. The cats – well, they just ignored us and went about their business. Still, I saw the benefit of felines on watch. The stable was clear of rodents. I understood their purpose as hunters and exterminators.

    While Levi shared my indifference for cats, we had a memorable time on one visit when we happened upon a litter of kittens in the barn. They were cute and their mother allowed us to hold them whenever we

MILITARY BRAT   Pete Masalin

visited. While visiting the kittens one day, we met a boy who, like us, had an interest in the litter. We quickly learned his intentions were the opposite of ours. One day we arrived to witness him choking a small grey striped tabby with his hands. Levi approached first, and I heard him shout, "Stop it!" He then pushed the boy which caused him to drop the cat. The boy ran to his mother who worked at the stable and returned with her immediately.

"What is the meaning of this? Why did you push my son?" she demanded of us.

"He was choking the kittens," Levi replied.

"I saw it too," I offered in support.

"Were you squeezing those kittens?" she asked of her son.

"No. I was just pettin' 'em, Momma."

"My son would never hurt those cute little kittens. You boys say you're sorry, and maybe you should just go home for today."

Our parents had raised us to respect the authority of adults, and we did not offer a rebuttal. We retreated towards the direction of our home although we did not apologize. I turned and looked back towards the boy and his mother. With her back turned, she was looking away from us, but her son, watching our departure, lifted his hand and flipped us off. Levi and I looked at each other, incredulous of his gesture. He was not a good boy. To the contrary, he was bad and possessed an evil streak we would discover on our next visit to the litter of kittens.

We came to find all the kittens dead. The mother kitten tried to no avail in resurrecting her offspring. They had been poisoned. Shocked by the sight, we wondered how this could have happened. Our answer was soon revealed. In talking with the stable hand's son who we previously found strangling the tiny mousers, he admitted to killing them with saddle soap. He was not remorseful and somewhat amused by his deed. Saddened by their death, Levi and I were moved to action and devised an immediate plan of retribution.

Our motives hidden, Levi and I encouraged him to join us as we explored and played in empty stalls. One stall had yet to be cleaned.

It was here that we exacted revenge. In the center of the stall was a rather large pool of standing water, rotted cedar mulch, horse urine and droppings. Having just moved from Hawaii, we convinced him of our accomplished surfing skills and our ability to teach him the same. On the ground, next to the stall gate, Levi spotted a large sponge used to clean stable equipment.

"This is perfect!" Levi shouted.

"Yeah, it's just like the one I used," I said.

"What? What do you mean?" the boy asked us.

"I learned to surf on a sponge just like this one," I explained.

"Really?" he wondered.

"Yes. Finn, why don't you put the sponge on the edge of the water so he can jump on it and surf to the other side."

I did as Levi instructed and directed the cat killer to step outside of the stall. "You'll need some room to run so that you have enough speed to surf across the puddle," I directed.

"This is going to be cool," he said, readying himself for his attempt.

Levi gave the final direction, "Run as fast as you can and jump on the sponge at the last second." With the boy in place, Levi counted down, "3, 2, 1 GO!"

He took off with determination on his face, raced to the stagnant, rancid water and leapt upon the sponge. Immediately, the sponge submerged. The boy's weight drove it to the muddy bottom while his momentum carried him forward. He was launched into the middle of the stable pond and crashed face first, murky, putrid water sopping his face. The splash swallowed him, covering his entire body. Levi and I didn't even wait for him to stand knowing that he would run to his mother. We ran home laughing all the way satisfied by our cunning and satisfied that justice had been served.

We finally tired of stable visits and confrontation with Pinky when a new arrival joined our household. Our neighbors, the Schmidts, had a dog that was soon to give birth to seven mutts. We begged our parents for

MILITARY BRAT   Pete Masalin

one of the puppies. We never had a dog before, and we were relentless in our pleas. Our parents were resistant at first, but finally acquiesced upon the arrival of the new pups. As neighbors, we were afforded preferential selection of the litter. We chose Cocoa, a predominately chocolate colored pup with highlighted tan eyebrows and lower legs. Another neighbor, the McMullins chose a sandy colored mutt with black markings and named him Pookie. As they grew, we enjoyed bringing Pookie and Cocoa together so that the canine brothers could stay connected.

Summer soon ended and school began. Hunters Woods Elementary School was at the end of our street and all the kids would assemble, forming a small platoon as we walked to school. Those furthest away would start off and would meet with others as we marched to school. We were more than two dozen strong by the time we reached the doors of our elementary institution. On the way home, we reversed the process and individual children peeled off as they reached their home.

On one such occasion, Gavin McMillan, whose home was first on our return route, ran to meet Pookie. We hadn't taken ten steps before we heard Gavin's anguished cry. Halted by his torment, we stopped, looked at each other and ran to the back of the McMillan home. Both McMillan parents worked, requiring that Pookie remain secured outside his home, his neck leashed by a rope on the back deck. Gavin couldn't wait to release his dog and play with him in the back yard. We thought perhaps that Pookie had freed himself and run off. What we discovered was far more unsettling. Gavin stood trembling as he sobbed looking upon his most revered friend. Pookie was still attached to his tether, but it was neither short enough nor long enough at the same time. Before us, we looked upon a stiff, half-grown pet, whose tiny hind paws barely reached the earth. It was obvious that he had struggled to maintain his breath, ultimately surrendering to fatigue, and strangling himself.

"Pookie!" Gavin cried out, desperately attempting to revive his friend.

There would be no response as Gavin released the dog's stiff body from its noose. We tried to help, not knowing what to do or how to console him. None of us had experienced such trauma before us.

"Get away. Go!" Gavin continued, as tears streamed from his eyes.

MILITARY BRAT　　　　　　　　　　　　　　　　　　　　Pete Masalin

He was considered a tough kid among our gang. Not quite a bully, but one who was always viewed as hardened, one who was not to be pressed. He did not appreciate our attention as it revealed a weakness in him. The girls of the neighborhood cried.

    I was unsure of how to react. My friend was suffering, and I had no idea how to console him. Mary Peterson ran home and collected her mother. Upon arriving, Mrs. Peterson hugged Gavin, and escorted him to her house where she called Mrs. McMillan to share the tragic news. Gavin did not join us on our walk to school for the next two days. The next few days, I remember being especially attentive and thankful for our dog Cocoa. He was part of our family, and we were all more appreciative of his presence.

    Soon, any thoughts of Pookie passed, and we continued our life of lightheartedness. At this time of my youth, there was much tension and conflict in the world, yet, for the army of children living on Paddock Lane, we were insulated from the strife of global events. Our country's involvement in Viet Nam was at its height; nevertheless, I don't recall any impact of the world's disharmony upon our daily life. We all were allowed to venture to our surroundings with the understanding that life's challenges ended at the limit of the neighborhood. We pretended to be engaged in great battles ourselves, throwing acorns and dirt clods towards equally divided armies at construction sites of new homes on our street. I had a pump air rifle that was intended to only emit an explosive sound when the trigger was pulled. I discovered that I could jam the muzzle into the ground filling the barrel with a compacted plug of earth. When fired, it was an effective weapon against my enemy.

    "Finn," Ted Peterson complained as I drilled him in the shoulder while he attacked with acorns. "That's not fair."

    It wasn't soon before the weapon suppliers of our armies recognized the imbalance and provided their offspring with air guns, ensuring parity on the battlefield. Détente was not beneficial to the harmony of our neighborhood. What would the children do if they did not have daily faux battles to occupy their time? These were days long before video games relegated the youth to soft drink and frozen pizza laden tables, controlling

MILITARY BRAT　　　　　　　　　　　　　　　　　Pete Masalin

young minds to plant their bodies in front of conscious consuming arenas inside their homes.

Our entertainment and our parents' leisure required that we engage each other between the school's final bell and family time at the dinner table. Amid skirmishes, we ate potato chips and drank Kool Aid provided by our mothers, ensuring sustainment as we battled. Somehow, we remained thin. The energy we exerted in our afternoons offset the caloric intake of fatty treats and sugary drinks.

To our parents' credit, we were never weighted down by the turmoil of the world. We never watched the news or listened to their conversations when they were certain to discuss adult matters. Our concerns were of greater merit; catching box turtles and hog nose snakes in the woods, exploring the endless pipeline behind our homes, construction site battles, kick the can at dusk, and occasionally throwing projectiles at Pinky.

Sundays were days routinely filled with television. At this time, families rarely possessed more than one TV. There were three major networks and a smattering of alternative local stations carried on Ultra High Frequency, UHF. UHF stations generally required a combination of tentative antenna manipulation and strategically placed aluminum foil. Black and White programs were a mainstay. I enjoyed the old Abbott and Costello movies and Creature Feature, showcasing The Wolfman, Dracula, and Frankenstein. However, on Sundays, after church, Leigh would monopolize the TV to watch Shirley Temple while mom made final preparations for our family dinner. There was no fair adjudication of this. None of her brothers' voices resonated in their protest. The road trip princess prevailed by executive decree. While we awaited supper, Levi, Ash, and I were relegated to watching Shirley Temple sing "Animal Crackers in My Soup."

All was amended by evening when the family broke from the dining room table, gathered in the rec room, ate homemade pizzas made on a base of English muffins, and viewed two important shows: Mutual of Omaha's Wild Kingdom followed by The Wonderful World of Disney. In some measure, all of America replicated this routine. In many ways, it was a simpler time, absent of today's distractions that facilitate segregation

MILITARY BRAT   Pete Masalin

of the family bond and destroy its unity; family gatherings mattered. Sunday was a day dedicated to family cohesion while the balance of the week presented times for the mass of neighborhood children to assemble in foolishness.

At each free moment, we all gathered to establish joint missions and every day the ventures were different. In the winter, we erected snowmen in each other's front yards. New homes continued to be built in the neighborhood; and as soon as the crews left, we raided the homes and pilfered scrap wood to build tree forts in our back yards. Each evening, supper time was the limiting consideration of our daily operations. It was expected that when mothers hailed their children for dinner, they would find the most direct route home.

There was no mistaking my mother's beckoning for the Makinen children. She purchased a cow bell as her signal for assembly. Once sounded, we had exactly five minutes to all be present, ready for our family dinner. We were not offered any variance; five minutes was all we were afforded – no excuses. Any delay was met with penalty. Punishment varied from denial of desert to the ever-feared wooden spoon. The severity depended upon our procrastination.

The wooden spoon was not the only instrument of correction, but its usefulness as a disciplinary measure was unmatched. We feared Mom's skillful wielding of it as punishment. It was a welcome sight when given to us as reward covered with cake or brownie batter. Presented to us dry, we knew we were in trouble. Its sting met our butts when receiving sentence for misdeeds. Levi was the last to incur this method of correction. The nature of his violation escapes me, but I remember the day he was taken to task for a serious breach. Mom took him to his room and began to whack his backside. It wasn't more than three paddles that the spoon broke upon his seat. I am certain that the force was not excessive, but rather the spoon had become stressed from a combination of cooking and discipline. Startled, my mother withdrew, and Levi's session ended. I don't remember any of us ever being spanked by a wooden spoon again, but the knowledge of its existence was ever present.

Chapter 8

Snapper Blues

My father's frequent changes of duty stations required by the Navy fostered a somewhat nomadic life for his children. We didn't just move. We transitioned to new cultures. New England was vastly different from Hawaii, and Virginia was foreign to both. Although each place was American, the dialects, traditions, and foods were foreign to each other. We had clam bakes in New England, Luau's in Hawaii, and Country Fairs in Virginia. Poi was replaced by grits. "Hey, brotha" became "Hi, y'all." Strangely it was an easy transition, and the experience allowed all of us to develop skills of adaptability.

Emphasizing this truth was our reuniting with our New England cousins. Their dialects were strange after years apart from them. The letter "R" was not often included in their conversations. We didn't play in the yard; it was a *yahd*. Their preferred mode of transportation was a *cah*. And when they were excited about something, it was *wicked pissah*. Our cousins in Maine were equally challenged. Upon our arrival for visits we would say, "It's great to see you." and they would respond with, "Eh, *yah*, so glad *youh heyah*."

Nevertheless, these were welcomed excursions north as we reconnected with my parents' history and our heritage. Dad traded his Impala station wagon for the latest Chevy model which included the welcomed luxury of air conditioning. Travel was no longer uncomfortable as we rode for hours along I-95. AM radio was replaced with FM. To be sure, there were times when the close proximity to siblings incited conflict; but for the most part, our travel was content. Still, her majesty, Princess Leigh held her tail gunner post along the way. We passed the time as we travelled, eating snacks Mom had so carefully planned. Our stops were only for fuel and relief. All of us were eager to meet with our relatives.

Over the course of the next several years, each summer's deployment was the same. Dad would take two weeks leave and we would head north. Our first stop was South Dartmouth to visit with the Whites. Ingrid White was my mother's sister who had married Theodore, a descendant of Peregrine White, son of Susanna White, born on the Mayflower as it anchored off Cape Cod. They were New Englanders of true historic

MILITARY BRAT   Pete Masalin

lineage. Their children, Chase, Rachel, and Anson were closely aligned with us in age, and we greatly enjoyed our times together. My mother's brother, Johan, would bring his family, wife Dorothy, son Donald, and daughter Macy from Duxbury to join us in great family reunions, providing us with long standing memories of mischief and adventure.

The parents would gather together with little concern for our welfare. South Dartmouth was a safe town, and we were granted liberty to wander the village freely. And wander we did. Prior to our arrival, Uncle Theodore would borrow many of his neighbors' bikes to ensure we had sufficient transport for our daily excursions. It mattered little where we went as long as we had a method of movement. Each day we would mount our bicycles and advance upon the small waterfront village with little concern for the inhabitants. Long before the cyclists typical of today arrogantly stall traffic patterns of hurried motorists, we, on our bikes, covered many roads as we leisurely travelled. Horns would blare, and we ignored them all.

"I know who you *ah*, Chase!" a frustrated driver yelled to the oldest of the White children. "I'm telling your *fahtah* what a jerk you kids *ah*."

Levi and I just smiled and waved at the concerned citizen, understanding that we didn't live in the town and felt immune to his rebuke. We were right. Still, Chase and his little brother, Anson, were concerned. "We *ah* in wicked trouble," Anson said.

"Anson, they're not going to do anything," Levi consoled. "Let's just go fish."

"Yeah, I don't live here," Donald added. And we summarily continued towards Padanaram Bridge.

Uncle Theodore's family owned a general store, The Packet, located in the village's center for a couple of generations. From The Packet, situated next to the shore, we could see people already positioned with their poles along the bridge's rail. We hurriedly parked our bikes and gathered important provisions from our uncle before joining other anglers. We arrived with all tackle necessary for fishing, but we lacked one important mainstay: rock candy. Uncle Theodore would reach into an open wooden barrel and hand each of us a stick, weighted down with

MILITARY BRAT Pete Masalin

a mass of crystalized sugar covering the top three fourths of a tiny pole allowing for an extended wooden tip to serve as the treat's handle. We all ran from the store to the middle of the bridge, causing a commotion and alarming the other fisherman with our arrival.

Immature Bluefish also known as Snapper Blues, schooled in the swift currents flowing beneath the bridge as they chased small baitfish. The water boiled beneath us as we cast our spinners into the bay. Within short order, our small cooler was filled with pan-sized fish to bring home to grill. Always hopeful, Levi, Donald, and Chase were serious fisherman. They continued to fish with determination that a record breaking lunker would soon bend their rod. Anson and Ash became bored, sat next to the cooler, poked our catch with their fingers, and threw dead fish at each other while complaining about wanting to go home. I found another source of amusement.

The day was hot, and the refreshing New England sea beckoned my relief. As Anson and Ash played with dead fish and the others fished, I took off my shirt and shoes. On impulse, I jumped the rail and did a cannonball into the midst of the schooling fish below. The water opened to receive me, and I was quickly immersed, followed by a towering splash. As I sank, the cool water surrounded me with refreshment. But arriving to the surface, I was met with displeasure.

"Finn! Get out of the water!" Levi demanded.

"Hey asshole! What the hell do you think you're doing? We're fishing here," an angry fisherman yelled. "You are not allowed to swim from the bridge."

"I'm not swimming; I fell," I replied.

"Yeah sure. Get your ass out of the water," commanded another.

"Get out, Finn!" added Chase. "We *ah* gonna get it."

Slowly, I made my way back to the bridge. As soon as I rejoined my cousins and brothers, we were sternly encouraged to leave by our competing anglers. I was ready to go anyway; Anson and Ash agreed. The others were disappointed by our early departure but satisfied with the size of our catch to bring home, and so we set off.

MILITARY BRAT   Pete Masalin

When we did make it home, Chase began to retell the story of how I ruined the trip by swimming. I insisted that I fell. Chase's protests fell on deaf ears. Fortunately for me, his concerns didn't matter to the adults. We were all home safely, and there was a more important matter to deal with.

"Quiet down, Chase! The Sox are on," Uncle Theodore admonished.

The Red Sox were playing, and everyone was involved in the game, watching it in the family room. It was the seventh inning with the Sox down by one. All attention was focused on the TV. Once again, circumstances had saved me from a proper and just rebuke. No matter, the Red Sox rallied to win in the bottom of the ninth and my fall from the bridge was never discussed again.

The grill was lit, the children played in the yard, and a pile of Narragansett Beer cans continued to grow in the kitchen trashcan as the parents relived the Sox game. Grilled hotdogs, Snapper Blues, corn on the cob and coleslaw filled our bellies that evening.

At least one night each summer, we went to Lincoln Park, an amusement attraction close to the White's house. We ran wild, racing from ride to ride. The park boasted of having the oldest wooden rollercoaster in the country, and to ride it you would know it to be true based on the sounds of wood rubbing upon wood as the cars traveled the course. At any moment, I thought I would fly off the rails to my certain death, but I found this to be the very draw that excited me.

Little did I know that the most danger came from a caged Ferris wheel. It wasn't the ride. It was the occupant on this particular evening. I found a porcelain piggy bank that someone had won at a carnival event and left it unattended. I carried it with me into a caged seat with Levi. As the Ferris wheel rotated, the individual cages would spin causing us to be inverted during the ride. In all my brilliance, I discovered that the cage was just wide enough for my ceramic prize to squeeze through the gap. At the apex of the ride and hanging upside down I let it go. I watched, at first with delight, as it sailed through the night sky only to be horrified as it slammed at the feet of a man as he waited in line. I never knew the result of the impact – and I had no desire for discovery or inquisition. When the

MILITARY BRAT   Pete Masalin

ride ended, Levi and I quickly exited.

As we walked through the park, Levi asked, "What happened to your piggy bank?"

I replied, "Oh no! I must have left it on the ride."

"That's too bad, Finn. Do you want to go back and look for it?"

"Nah. It's OK. I didn't like it anyway."

While it often seemed that I ran wild, and I mostly did, there were moments when the character of my parents' imprint upon me was revealed. The Whites lived midway on George Street, between Russells Mills Road and Elm Street. Traveling to and from my cousins' house, we often passed an older man sitting in front of his home, on the corner of George Street and Russells Mills Road, shaking uncontrollably as he sat in a chair watching traffic.

One day, I walked up the street and timidly approached him. I introduced myself, and he, likewise, welcomed me to his yard. Bill had been a lineman and was suffering from Parkinson's disease. He lived alone with his wife. He had three boys who had long ago moved away and whom he hadn't seen in years. He shared stories of the town he loved and his years repairing and installing phone lines. I met his wife only briefly, and she left us alone to visit. I remember feeling good in sharing time with Bill. I didn't pity him. I genuinely enjoyed hearing his stories. I would return to the White's house and share what I had learned with everyone.

My time with Bill taught me how we can all learn something from everyone if we will only listen. The following summer, we all returned to visit the Whites at their George Street home and I noticed an absence. Bill no longer watched traffic from his doorstep. He had passed away. My visits with him were a defining moment in my development as a child, for it is not only family that contributes to who we are, but also the value we place on people we meet in our lives.

Following our visit to Massachusetts, we would venture to Camden, Maine, to visit my father's sister Sarah and her family Uncle Seth Parson, and cousins Aaron and Tom. Camden was a sleepy coastal town, born of

MILITARY BRAT   Pete Masalin

fishermen and the textile industry. The residents were representative of most Americans of the day. It was "Mayberry" in a way. The postal carrier walked door to door delivering mail while carrying butterscotch Lifesavers and distributing them to cheerful children he encountered along his route. Weekday deliveries of bottled milk and orange juice arrived each morning to the back doorsteps of cedar shake sided homes. The Parson's home was modest but welcoming. Our arrival required creative sleeping accommodations. My cousins would surrender their room and twin beds for my parents; Leigh and Ash took to the floor on bedrolls. Aaron and Tom would sleep on the floor of their parents' room, while Levi and I would roll out our sleeping bags and slumber in the mudroom of the side entrance to the home.

Camden didn't offer the excitement of our visits to South Dartmouth. Sarah was very protective of her two boys and limited their ability to join Levi and me on daily recon patrols of the surrounding area. The Parsons lived on Gould Street which sloped modestly from Mount Battie to the Megunticook River. One day, I walked down to the tiny convenience store nestled on the river's bluff at the end of Gould Street. Drawn by thirst, a drink unknown to me, prominently displayed in the cooler, became the focus of my attention. Dad had convinced me that Moxie was the best soft drink of all time. He drank it in his youth; and reflecting on it now, I realize why it never gained popularity across the country. It was a beverage that puckered even the sweetest of lips. Caramel in color, one would think that they were about to sample the king of colas; however, upon its first meeting with my tongue, an overpowering influx of licorice, ginger and alum overwhelmed my taste buds. Still, I was drawn to it, if for no other reason because Dad drank it, and I wanted to be like him. I grabbed my Moxie, paid for it at the register, and headed to the shore of the Megunticook River, planning to cool my feet in its flow.

The river was not wide and was more akin to a stream, racing a short distance from its source of Lake Megunticook, then exiting the land over a cascading waterfall in the heart of Camden and into the sea. There was a crisp crackle of water as it splashed around and over dark boulders. Aquatic plants danced in the translucent crystal, clear currents among a rocky stream bed. Sipping my Moxie upon the shore, I was hypnotized by

MILITARY BRAT   Pete Masalin

my surroundings and my solitude as I consumed it all. I was alerted from my peaceful trance by a disturbance under the Washington Street Bridge. My curiosity heightened, I moved to inspect it more closely. As quickly as my legs would carry me, I ran to Aunt Sarah's house.

"Levi!" I yelled.

"What?"

"C'mon. There's fish in the stream!"

Uncle Seth laughed. "Finn, there aren't any fish in the *rivah*. That tannery killed them all."

"Uncle Seth, I saw them. They're there."

Only Levi was stirred. He jumped from the couch and joined me as we ran through the mud room back towards the river. We hustled to the spot under the bridge where I witnessed fish enjoy the sunlit current of the cool waters lapping boulders in its path. Returning to my Moxie can, I raised it and finished its contents.

"Finn! Look at that. Fish!" Levi excitedly yelled.

"No shit, Sherlock." I didn't understand the term, but knew it was used to expose the obvious. "That's what I was telling everybody. Nobody believed me."

We ran back to the Parson home, grabbed fishing poles, and a lifelong secret fishing hole was born. Each summer, Levi and I fished the Megunticook River. We would land fish; Rainbow Trout, Brook Trout and Smallmouth Bass, carefully carry them to the Megunticook Store, weigh them in the vegetable scale, and release them. None of the locals believed us. One day Levi caught a Smallmouth measuring 24 inches and 6 ½ pounds in a narrow, slow-moving pool. It was so large that he was mocked in the small general store.

"Where d'you boys catch that?" one shopper asked.

"Right there," Levi responded, pointing to the river.

"No, you didn't. That tannery killed everything in that *rivah*."

"Mister, he caught it right back there," I insisted.

"No, he didn't." The man then walked away.

We didn't know what to say. We didn't care. We fished a stream of such abundance that we never left disappointed. From the dam of Lake Megunticook, we followed the flow of the river as it progressed past shoreline scenery of mobile home parks, retired mills, a tannery accused of killing all life, and the darkness in a tunnel beneath the traffic of Main Street Camden until we stood at the falls of fresh water crashing into to the seawater of Camden Harbor. Along the way, we caught fish the locals never realized were before them. They never believed us.

One day we were under the town of Camden, wading through the shallow rapids that wandered below Elm Street. Levi and I stepped carefully in the darkness so as not to stumble and crash into the water causing our intended catch to scatter. As we entered the tunnel, some of the natives must have witnessed us disappear into the shadows. There was one store, The Smiling Cow, which maintained a hinged panel in the floor accessing the river. I never knew why it was there, but as a child, I remember discovering the secret hatch under a floor rug. I opened it each time I visited. "Shut that door!" was always directed my way every time I visited. On this occasion, I was on the opposite side of the portal. In front of us, a crack of light appeared, followed by a slow opening of The Smiling Cow's river entrance. A head appeared. "What *ah* you kids doin' down there?" echoed a stranger's inquiry.

"We're fishing," I replied.

"There ain't no fish in that *watah*. The tannery killed 'em all," said the man.

How many times were we going to hear the same proclamation? It was a common belief.

"We know," responded Levi.

"You boys be careful." The man then closed the door.

It wasn't two minutes later that Levi hooked a fish bending his pole to its limit.

"I got one! I got one!"

MILITARY BRAT   Pete Masalin

I stopped in my tracks, watching Levi fight for his catch. In the dimly lit cavern, I was able to see small flashes of color of the fish's side as it fought for freedom. Levi's battle lasted at least five minutes. Quite lengthy considering our close quarters of battle. Finally, exhausted from the fight, the fish relinquished his effort, and Levi, smiling broadly, lifted it by its gills to show off his trophy – a beautiful 5-pound Rainbow Trout. As far as the locals were concerned, there were no fish in the Megunticook River, and the two Makinen brothers agreed not to change their mind. Levi placed his prize in his creel, and we headed to the Parson home. That night, Aunt Sarah cooked us all fresh fish from a river that at least one native, Uncle Seth, now believed had fish.

Summers with my cousins were always fun, but most importantly they were memorable and demonstrated the great love and importance of family. Our times together rarely required much in terms of money. In fact, money was the least contributing factor to our amusement and affection. We had each other and that was enough. I hate baseball; however, I still follow the Red Sox. Lobster, blueberry pie and *Fiskeboller* - a Norwegian fish meatball in a cream sauce - all bring back favorable childhood memories with my cousins. Even today, I return to fish the same "honey holes" and secret streams of my youth with my brother Levi and cousin, Donald.

Chapter 9
Monkey Business

Our time on Paddock Lane was brief by typical standards. We lived in the neighborhood for only two years before we were on the move again. It wasn't the Navy that caused our displacement, but the allure of a new waterfront home. I wasn't sure what to expect of the last summer in our stately columned home. We were leaving a community pool, not more than a three-minute bike ride from my house. I would enter a new school and leave my friends. Nonetheless, excitement was never far from my side.

Two weeks before our move across town to Lake Anne, a neighbor's pet monkey escaped its enclosure. Everyone knew Spanky, a spider monkey owned by Mr. Toth. As was typical, all the children were outside running wild from yard to yard. Phil Peterson ran to the group from his house screaming, "There's a monkey on my porch! There's a monkey on my porch!"

"Really?" one in the group questioned.

"Yes. I swear," Phil responded.

We all ran to his house and enveloped his back yard. Startled, Spanky jumped from the rail to the ground and our small squad pursued him on foot. It was a valiant effort, but the simian was too agile and quick to be captured. Our chase lasted at least 20 minutes as the monkey fled. He would pause atop a small dogwood, and we would shake it until the terrified creature leapt to a fast escape. Finally, he climbed atop a tall oak tree where he rested to catch his breath. Safely separated from our grasp, he looked down upon us. His breathing was quickened, and fear was in his eyes. From below, we yelled and threw stones in his direction, but he was much too high for us to reach.

By now, the commotion had stirred many of the mothers who stayed at home with their children. One mother, I know not who, called the dog catcher to arms. We knew the monkey to be Mr. Toth's pet and pointed the animal control officer to his house; however, Mr. Toth was not at home. We observed as the officer left Mr. Toth's front door, arrived at his vehicle, and pulled out a rifle. He loaded the chamber with a dart and moved to a position below the tree with a clear view of Spanky.

MILITARY BRAT   Pete Masalin

We all stood in silence. Bang! The rifle fired, and I watched Spanky jerk upward as the projectile hit its mark. The furry primate screamed at first, pulled upon the impalement to no avail, and began to wobble. Within seconds, it lost its footing and tumbled to the ground. As he plummeted, he grabbed a small branch which quickly broke off, remaining clenched in his fist as he hit the ground. Some of the girls cried at the sight. We watched as Spanky's limp body was stuffed into a black cloth bag, placed in the trunk of the animal control vehicle, and driven off. Standing at the location where the animal landed, looking solemnly at the blood-stained branch it had carried to earth, I felt responsible for the creature's misfortune because of our chase and the ultimate outcome. Sadly, I never knew what became of Spanky as we moved soon after that day.

The benefit of moving frequently was that we Makinen children easily made new friends and this move was no different. Our orders in hand, it seemed just as quickly as we deployed, we assimilated into new neighborhoods. There was no sense of loss of friends left on Paddock Lane as we joined a new legion of youth residing in the Moorings Cluster subdivision. Levi, as one of the oldest among us, assumed a leadership role. I, in the middle bracket, remained free of responsibility, but a valued member among the new platoon.

Our new home on Waters Edge Lane provided us with unfamiliar accommodation, a townhouse. No longer did we have a large yard. In fact, there was very little yard at all. We only had a backyard and no side or front lawn. What we did have, and I came to enjoy it immensely, was a lake.

It was appropriate that I was born an Aquarius. Even before I could swim, I was drawn to the hypnotic force of water. Its power has never left my desire. I want to be near it, smell it, and immerse myself in it. Years later when my wife was near death, I would visit the ocean water of Sullivans Island, South Carolina, and swim past the breakers and allow my tears to mix with the seawater. Water comforts me, and it was in my youth that I discovered its importance and my dependence on it. I thank my parents for showing me this gift and ensuring that it was always nearby. They were the children of fishermen, drawn to the sea, and they ensured that their heritage was within me as well.

MILITARY BRAT   Pete Masalin

From my birth until I left home for college, I would reside in seven different homes. Six of those years, longer than any other of my previous residences, the house on Waters Edge saw the greatest evolution in me. It served as my incubator as I transitioned from grade school juvenile to high school teenager. I learned many valuable lessons through the years near the waters of Lake Anne. Many who witnessed me develop would argue that I lost a healthy respect for fear and common sense, but in truth, it was in these years that I grew in my confidence as a risk taker and adrenaline junkie.

I had a full summer before the commencement of fifth grade to meet and integrate with my new comrades. Most were green in their experiences, trapped by overprotective parents and the security of familiar surroundings, having rarely travelled outside a 200-mile radius. Their caution and timidity thrust Levi and me into the role of coach, teacher, motivator, and Field Marshall. As *Old Salts*, Levi and I were able to stir our friends into actions that served them well in their personal growth. I am certain their parents had a different view, but they never witnessed and, even today, are probably unaware of the many achievements we enjoyed in the years we patrolled the neighborhood.

The first summer saw the erection of a basketball hoop along Waters Edge Lane, in the central part of the subdivision. Many in the homeowner's association objected, but a majority vote ruled, and it remained in place. We painted a half-court configuration on the pavement and, again some protested, but it was too late. The court, centrally located to our homes, served as an assembly area for our unit. We played pick-up games and HORSE; however, the court served primarily as command post where plans were hatched, and orders dispensed. Our parents only saw the basketball venue. Never could they have realized that it was the command center of all our activity.

Although allergic to bees, I would lead assaults on reinforced yellow jacket hives nestled in ten-foot-high retaining walls along the lane. The walls buttressed the neighborhood streets as the terrain fell from the community entrance towards the lake. While on patrol, as the sun faded, we noticed a line of hornets returning to their fortress. Seeking to rid our homes of danger, we began preparing for an assault. Of course, we

MILITARY BRAT   Pete Masalin

could have informed our parents of the nuisance, but that would have sabotaged our planning. In the twilight of that evening, we met at the CP, calculated the attack, and dispersed until morning.

Smoke bombs were easily available, and we all had them. The most common ones were colored spheres, 1 ½" in diameter with a single fuse at the top. Red, blue, yellow, green, purple; our envelopment of the Yellow Jackets would be a glorious display. The time of attack was planned to ensure that adults going to work that day would be absent from the area as we assaulted minimizing the likelihood of intervention.

"Finn, I got green and blue," said Pat Swinson, holding up his munitions.

"I got red," yelled his little brother Tim as he approached.

We all met at the CP, inspected our collective weaponry, and moved into position. Levi started the siege by placing two smoke bombs at the primary entrance of the hornet's citadel. Once lit, billowing smoke engulfed the scene. Still, more munitions were directed, placed tactically into position, and ignited. By now we had stirred the entire colony, and they acted to protect their home. We were a safe distance away when a confused swarm, slowed by the smoke, deployed countermeasures.

"Cover me!" I yelled as I approached the hive.

"Finn, what is that?" asked Pat.

"It's a secret weapon," I replied.

As the smoke waned, I advanced with a can of WD-40 and a lighter. I raised the can and placed the lighter in front of the nozzle. Simultaneously depressing the can's actuator and flicking the lighter, the aerosol contents burst into flames, providing me with a flame thrower to overtake the onslaught. Moving forward, the heat cleared my path of bees. What happened next was unexpected and dangerous. I had not fully considered my choice of weaponry and its potential for collateral damage. Built of creosol railway ties, the retaining wall ignited as the flames of my handheld torch reached the wall. The remnant-colored smoke from our smoke bombs was overwhelmed by a thick, black toxic cloud. We backed off, stunned by the enormity of the fire.

"Oh my gosh! What have you kids done?" screamed Mrs. DeSoto as

MILITARY BRAT   Pete Masalin

she emerged from her house, alarmed by the thick black cloud.

We all scattered, along with her tomboy daughter Millie, an accompanying soldier in the wasp attack. As we fled, Mrs. DeSoto demanded we stop. We did not. Securing an observation post on high ground, we watched as the blaze slowly died. Relieved, we slowly descended the hill towards Millie's mom. She was furious, and it was to our benefit that Millie was with us. Seeing her daughter within our ranks, Mrs. DeSoto directed her daughter home, spanking her as she went. The rest of us were spared her wrath.

"C'mon," Levi directed. "Let's go see what we did."

We approached the hive with caution. Hundreds of tiny hornet carcasses lay on the ground. Their wounded tried to recover and retreat back into the safety of their hive to no avail. The heat and smoke had decimated it. We all smiled and congratulated each other. We had gone into battle together and defeated our foe. Not one of us received a sting from the swarm that had emerged in defense of the nest. In fact, our only casualty was Millie and that was at the hands of her own mother.

Returning for supper, I walked by the family room and listened to a news anchor report of the ongoing conflict in Viet Nam. I never paid attention to the reports; however, it was sometimes hard to ignore the images in print presenting some of war's horror. After our flame filled assault combined with the day's news, I was reminded of an AP picture widely distributed and seen by most around the world. The historic photo shows a sky fully consumed by smoke in the background. Children fleeing the onslaught were in the foreground, their faces displaying terror as they raced to safety. One girl had her clothes vanquished by the flames of Napalm. Soldiers were immediately behind them ushering them to safe harbor. There were no moral or political thoughts in my contemplation. I made no comparative analysis between Levi's and my battle with hornets and a war half a world away. It did, however, cause me, if only for a moment, to reflect that our soldiers were engaged in conflict. In my contemplation, I never considered that I would be anything but a military man. My dad was in the Navy, and I was proud to see him in uniform.

MILITARY BRAT   Pete Masalin

    Yellow Jackets weren't the only neighborhood menace requiring the protective action of our patrols. One evening, Levi and I exited our back door to properly secure the family canoe used earlier that day and left on our shoreline. As we carried it to its dockside mooring, we both noticed shadows of activity in the adjoining townhouse. Silhouetted on the downstairs curtains was the image of a man and a woman I thought to be wrestling.

    We quietly advanced to further assess the situation. Levi's eyes grew large as he peered upon the backlit drapes. I had just recently completed my fifth-grade sex education classes, and I soon realized that they weren't wrestling. Mrs. Tomlin had recently divorced, and as she straddled the man beneath her, my classroom instruction manifested itself in real life before me. Levi and I, mouths agape, watched in astonishment at the activity before us. Frozen in place, we stared a short while longer until I was compelled to bang on the window. As quickly as my knuckles pounded upon the glass, Mrs. Tomlin and her suitor jumped from the bed.

    "Run!" I shouted.

    "You idiot," Levi protested as we ran around the row of townhomes to our front door.

    Entering our home, winded and laughing, we drew Mom's attention to us. "What's so funny, Finn?"

    "Levi busted his butt coming up the hill," I covered.

    "Well, you boys get ready for bed."

    I went to bed, but hardly slept. I had developed a friendly relationship with Mrs. Tomlin. She was born in Germany, and as a young lady, married a US soldier who had been stationed in Stuttgart. In the early days of cable TV, she had her own children's show. She enlisted me as her helper for the show to seat toddlers and select a book from a toy box for her to read as they sat and listened.

    One Halloween, too old to trick or treat, I stopped by as she handed out pretzels to the costumed children visiting her front door. At this time, her husband had left her, and she was alone in her house. She was happy to have the company. In between visitors, we would talk as she

MILITARY BRAT   Pete Masalin

drank white wine. Finally, she encouraged me to have a glass with her. At 13, I had never had alcohol before, but the Riesling tasted good, and I really didn't have any other activity pressing for my attention. One glass passed easily and the second was equally pleasing. Finally, the knocks upon the door ceased. I finished my third glass and walked the short distance to my house. I suppose that her European culture never halted her thought of serving wine to a minor. She had no children, and when she was my age, wine was a common beverage for teenagers in Germany. I was lightheaded but happy. I remember sleeping very well that night.

Word of our discovery quickly spread among the platoon. One evening, we all gathered in front of Mrs. Tomlin's home. We were cruel. The hornets, with their close proximity to our command post were a real danger. She was not. Still, we were relentless in our personal assault. In the darkness of night, we rang her doorbell and ran. She would crack open her door and shout that we leave her alone. We did not, instead, we continued multiple assaults of "Ding-Dong Ditch It." It was shameful and as a parent today, if I caught my children participating in such abuse, they would never see the light of day.

We angered her to rightful defense and action. Mrs. Tomlin emerged from her house, iron skillet in hand and captured a member of our party. David Lebowitz was one of the weakest among us; and as we scattered, he was too slow. She grabbed him and pulled him into her lair. In an instant, our perceived strategic advantage had been lost. David was a prisoner, and we all were scared. We could not enlist the aid of our parents for fear of their wrath as they discovered our heartlessness. We floundered for a while, fearful of David's fate. Finally, Levi devised a plan that we thought foolish, but hopeful that it would secure David's release. My parents were not at home, and we all gathered in the kitchen as Levi placed the call.

"Mrs. Tomlin," Levi stated, trying desperately to mask his prepubescent voice as that of Mr. Lebowitz. "I know that you have kidnapped my son. I demand that release him before I call the police."

"Your son and his friends are tormenting me," she pleaded in her thick German accent.

"You have two minutes to release him before I call the cops."

Two minutes later, her front door opened, and David exited to a welcomed reuniting with us in the street. He had been released without incident. Shortly, she appeared in front of her house. Visibly shaken, she asked, "Why are you children tormenting me?"

I approached her and said, "I'm sorry, Mrs. Tomlin. I will talk to everyone to tell them to leave you alone."

Not knowing that I was part of the lynch mob, she replied, "You're a good boy, Finn. Thank you."

We dispersed, and I left, ashamed that I had been so personally vicious to someone who trusted me. It was a valuable lesson in my youth. I discovered in me the ability to eviscerate people beyond effective retaliation. It was a skill that I would use again, but only in defense of a transgression against me. I did not like that I had used this trait against an innocent party, and in the years to come, I slowly learned to try to disarm aggression of no importance with kindness and humor. This is not to say that I have mastered my de-confliction with others fully, for even today, I can sometimes be an asshole.

Many factors influenced our planning including popular music of the day. While playing HORSE, we all were discussing the evening's plan for a campout behind the Forrester's house. In the conversation, we spoke of dinner plans and swimming in the lake. It was 1974 and one of the most popular songs on the radio was "The Streak' by Ray Stevens.

"How 'bout we go streaking?" Levi suggested.

"Really?" replied someone.

I remember Ron Forrester, the oldest among us say, "That's a great idea."

I concurred as did a few others. Jake Nicholson protested, but it wasn't long before reasoning won him over.

"If you don't go with us Jake, you can't camp with us tonight," I encouraged.

"Yeah, and you can't play basketball here anymore," Ron insisted.

Persuaded, Jake joined us as did everyone else. Later that evening

MILITARY BRAT   Pete Masalin

we ate burgers and dogs cooked by Mrs. Forrester. While she cooked, we finished setting up camp, followed by a swim in the lake. The sun set as we ate our meal on the deck. Rations complete, we made our way to the bivouac site and told stories until we were certain that parents were in bed. Under the canopy of darkness, we all disrobed, wrapped our waists with towels, and set off on patrol.

Traveling with much stealth, we made our way to the busy thoroughfare of North Shore Drive. We took our positions and waited. As several cars approached, Levi gave the signal and we all advanced. We removed the towels serving as our loincloths, draped them as hoods over our heads to avoid detection and dashed quickly across the drive. Horns blared as cars braked to a stop. We all laughed as we mustered to a preplanned rendezvous point. All made it except one - Jake. The one who had earlier protested lay prone on the asphalt, his towel before him. He stared at the headlights, frozen if for only a moment. In one motion, he grabbed his towel, jumped to his feet, and joined us on the run as we retreated back to our camp.

Mid-way home, we saw a target of opportunity. Set in the back yard of a neighboring subdivision was another campsite of two tents. Slowly we approached and discovered four sleeping occupants. Levi and Ron huddled and whispered while attempting to formulate the next plan of attack. I chose my own plan and sprang into action. Naked except for my cloth covered head; I entered one shelter and pulled down a tent pole.

"Finn!" I heard as I exited.

"Run!" I yelled grabbing the other tent's support pole. It too fell as we fled.

Awakened by our ambush, the campers screamed, and flood lights lit beaming upon us. The camper's parents stared out of their bedroom window only to witness the bare pale bums of boys disappear in the darkness. We ran all the way to the Forrester's back yard, stopped, and stood silently except for the sound of air entering and exiting our heaving chests.

My time on Waters Edge Lane shaped in me an understanding of commitment to loyalty. The children of the neighborhood were committed

MILITARY BRAT   Pete Masalin

to each other, and we protected one another. This would be witnessed on nights when we were directed to stay inside when our parents were away. We all knew the vehicles belonging to the adults: color, make and model and, very importantly, headlight configurations. While we played, one would be assigned guard at a vantage point that provided us with early warning. As cars approached, the guard could identify each car as friend or foe well in advance and alert us to a foe's approach. The system was never detected, and we all enjoyed extended times of play on many evenings.

In my mind, I hold memories of wild stories too numerous to include in this recounting of misguided missions gone awry. Yet in all of them, they served as character building exercises that would forge my temperament and develop my traits. As I grew, I became bolder and less risk adverse. I thrived on adventure and enjoyed a body fueled by adrenaline. It was not recklessness. It was the exhilaration I sought. I learned to recognize boundaries, their limitations and for the most part, pushed them to the edge; however, I sometimes extended them beyond the limitations I perceived in myself.

As a group, we all lived by one unifying principle; if you're caught, you acted alone. Whether throwing snowballs at police cars, streaking or a simple game of Ding-Dong Ditch It, I don't remember anyone who was apprehended ratting on another member.

It may seem that we all were a unit of terror upon our neighbors, but in truth, most of our antics were harmless pranks that often provided comedy to our parents. I remember settling into our tents in the Forrester's back yard after our naked patrol through the streets of Reston. Mrs. Forrester came down from the house to check on us.

"Hey boys, how's it going?"

"Great," we all responded.

"I was just talking to Mrs. Duncan. She told me that when she was driving home, she saw a bunch of kids streaking. Do you know anything about that?"

"Nope, nope. We were all here telling ghost stories," her son replied.

"That's great." she stated, turning away, and making her way back to the house. As she left, we could all hear her laughing before shouting to her husband, "It was them!"

As frivolous as our life often seemed, we all witnessed many episodes that taught us about the seriousness of life. As we all aged, so did our understanding of world events and life in general. Amongst the carefree days that normally filled our lives, we were passive observers to tragedy and sober moments that also helped define our character. Sometimes life is not fun.

Chapter 10
Casualty in the Ranks

In the autumn of 1971, the Sampsons moved into a home situated on the slope above us at the end of Moorings Drive. Charlie was the only child of Louise and Mike. The Sampsons had lived in Reston for many years and had decided to move to a lakefront community to enjoy the peaceful setting. Charlie was an accomplished athlete at Herndon High School, lettering in the three big sports, baseball, basketball and football, where he won regional accolades as a wide receiver. He was cool. He had his own car, was popular, and often was accompanied by the town's most beautiful girls. While much older than the rest of us, he was cordial to the young men of our company. We respected and admired his bearing and willingness to spend time with us. We aspired to be like Charlie.

The back yard of the Sampson home lay directly across the street from my house. One day, I opened my garage door and emerged dribbling my basketball towards our CP. Charlie was mowing his back yard and spotted me.

"Hey Finn! Where you headed?" he asked.

"Down to the court to play some HORSE."

"Mind if I come along?"

"Really? Sure!" I said.

As soon as I was within audible range, I yelled to my peers, "Hey! I got Charlie with me."

"Finn said it was okay if I played some HORSE with y'all. Is that okay?"

"Sure, Charlie," was the collective response.

Charlie could have easily beaten us all, but he was a young man of great character. He toyed with us as he extended the games to the very end but ensured that he was never the victor. Most times, he eliminated the best players among us to ensure that the weakest won the game.

Our parents all had signals to assemble us for dinner. Some mothers would just come out and call their children's names. Mrs. Forrester would blow a whistle, and my mom would ring her cow bell. Whatever the signal, they all seemed to beckon simultaneously. We all knew that Charlie could

MILITARY BRAT   Pete Masalin

have beaten us all without effort. Still, we enjoyed our "victories" over him. "Good night fellas. Thanks for the game. You all beat me fair and square," Charlie said smiling as we all dispersed.

The school year passed quickly. In June of 1972, Charlie graduated, and we all watched and waved goodbye as he headed out to army boot camp. He had been recruited to play football at the University of Virginia but decided to enlist as his father had once served in defense of his country. As a young man, Mike Sampson enlisted in the Marine Corps during World War II. Highly decorated for his actions at the historic campaigns of Guadalcanal and Iwo Jima, Charlie was proud of his father and wanted to carry on the tradition in Vietnam. Mike was proud of his son and smiled as we all lined the street, watching their departure for Army boot camp. Mrs. Sampson was not as eager to celebrate with us. She stood silently and blew a tear-filled kiss as the car crested the hilltop and disappeared. It was the last time I would see Charlie.

The following April, our neighborhood was abuzz. We had a mix of families both for and against the war, but we were all united in excitement for the return of Charlie. Two weeks before his return, Mrs. Sampson shared the news of her son's return from a six-month deployment to Vietnam. Plans were made for a gathering and celebration at the community park the last weekend in April.

One week before the planned party, my mother solemnly entered our house. My father knew.

"Susan, is something wrong?"

"I just spoke with Louise who was in tears. Charlie won't be coming home."

Incredulously, my father asked in hope that the obvious was not true, "Did he get extended?"

"No. He's dead," Mom wept. "John, he's not coming home."

Stunned by the revelation, Levi and I just looked at each other not knowing how to respond or what to say. Charlie was the neighborhood's representation of all we wished to become when we were older. In so many ways, he was our mentor, and now he was gone.

MILITARY BRAT   Pete Masalin

    In the months to follow, in the hushed conversations of the adults, I was able to learn of Charlie's death. True to his nature, he ran full throttle and never shied from challenge or obligation. His return was secure, yet just as he was with us when playing HORSE, he considered those around him first. It was his demise. One week before his scheduled date of shipping home, he was afforded dispensation from front line duty. Charlie did not want any special consideration and volunteered for one last assignment. The award citation speaks to Corporal Sampson's devotion to country and heroism for his fellow soldiers as he selflessly sacrificed himself for his comrades. The award provided no comfort for Louise, and she threw the citation in the trash. Mike Sampson's loss forever altered his perceived value of heroism; he would rather have his son and lineage before him.

    I learned that war is cruel. However, its sting of casualty is not fully learned unless it is personal. It is easy and vaunted to revere those who have fallen for a just cause as long as those who are felled are not your own. Even so, my desire to one day be a soldier never waned.

    Two years later, Saigon fell. The United States absorbed an influx of refugees spanning the spectrum of socioeconomic classes. The elite of South Vietnam were joined with the working class as they sought protection and liberation from the certain suffocation of communism as the North swallowed the South. One such family landed at the small waterfront subdivision of Moorings Cluster. General Huy Nguyen, with his family of six, settled into a home two houses removed from the Sampson's. General Nguyen, "Guy", had held a high position within the South Vietnamese Army. He and his family were certain to have been executed had they stayed. Our government provided him with the resources to establish his family in Virginia and rebuild his life. It would not be the plush life to which they were accustomed, but it would afford them a chance to assimilate and begin anew without the fear of torture and death.

    They were the most accommodating neighbors I had seen. Friendly to all they met. Guy was particularly outgoing, serving on all work details when our association gathered together to landscape the neighborhood. They were thankful to be "Americans." Neighbors welcomed them with

MILITARY BRAT   Pete Masalin

gift baskets of food and extended hands – except one. Mrs. Sampson saw in the Nguyens as the enemy responsible for her Charlie's death. Never mind that Guy had been on the side of the "good guys." Louise saw in him the evil yellow man that killed her son. Her husband Mike, while not as obvious in his mistrust, understood his wife's misgivings. He still struggled with all Japanese, as they reminded him of the ferocious enemy that killed many of his friends on battlefields in the Pacific so many years before.

The remembrance of a war that divided our country was ever present at neighborhood gatherings. The air of tension was palpable between the Sampsons and Nguyens. There was no bridge that could bring these two neighbors together. The scar of loss was not one sided. The Sampsons had lost their only son. However, it could not be diminished that the Nguyens had lost everything; the home they loved, family members they cherished, their language and culture were forever gone. I learned in my observation of this small sampling that war, while it may produce an ultimate winner, everyone suffers loss.

While Charlie's death resonated with all of us, even though he had been gone for some time and we were not witnesses to his passing. It is another matter to observe a death before you, even if the departed is someone unknown. As was often the case, we all lived in the refreshment of Lake Anne in summer months. Just three months after Charlie passed away, we were all witnesses to the unforgiving depths of the lake to those who can't swim. We lived on the shores. We swam like fish, comfortable with the warm waters of July. On the other hand, there were many visitors who rented canoes and paddled upon the lake who did not have the same comfort of emersion as did we.

On a bright, sunny Fourth of July, an armada of visiting young adults in canoes passed in front of us. As they progressed, they began roughhousing between vessels. Unstable, one canoe tipped launching a young man into the lake. I remember he was wearing a pale blue tank top, jeans, and boots. For a short time, he struggled. His friends laughed as he grasped for a saving grip to secure his safety. My last vision of him was the extension of his paddle as he slipped to the depths beneath him. The paddle, free from his grip, popped to the surface.

MILITARY BRAT   Pete Masalin

"Tommy! Tommy!" his girlfriend shouted.

In desperate measure, his friends dove into the water to search for their friend. Lake Anne was a murky body of water that limited visibility beyond two feet. The depths fell fast from the shoreline and their position was at least five fathoms. After ten minutes, the realization that their friend was gone set in and they made their way to our shoreline. Mrs. Nicholson provided them all with towels as they waited for the rescue team to show up. Huddled together, I could hear their audible cries of anguish and witnessed their trembling bodies.

The divers were unsuccessful at finding Tommy. Two recovery boats were launched, pulling a line with grappling hooks. Six hours later, a body was recovered. Levi and I stood on our balcony as we watched a young man's body retrieved from the dark waters behind my house. The hook, ahold of his leg, brought him to the surface left foot first. I watched the recovery team grab his boot covered ankle and slowly raise him into the boat. Exhausted by torment, his friends had been silent for hours. Once pulled into the boat, the shore, lined with Tommy's friends, erupted in loud weeping and screams of anguish. The women of the neighborhood were positioned nearby and did their best to comfort those who were grieving. It had been a long day. Earlier, it was expected that there would be a great celebration among neighbors reveling the Nation's Birthday. All festivity was cancelled as families retreated to their homes and reflected on the somber events of the day.

"Dad, are we going to watch the fireworks?" I asked.

"Not tonight, Finn."

"Shut up, stupid," Levi directed towards me.

My dad gave me a hug and said, "I love you, Finn."

Chapter 11

Close Quarters

Life within the Makinen home often mirrored the foolishness and mischief we created outside its walls. There was, however, a bond between us greater than that within the neighborhood platoon. Our house was full of love. Susan and John ensured our needs were met, but not before looking after one another. My father served as a great example of what it is to be a man and husband. He honored his wife, and she honored him back. What a blessing it was for the Makinen children to grow up around that kind of love. Quietly, without saying a word, our parents taught us how we were to behave in our marriages. It was one of the most valuable lessons I learned growing up, and it served me well in my own marriage.

Each night during the week, my father would return home from work. He would arrive through the front door, look at his wife and say, "Would you like a drink?"

"Sure," Mom responded. "How was your day?"

"Great. Let me get us a drink and you can tell me about yours."

"You won't believe what your son, Finn, did today," she said.

Dad smiled and headed downstairs to the bar. "Can't wait to hear all about it."

Within minutes, my dad met my mom in the formal seating area on the second floor of our three-story townhome. Manhattan for Dad and a whiskey sour for Mom, they reclined on furniture that we were never allowed to occupy. Each evening, they set aside an hour to talk and decompress from the struggles of the day. Our small fireteam of four was given strict orders to never interrupt their quiet time together. We never did. After their time together, we would all gather for dinner as one family. We would sit at the table until our plates were clean. Mom required that we ask permission to be dismissed from the table when we finished our meal.

"Takk for mattin," we each would say in Norwegian.

"Velkommen," was my mother's reply.

After every meal, we would all rush from the table to do our homework or watch TV, except one. One would remain to be "Lena," maid for the

MILITARY BRAT   Pete Masalin

night, whose detail required clearing the table and doing the dishes. Lena was the name Thyra Ofstad had ascribed to her daughters Susan and Ingrid when they were young and assigned the same duty. Johan was the only son and was spared KP. When it came to our assignments, Mom was more progressive in her beliefs of "woman's work." Leigh, the only daughter among us, was not held to the stereotype, and we all took turns being Lena. Somehow this progressiveness never translated to "man's work," and Leigh never cut the lawn.

What stuck with me, watching my parents interact year after year, was that love is work. Love is also commitment. And love is rewarding. However, most of all, love will complete both the husband and wife. It will be the sustaining glow that lights the couple's path as they progress through life. Both are stronger together than they ever will be apart. That is the beauty of marriage, and it was on full display when watching Mom and Dad.

While within the home, love was amongst us, it was no assurance of contentment between siblings. Fratricide was a common occurrence often sought out by my pranks. I enjoyed a good disruption to order, and my younger siblings were easy targets of opportunity. Levi was rarely, if ever targeted. He was my bunkmate and watched from the sidelines as I formulated plans against Leigh and Ash. The truth is I was better at devising mischief than he, and Levi could observe fully and laugh at the outcome without the threat of discipline when caught. He could always deny culpability but enjoy the results of my strikes upon the two. Frankly, Levi was sometimes instigator, quietly encouraging me into action.

Our parents went to dinner with friends the night of Tuesday, March 4, 1975, and left the four of us alone. Levi was old enough that it was felt that babysitters were no longer required. Following a dinner of Swanson chicken pot pies, we assembled in the TV room. The ABC Movie of the Week, *Trilogy of Terror*, was anxiously awaited by Levi and me. There would be no Shirley Temple. Leigh and Ash would have to watch the selected movie of the night. The feature was segmented into three short stories, *Julie, Millicent and Therese*, and *Amelia*.

Amelia involved a woman living alone who had acquired a strange

MILITARY BRAT
Pete Masalin

doll fashioned as an aboriginal warrior with a spear and sharklike teeth. Ultimately, the doll desired to possess the woman's soul and does so after a fierce struggle. While watching the movie, Ash fell asleep on the sofa; however, Leigh was petrified, but unable to turn away from the drama. Near the end of the viewing, I was able to break away and coordinate a ruse upon my sister. In the next room, I turned on the cassette recorder so that it would record while I returned to the TV room. For ten minutes, I let the machine record silence before returning. Once I returned to the device, I began whispering close to the microphone.

"Leigh, we want your spirit. Leigh, we are going to get you. We want your spirit. You cannot get away. We want your spirit."

I recorded myself, repeating the chant, filling at least three minutes of airtime to accommodate my scheme. Before the movie was over, I had discreetly attached fishing line to a rocking chair across from Leigh's bed and strung it a distance across and outside her room. In the rocker, I placed a life-sized baby doll such that it was peering from the chair to her bed. I secured one of her other dolls as a prop to my plan. The movie ended, Levi roused Ash from his slumber, and directed him to bed. Leigh was soon to follow as I closely watched her. As she brushed her teeth, I placed the recorder under her bed and pushed "play." She exited the bathroom, headed to her room, said goodnight, and closed her door. The recorder playing, I had ten minutes to spare. With fishing line, I quickly attached one leg of the doll I had captured to the outside door handle of Leigh's room. I positioned the doll on the banister of the staircase in front of her room and paused for the signal.

From my position outside her room, I grabbed the line attached to her rocker and waited until the hushed callings of my recordings sounded. "Leigh, we want your spirit..." Immediately, I pulled upon the string setting the rocking chair in motion. Lit by the shining glow of moonlight, the cold stare of her doll gazed upon her as it swayed back and forth at my urging. Leigh screamed and jumped from her bed. She rushed to her exit, only to be met by a flying figurine as she threw open her escape. There were more screams and terror from Leigh as I laughed so hard that I had to catch myself for fear of falling down the staircase. My mission completed, I retreated to my room for bed.

"Nice, Finn," Levi said wryly.

I don't know if my parents ever were aware of the event, but if they were, I don't remember being counselled.

Ash's position as the youngest of the Makinen squad assured him no protection. In fact, there were occasions it served as a liability for him and offered easy victory for me in my efforts against him. Many years after I learned the truth of Santa, I leveraged Ash's belief in the myth to my tactical advantage. One Christmas Eve, I awoke in the middle of the night. I quietly slipped downstairs where our stockings had earlier been stuffed with candy and gifts from Santa.

There was no mistaking one child's stocking from another. My mother, employing the Norwegian techniques of knitting passed down from her mother, meticulously fashioned individual stockings for her children. The patterns mirrored the Norse sweaters and mittens Mom and Mor Mor made for us each year except for the seasonal Christmas design incorporated into the grossly oversized stockings that hung on the mantle. They were beautiful and easily distinguished between us.

Making my way to the fireplace, I unhooked Ash's overstuffed yuletide sock and assessed its contents. Stealth was required as his stocking was adorned with small bells. Carefully paying attention not to alert my family resting peacefully in their beds, I transferred most Ash's gifts from his stocking to mine such that his was visibly hollow while mine was stuffed and stretched beyond capacity. Quietly, I snuck back to my bed and awaited the morning.

No sooner had the sun arose before Ash and Leigh rushed the morning gifts from Santa. Levi and I soon followed.

"Wow! It's just what I wanted," Leigh yelled.

I knew not what she received, nor did I care. I looked at my stocking and admired, "Santa loves me the best. I was the best kid all year. Look at my stocking."

Ash looked at his stocking and was silent at first. I looked straight at him and said, "You're not a good boy and Santa knows it."

He ran to my parents' room crying and shouting, "Santa doesn't like me!"

MILITARY BRAT   Pete Masalin

Mom comforted him. "What are you talking about Ash?"

"My stocking is empty."

"It's okay, son," Dad interjected. "Come with me. We'll sort it out."

Ash and my parents joined us in front of the fireplace. Dad assessed the situation and asked us if we knew how the stockings got "all mixed up." Of course, Levi and Leigh had no idea of how the disparity occurred. I just shrugged my shoulders and said nothing. Mom and Dad needed to preserve the illusion of Santa for Ash and possibly Leigh. Quickly surmising that I was the culprit, their dilemma required caution so as not to reveal Santa as a fraud. They were careful in calling me on the carpet and restoring Ash's faith in Saint Nick. Dad pulled me aside and counselled me so that order could be restored.

Lovingly but with obvious intent, he whispered to me, "You tell Ash that Santa somehow made a mistake, help him pick out the things in your stocking that belong in his or I promise you, there will be hell to pay. Do you understand me? You will never get another gift from Santa."

Hearing my father's direction, I looked at my little brother and said, "Hey Ash. I think Santa must have been in a hurry. Some of your stuff is in my stocking. Come over here and let's sort it out."

Santa's gifts were now evenly divided among us, and order was restored. Ash was enjoying his Christmas morning, and I was taught another valuable life lesson: Don't be greedy. In the following years, I still made my Christmas Eve raids except that I was more discreet in my pilferage. I took smaller portions of the treats within the stockings so that any absence would not be detected. And I not only gained from Ash's hanging sock, but Leigh's and Levi's as well. It could also be said, that when Peter Cottontail came to town, he was more generous to me than my siblings in filling our Easter baskets. I never boasted of my favorable position, ensuring that the imbalance remained undetected by any of my family members.

In the quiet times of the household, I also tried my hands at science. A small wooden case, stored in a kitchen drawer provided me with a real test. An acquaintance of Howard Carter, the archeologist who discovered

MILITARY BRAT   Pete Masalin

King Tut's tomb, was a friend of my father's mother, Olive. He provided her with a handful of petrified peas from the burial chamber. For years, the shriveled peas had remained with our family, protected by the small box. A grade school science assignment moved me to action – I would grow Egyptian peas. I gathered soil from outside into a flower box and carefully planted each seed beneath the dirt. I took my project to school, placing the experiment on a windowsill in the classroom. Each day, I watered my crop expecting ancient sprouts to appear. Two weeks passed without growth. Finally, I took my project home disappointed at the result. As I entered the door, Mom asked me what I was carrying.

"Peas, Mom," I replied.

"Peas? What peas? All I see is dirt."

"Yeah, those seeds in the drawer were no good."

"What!" my mother shouted. "Oh, Finn, you didn't take those old peas from the drawer, did you?" she asked as she made her way to the kitchen.

Angry, Mom sternly spoke, "You wait until your father gets home. Those were his mother's."

"Don't worry, Mom. They weren't any good," I reasoned.

"Finn, your father will deal with you. Go to your room and wait for him to come home."

Growing up, I learned it was better to get the "wait until your father gets home" late in the day. Spoken to me early in the day, the anticipation of his arrival lingered longer and destroyed the balance of my day while watching the clock and contemplating his appearance. Hearing it late in the day, my agony of thought was sufficiently lessened and for the most part, I had already enjoyed my day. Still, there was no recovery from my sad farming skills and the loss of a family heirloom. I was adequately and rightly punished. My siblings enjoyed a lighter week as I assumed most of their chores.

Almost all shenanigans in the house came without casualty; however, on occasion, a corpsman was required to tend to the wounds. Leigh once crawled under the coffee table to pet our resting dog, Cocoa. There is logic behind old adages. Leigh validated "let sleeping dogs lie." As she entered his territory, he was startled and responded by ripping into her lower lip. Leigh went to the infirmary with Mom, and Cocoa went to the vet with Dad. We never saw our first dog again. My father came home without him, explaining that Cocoa went to sleep. That was it.

Ash would encounter a similar fate while visiting friends in Annapolis. While calling on a classmate of my father, Captain Hartman, Ash went out back to visit their family dog. As he bent down to pet Rex, the animal lunged to his face pealing down the flesh of his forehead and nearly severing his left ear. 144 stiches later, Ash returned home.

"You look like Frankenstein," I exclaimed. "Cool."

"Be quiet, Finn," my mom directed.

His injuries from the dog were more severe than his encounter with me when I tried to teach him a flip. With my parents gone, I encouraged my little brother to learn how to do a front flip. Standing before me, I instructed him to place his hands between his legs. Grabbing his wrists, I told Ash to tuck his legs when I pulled.

"Are you ready?" I asked.

"Yup."

I pulled with all my might. Ash did not bend his legs as coached, instead keeping them extended. The force of his heels slamming upon the hardwood floor emitted a loud thud. Writhing in pain I tried to comfort him, "You idiot. I told you to tuck."

Following their night out, my parents returned to discover their youngest unable to walk. The story of the mishap was unclear to them as we tried to explain what happened. Together, they took him to Walter Reed Hospital, and I awaited their return. They needed not state, "Wait until your father gets home." I knew the drill. X-Rays revealed a fracture in the most unlikely position. Ash returned with a cast, and again I was assigned "extra duties."

Chapter 12
An Entrepreneur in the Making

My experience with Ash demonstrated that I would never be an effective circus trainer, and my skills as a scientist revealed in me failure as a future farmer. Fortunately, the many opportunities I was afforded to perform extra duties helped me develop a work ethic. Working from my home office on Waters Edge Lane, I developed entrepreneurial skills that showed promise. We would scavenge the construction sites close to home for soda bottles that, when returned to the local Safeway, would pay five cents per bottle. Levi and I would spend hours on weekends in piles of construction debris and mining in random mud pits while searching for discarded glass bottles to evenly divide when we got home. I would save my allowance of fifty cents per week in a clay piggy bank. Slowly, I amassed a small fortune for a young man of my age.

Walking through my neighborhood one Saturday, I came upon a neighbor's yard sale where a Toro push mower was offered. I ran home and emptied my reserve to purchase it. With my acquisition, I started a lawn care business servicing townhomes in my neighborhood. End units were a premium as they offered more property to cut and garnered a higher wage. Service was made simpler when I contracted adjoining units and cut them on the same days. Interior townhomes were $1.75. The end units each paid $2.50.

This was at a time when gas shortages caused long lines at the pump and control measures were enacted by the government. During morning commutes, car owners were directed to alternate days for fueling. One day, if your license plate ended in an odd number you were authorized to visit a gas station and fill your car. The next day would be for plates ending in even numbers. When my lawnmower gas supply dwindled, my dad would fill my gas can on one of his prescribed days. The price of fuel rose steeply, and I went to my customers with a price increase to accommodate my rising costs. My increase was modest; twenty-five cents and I received no argument except for Mr. Schmidt who owned an end unit.

Knocking on the door for payment after cutting the Schmidt's grass, he opened it to greet me. "Hi, Finn."

"Hi, Mr. Schmidt. I just finished your lawn."

MILITARY BRAT — Pete Masalin

"Okay. Here's $2.50. Will I see you next week?"

"Yes, sir. But about the price. With gas going up I..."

Mr. Schmidt interrupted me, "You're not raising the price, are you? I think $2.50 is more than enough."

"I was only going to raise it a quarter 'cause I am spending more money for gas," I responded.

"You're not spending a quarter more on my grass though. There's no way," he declared.

"I think it's fair, sir."

"Finn, I'm just going to have to find someone else. Here's your $2.50. Goodbye," Mr. Schmidt said as he closed the door on me.

Over the course of the next two weeks, the summer thunderstorms that frequently visited the Virginia skies in the evenings were particularly heavy. One Saturday, my lawn duties finished, I walked past Mr. Schmidt's well overgrown lawn on my way to the drug store to get a Nehi and chocolate sundae. My belly full, I made my way back through the neighborhood and was met by Mr. Schmidt in his car as he was returning home.

"Finn! Can you cut my lawn tomorrow? I've been thinking about it and $2.75 seems fair."

"I can cut it after church tomorrow, if that's OK with you Mr. Schmidt."

"That would be great, Finn. Thanks a lot. My wife has been on me to get it cut."

After two years in the lawn care industry, a new startup venture was on my horizon. Dad brokered a sale of my old Toro on the Pentagon Bulletin Board. It had been a sound investment. I purchased the lawnmower at a garage sale for $25, put it through its paces, and my father was able to get $50 for it. John Makinen expected no commission from his son, and I cleared 100 percent profit on the machine.

That July. the Makinens deployed to Martha's Vineyard for some R & R with the White and Ofstad units. We all rented bikes and set out to patrol the island. The weather that day started clear, but quickly changed to driving rainstorms in the early afternoon. In a frenzied three-mile dash for shelter, we all pedaled fiercely along the side of the open road. A flash of green caught my attention, and I jumped from my bike to retrieve it. Levi and two other cousins had missed it as they rode ahead of me. Before them, I had witnessed at least three other individual riders pass the spot as they pressed against the weather. Reaching down, I grabbed a wad of soaked and folded bills. Realizing my new prosperity, I jumped up and down screaming as my bike lay in the road. "I found over 50 dollars! I found over 50 dollars!"

Fearing distress, my father approached not knowing whether or not I was injured. As he drew near, he could hear my exclamation and became relieved.

"What's that, Finn?" he asked.

"Dad. I found over $50!" I repeated.

"Let me see."

I handed him the money. It was just a clump of bills, no wallet or identification. It was obvious that some tourist's misfortune became my gain. With no way to locate or identify the owner I would be able to add to my assets. By now, all the families had gathered around me. No one paid much attention to the rain, instead we anxiously awaited my father's count.

"10, 20, 40, 60..." Dad began to laugh. "...80, 90, 95, 100, 105, 110, $111."

"Wow, Finn! That's quite a find," my Aunt Ingrid shouted.

"I know. Let's go buy everyone lobster," I stated.

"Don't let that money burn a hole in your pocket. You need to save it," Dad instructed.

"But Dad..." was all I could say as he cut me off and reminded everyone that we needed to get on our bikes and return to town. Most of my extended family was happy about my discovery; however, I could see it in the faces of some of my cousins - disappointment that they were not more observant or ahead of me on our hurried sprint for cover. Since that day 111 has always been my favorite number.

Returning to Virginia significantly wealthier than when I left, I contemplated how to best invest my newfound fortune. I had just finished a yearlong photography class at Herndon Junior High School and with that knowledge; I decided to purchase a camera and photo lab equipment. Soon after receiving my equipment, I made a makeshift darkroom in the downstairs bathroom. Only skilled in black and white photography, I canvassed the neighborhood to offer service in producing family portraits. To my welcomed surprise, many of the neighborhood families were interested, and I earned enough money return the cost of my equipment and provide modest income to a lad of my age.

Chapter 13
Mountain Men

John Makinen always provided for his family, and this was true when it came to leisure. Growing up during the Depression, a young John never contemplated family vacations. Such thoughts were foreign in the small fishing village of Camden, Maine. There were few days of relaxation at a time when everything and everyone was focused on the survival of their family. A day off meant a day short of provisions. Still, he enjoyed his time free from labor. In his youth, he worked his grandfather's fields, high on the coastal mountains overlooking Penobscot Bay.

He was child, yet he performed as a young man laboring on the farm. He never complained, and he especially loved his time at the table with his grandfather. Fresh from the fields, his grandmother, earlier in the day, would rake blueberries from slopes covered by wild vines full of the dark purple berries and make a pie for an after supper treat. Dad sat at the table, demolished the slice before him, and lifted the plate to lick the sweet syrup and residue of the succulent pastry. Even at five years old, he would sit with his grandpa and rest in the quiet, dawn lit kitchen to enjoy a cup of coffee before heading to the barn to feed cattle. No matter how brief, my father understood the value of peaceful, soul restoring times with family. Dad made sure that we would come to realize and value the same while requiring that it was not without our involvement and labor to fully appreciate its worth.

My father bought a piece of property in the Shenandoah Mountains where we would build a vacation home. Tucked away high atop a mountain peak was a corner lot fronted by gravel roads. On weekends, Dad served as general contractor, and it was determined that Levi and I were old enough to be his general labor. The three of us would ride just over two hours on Friday and return on Sunday after a weekend of building. "Boots" was a local carpenter, electrician and plumber who served as foreman in the construction of our prefab A frame home.

"Hey, boys," Boots said upon our first meeting. "Y'all ready to work?" His cigarette dangled loosely from his lips, bouncing up and down as he spoke.

We just looked at him and nodded.

MILITARY BRAT   Pete Masalin

"This is my son Billy," he said as he introduced us to his boy who was close to us in age.

Billy wasn't that bright, but he was a fastidious worker with plenty of stamina. Boots had him well-trained. Both father and son sported a closely cropped flat top and the skin of Boot's neck was weathered much like the skin of an elephant, thick and deeply wrinkled from years of exposure.

Quickly, the house was erected. Trucks delivered entire walls, that when off loaded, were immediately stood up and braced for assembly. It seemed as though the entire structure was framed in mere hours. Levi and I labored as *go-fers*. "Finn, grab me a hammer." "Levi, fetch me the 10 penny nails." We crawled under the elevated ground floor to fill its cavities with insulation causing us days of irritated and itchy skin. We painted. We removed trash and lifted lumber.

Although Ash didn't always accompany us on our trips to the mountains, by the time the house was half complete, he joined our work detail for full duty. He was getting older, and Dad considered him to be a valued member of the team. To Levi and me, he was our go-fer's go-fer. Ash was our Gunga Din. At the job site we barked commands; "Ash, grab me a Mountain Dew. Ash, go get the hammer." He actually had a cheerful attitude about it all as he no longer had to spend weekends with Princess Leigh and Mom.

He was a good sport even when Levi and I sent him on impossible missions. We would send him off to the station wagon in search of a left-handed monkey wrench or a wood stretcher, and he would spend an hour looking for both. In the meantime, Levi and I would smirk and laugh as we watched his futile efforts in search of the unattainable. Our father didn't know the source of jocularity, and we certainly would never reveal it to him. Of course, this would result in extra assignments for us both because Dad felt, if we had time to mess with Ash, we had idle time on our hands. Our attempt to toy with Ash backfired, and we quickly learned to be more discreet in our frivolity.

Dad worked us during the day, but we enjoyed quiet times with our father as we broke for lunch to restore our energy with homemade corned

MILITARY BRAT   Pete Masalin

beef sandwiches and pork rinds made fresh at the local market. John Makinen loved his sons and our time with him brought great satisfaction and joy to his heart. We didn't understand it then, but we understand it now. At the time, we thought of Saturday morning cartoons lost and missed hours with our friends. What we now know is that it was our time together, through toil and tarry that created in us great memories and bonds never to be lost. I will never forget our Sunday trips home with stops for a well-deserved meal of hamburgers, fries and grasshopper shakes at the Tastee Freeze in Mount Jackson, Virginia.

The home completed; my father christened it as "The Crow's Nest" keeping in tune with his nautical roots. It was a modest two story, four-bedroom house resting high on a mountain peak. For years, we enjoyed weekend and extended trips to a simple home, free from the distractions of our life in Reston. We had no TV, dishwasher, phone or garbage disposal. The Crow's Nest forced in us peacefulness in family bond and solitude. They were good years. We all became avid skiers and maintained more freedom to roam the Blue Ridge Mountains than we had in the suburbs of DC. Levi and I became mountain explorers, fishing isolated cold-water streams and highland lakes teaming with trout.

On one such journey, Levi and I came upon a farm roughly two hilltops from our home. Spying a farmer in the field, I became interested in who he was. Levi was more cautious and encouraged us to leave. He did, and despite his protests, I stayed. I met Grover Barrow who invited me to his home for saccharine laced sweet tea and homemade hard candy with his wife, Mary. An hour later, Levi and my father knocked on the Barrows' door curious of my whereabouts. Satisfied that I was in no harm, Dad and Levi joined us for tea and conversation. A friendship between our families was immediately solidified. Growing up on a farm, my dad and Grover spoke for some time as I filled my face with more candy. Finally, we arrived back home to an anxious mother who grew concerned of the absence of her three men.

Mr. Barrow and I developed a unique rapport for having such a disparity in age. He had served in Patton's Tank Corps, and I enjoyed hearing his stories of World War II. Each visit, I would stop by for a quick visit and of course, tea and candy. In the family room of their home,

| MILITARY BRAT | Pete Masalin |

Grover Barrow was most proud of a picture of his father and a team of horses pulling logs on the property he now occupied. I told him of my interest in photography and how we could replicate the picture with his two tobacco consuming workhorses for a portrait of his own. His horses weren't good for much, but they loved chewing tobacco and could be coerced to do just about anything for a mouthful.

One day, with camera in hand, I visited Grover for a photo shoot. He assembled his horses with the very rig that was his father's, and we headed to the same wooded parcel of his father's picture. Before us was a felled tree trunk. Grover hitched his team and struck a pose resembling that of his father's. Three weeks later, I returned to present him with the finished product, neatly positioned in the antique frame he provided, and watched him smile as he hung it reverently next to his father's photograph.

With school recessed, we spent many extended visits at our mountain sanctuary. On occasion, cousins would join us on these journeys. As with siblings, harmony did not always reside continually during these visits. One summer, Donald Ofstad joined us for a weeklong visit. Generally, we all meshed well together. Donald, Levi, and I liked to fish and roam the woods. However, there was one day when Donald had a meltdown. To this day, none of us remember the cause, but we do remember the outcome. Donald became quiet and introspective. He refused to speak.

"Donald? What's up?" Levi asked.

"What's the matter?" I added.

We received no acknowledgement from him. In fact, he became more entrenched, refusing to lift his head and look at us. We enacted the logical steps of encouragement to break his silence.

"You're being a jerk," I declared.

"What's wrong with you? Cat got your tongue?" Levi questioned to roars of laughter by us both.

We continued to offer support. David was unmoved. Finally, he made his way from the house to the wooded mountainside adjoining our house. We watched as he disappeared into the thatched forest. Finally, after several minutes we decided to retrieve our cousin. As we approached, he sat silently, illuminated by a narrow beam of light shining through the treetops.

"Hey, dork," I encouraged. "C'mon. Let's go back to the house."

Donald was unmoved.

Levi offered his own encouragement as well. "Hey stupid. You're an idiot. You know there are bears out here."

Still locked in protest, Donald did not waver. He sat silently as I picked up small twigs and built a tiny structure upon his head. Levi joined in as we completed a miniaturized log cabin on his scalp. Throughout the entire process, Donald did not flinch. Finally, complete in our construction, Levi and I stepped back to admire our work.

"Look! It's Little House on the Fairy!" I declared paraphrasing a popular title for a TV show of the time.

Slowly at first, Donald began to chuckle before losing control. His amusement grew and caused the stability of his cranial foundation to falter, crumbling the carefully aligned stems to scatter as he laughed. The cause of his discontent was a mystery long forgotten. We all laughed and returned to the house, amused as we retreated home. These were days of our youth that endeared us to each other. Donald, Levi and I still join together for an annual trip to fish the secret watering holes of our childhood.

For more than a decade, we visited the Makinen mountain home for R&R. In that time, we grew older and closer as we explored that which our father had provided. We spent Christmases together away from the hustle and bustle of suburbia. We learned to drive on mountain roads far faster than common sense should have allowed. We marveled at the beauty of transition as the canvass of color cascaded on the hills of fertile Virginia soil in autumn. We ran wild in the wilderness, but we were tamed by our quiet time together as a family.

Chapter 14
End of the Dynamic Duo

My advancement to high school steered a path of significant growth in intellect, independence, and most noticeably, body. I arrived as a prepubescent freshman, five feet, two inches tall and a meager 104 pounds. I grew six inches during my freshman year, peaked my senior year at six feet two inches and extended two more inches in college. It was also a time when Levi and I grew more distant. As a senior, he had little time for his freshman brother; and most prominently, our circle of friends became our focus of social activity. Never mind that Levi could drive and I had to rely on Mom to carry me to activities.

Herndon High School was a large school housing more than three thousand pupils. As was typical with teens, personalities and associations blossomed among the wide array of generalizations. While some students remained neutral, most kids aligned themselves with one of three major characterizations: freaks, nerds and jocks. The freaks were the next evolution of the 60s hippies. Dressed in bell bottom jeans and army jackets, they often reeked of marijuana residue that clung to their clothes as they raced from in-between class toke sessions, secreted in well-hidden crevices on the campus.

The nerds were easily identified as caring nothing about fashion and were driven primarily by good conduct and studiousness. They were easily picked on then, but it never dampened their desire to excel in academics and rigorous study. The truth is most of them have probably excelled in adulthood to great reward. As proof of this dynamic, I offer the names of Jeff Bezos, Bill Gates, and Elon Musk. All these men were considered nerds and all of them are among the world's richest men. Proof that being a nerd was not a detriment, but the foundation of great success.

The jocks were the athletes of the school, and it was with this group that I most closely aligned. I participated and lettered in many sports; however, my rapidly changing body allowed me to transition to other sports as I grew. In my freshman year, I played soccer and was on the state champion gymnastic team. I continued this in my sophomore year while adding swimming as a filler sport in the winter. As I grew, it became more challenging to hurl my body through the air as is required for most tumblers. I withdrew from gymnastics in favor of track and football. The truth was that I found these sports more appealing, and my now larger frame was better suited for both. Running track, I competed in the 440-yard dash and hurdles. As a member of the Hornet football team, my position was as wide receiver.

Sports were always a part of Makinen life. My father was a gifted baseball player with the promise of a professional career. Sadly, at the time and in his prime, professional sports did not offer the financial gain that was afforded that of a naval officer. His choice was Annapolis.

Dad encouraged his sons to play baseball in their youth. I think he was somewhat disappointed that none of the Makinen boys took to the game. Even so, whatever the sport, John Makinen stood on the sidelines cheering us on and encouraging us even in our losses and failures. Sports taught us all how to compete, how to work as a team. Within me, it sparked personal goals for fitness, strength, achievement, and most prominently, a drive to best the foes on the playing field before me.

High school friendships became influential in teenage development. It was a time where I, like most, stretched the boundaries of independence. As such, the bond between friends who similarly tested and stretched the limits of parental control, grew strong. Extracurricular activities drove a wedge between family dinners together and my dependence upon my family grew weaker. Levi had his friends and I had mine. Leigh and Ash were too young to be trifled with; after all, I was in high school. It was a natural and correct process of growth. Mom was more resistant to it than Dad; but as with all parents, there comes a time when they must let go with the hope that they have provided a foundation to guide their children. Susan and John Makinen did. It wasn't perfect, but it was good. We made mistakes, but our achievements were greater, lifted by their leadership and example.

The summer after my freshman year, a significant change in the rank structure of our unit occurred. Levi became a casualty of his age. Graduating in early June, it was Levi's shortest summer ever as he left for The Naval Academy a month later. It seemed appropriate that on the most patriotic day of the year, July Fourth, John Makinen stood tall watching his son matriculate into his Alma Mater. How could he not. Levi

MILITARY BRAT   Pete Masalin

walked, mirroring the steps his father marched 26 years before. It was a great family moment.

    Truthfully, I wasn't sorry to see Levi go. I had all my friends in addition to receiving a promotion as senior offspring among those still at home. The reward: my own room. It was the most prized bedroom in the entire house. Located on the ground floor of a three-story townhouse, I had my own bathroom and no other chambers nearby. The third floor housed all other sleeping quarters. With this in mind, I watched as Levi appearing uncertain and lost, swore his oath to country and was ushered away by his cadre. He looked back at us one last time. I returned a glance, smiled, and said, "See ya!" I was top dog now.

Chapter 15

License to Drive

I adjusted quickly to life without a big brother around. With Levi learning to march, shine shoes, and generally get yelled at while residing on the banks of the Severn River, I was integrating into a newly formed platoon of mischief makers and friends. While the summer before our sophomore year required our mothers to carry us to areas of assembly, life would soon change as we each obtained our driver's license on or near our sixteenth birthday. Life is forever altered once a young man discovers the freedom behind the wheel of a car. Cutting more dependence from our parents further delineated our separation from childhood and turn towards manhood. Still, it could be stated that we lacked the maturity and temperance of young men. Eager to prove ourselves manly, we made juvenile decisions that for some proved deadly.

Some parents gifted their children with cars for their sixteenth birthdays. Others such as me had to beg for use of the family station wagon. These were the closing days of America's fascination with muscle cars. Even our 1972 Ford Gran Torino station wagon, powered by a V8 351cc Cleveland engine possessed more horsepower than was necessary for a family car. Some of my friends owned the fastest legal street cars of the day; GTO, Camaro, Trans Am, Firebird, Barracuda. One only needed to walk the high school parking lot to see numerous street sleds of speed.

Not everyone was satisfied with their stock from the factory provisions. Jason Wyatt owned a 1969 black Chevelle. The original engine, a big block, 396cc V-8 was powerful enough when delivered from the factory, but it was not enough for Jason. He and his father spent considerable time and money adding to the horsepower and torque of the beefy Chevy. During my high school years, it was easy for us to find roadways that were lightly travelled or empty. One night, while riding with Jason, we decided to push our adrenal glands.

"Finn, let's go check out the airport."

"Sure," I replied. The airport was Dulles Airport, now a bustling hub supporting the greater DC area was, at the time, remotely situated a great distance from the Nation's capital adjacent to farmer's fields and cow pastures. Nighttime activity on the runways barely justified late hours of operation. Once entered, the access road provided no exit, requiring any driver to travel fully to the airport in order to return to the exit at the point of entry. Traffic at night was always light and the road was straight. We entered the access road from Wheile Avenue, and Jason accelerated down the ramp.

"Watch this, Finn!" Jason said, stomping on the accelerator.

50, 60, 70. The speedometer climbed as my shoulders and head pressed back upon my seat. We were nearing 100 MPH when Jason looked at me and laughed.

"Check this out," Jason warned as he pressed harder on the gas pedal.

I looked at the speedometer and as the red needle hovered over the number "120." Already traveling more than twice the posted speed limit, I couldn't imagine we could gain any more speed. Suddenly, my head pressed even harder against my seat. "This is crazy!" I shouted as I laughed.

We raced down the straightaway. In the distance, I could see the red taillights of one lone car journeying towards the terminal. As we got close, I imagined what must be going through the other driver's mind. Looking into his rearview mirror, he could see the muscle car's headlights approaching at a speed not likely to be believed. How confused he must have been trying to discern what was trailing and approaching him at such a rapid rate. The mystery was revealed to him in a blur of black and the roar of a screaming engine. I estimated that we overtook the other traveler at a rate more than 80 MPH faster than he was travelling. My heart raced and excitement filled my veins. At the time, I didn't realize how stupid we had just been and the danger we had placed upon ourselves and others. The thrill was exhilarating; however, it would be the tragic events of others that would cause me to apply the reasoned brakes of temperance. Speed kills and maims. My drag racing days soon ended.

My automobile adventures aside, weekend nights would often find boys with massive, fast cars, speeding through the tree-lined back roads of Northern Virginia. It sometimes proved to be a deadly combination. Bobby Danning and Trey Smith served as a wakeup call for many of us.

Bobby and Trey travelled alone down a darkened, winding forest road.

MILITARY BRAT   Pete Masalin

Fueled by alcohol, their judgment was grossly impaired. When mixed with oversized engines and egos, disaster was invited as a passenger. It was estimated at the time their Challenger left the road they were speeding at a rate over 90 MPH. A solid oak tree met the passenger side door where Trey sat. As the car impacted the tree, it split along the dashboard sending the front half sailing into an open field while the rear section rested next to the tree trunk. Two young men sat motionless as they slumped forward, restrained from spilling to the ground by the seatbelts strapped around their waists. Safety belts intended to save lives proved to be insufficient in protecting the passengers; Trey was killed instantly. Bobby survived, but never regained consciousness. His mother's last memory of her son was watching her beautiful boy, disfigured and swollen, gasp for his last breath as he expired.

When I finally bought my first car, my parents had no concern. I performed a lot of odd jobs for an older neighborhood couple. While finishing up a yard project, Mr. Bentley pointed out a car parked in front of his house. "How would you like that car?"

"Really?" I asked.

"Sure. Why don't you give it a spin?" directed Mr. Bentley.

I took off, driving the car for a ten-minute test cruise. When I returned, I inquired about the price of the car.

Encouraged by his wife, he asked, "How much do you have in your wallet?"

"$5," was my answer.

"Well, you know what? That's exactly what we we're asking for it. It's yours." And he threw me the keys.

That evening, I told my parents I bought a car. They were incredulous. A car was not something that I ever thought I would own in high school, and it certainly wasn't anything they had intended for me. However, I was now the owner of a four-cylinder, four door sedan, 1963 Hillman Minx. Not quite the muscle car of my peers, but no matter, I wasn't riding the bus, and my folks knew I would not be challenging any of my friends on the back country roads and highways.

MILITARY BRAT   Pete Masalin

My appetite for racing waned, but not my desire for adrenaline. Mostly, I fulfilled my adrenaline rushes with pranks offering excitement without the risk of death. To be sure, if I was caught along with my squad mates, there would be punishment but not bodily harm. Our missions required stealth as we executed our provisioning, movements, and attacks of our objectives. Friday and Saturday nights, we would rendezvous at the Jack in the Box and complete our operation order.

A new Sheraton Hotel opened and provided us with a source for requisitions. These supplies were the limiting factor in our missions. In addition, concealment of the acquired ammo dictated that these of these types of activities be completed on cold evenings. To properly complete the task, much toilet paper would be required. Our money was too important to us to be spent on such munitions, but the hotel had an overwhelming supply. Our goose down jackets, stuffed with feathers, masked our expanded girth, and provided us with cover. These jackets were bulky and made it difficult for the hotel staff to discern our larceny.

The squad would divide into mission-oriented units, getaway transportation, sentry and assault. The assault group was further divided into smaller objective teams in order to raid as many bathrooms as quickly as possible. While stealth was required, speed was an essential element in avoiding detection. I always volunteered for the assault units. The thrill was always great, but I must admit the rush when being discovered and the subsequent chase and evasion was greater. The squad members maintained integrity and loyalty. One overriding directive was that if a member was ever caught, he would never reveal the names of his unit. I never did get caught. None of us did. This taught me the value of proper planning, coordination and execution: teamwork at its finest.

Nadine Hanson was easily considered one of the prettiest girls in our class. Any of us would have thought ourselves fortunate to be her suitor. None of us ever were. Nadine was always pleasant to us; however, she preferred more mature men at least two years our senior. Our stockpile fulfilled, we sat at Jack in the Box planning the evening's mission.

One of my best friends, Chuck Wilson offered, "Let's go get Nadine's house!"

"That's a great idea," Tommy Hanson replied.

Grant Harris, who had been rejected by Nadine, seemed particularly eager as we raced to the cars to attack. Our reinforced squad of 15 made off in three vehicles. Rob Yaeger drove his mom's Pinto; Chuck had the family Bonneville station wagon, and Jason Wyatt was driving our combat vehicle of choice: a custom Chevy van. The van could carry the most soldiers and offered a rapid troop deployment with its dual opening side doors.

"Follow me!" Jason directed.

We all said in unison, "10-4."

As we approached Nadine's street, we switched to tactical operations protocol; radios and headlights were turned off. We passed by Washington Redskin's quarterback Joe Theisman's home on the right and crept silently to an embankment providing defilade for our vehicles. We exited the cars and assembled.

"Is everybody ready?" I whispered.

Everyone nodded and we dispersed surrounding the Hanson's home. All at once, streamers of toilet paper filled the air gently laying long white tails through leaf bare branches. The only sound was the thump of tightly bound rolls as they ended their trajectory upon the frozen ground. All was well until I decided to climb atop the roof of the house.

"Finn, what are you doing?" one of my accomplices questioned.

"I got this!"

It was my desire to reach even higher among the treetops. I grabbed an awning and pulled myself up. I was achieving great success as I hurled my ammo. Unbeknownst to me, the weight of my footsteps upon the roof was enough to create a muffled sound that transcended the insulated attic crawlspace. Alerted, Nadine's mother quickly rose from her living room sofa and moved to the front door. Suddenly, the outside floodlights lit the battlefield. My comrades fled as I assumed a prone position on the roof. I was trapped. Mrs. Hanson' appeared below me with a flashlight in hand. I retreated to the opposite side of the roof's peak to avoid detection. She circled the house and shined

MILITARY BRAT   Pete Masalin

the light upward to the shingles. As she moved, I low crawled to avoid detection. It worked, and she retreated into the house. My friends made one pass attempting to collect me, but it was unsafe for me to try to rejoin them. They departed not knowing my disposition. Had I been captured? Was I hurt? Would I be interrogated? A half hour later, I lowered myself and walked home, narrowly avoiding a breach of my curfew.

The next day, Mrs. Hanson, a good friend of my mother, called to tell her of the events of the previous evening. When my mother first recounted the occurrence, I was certain that I had been discovered.

"Did she say who it was?" I asked.

"She said she didn't know, but she said whoever it was they got her pretty good."

My fears abated, I stated, "I'll ask around to see if I hear who it could have been."

"Mrs. Hanson told me someone was on their roof. These kids. What's wrong with them? I tell you Finn, I don't know what this world is coming to."

"That's crazy, Mom."

After breakfast, I headed to the Hanson's house, secure in my mind that we had not been compromised. I stood in awe of the job we had completed. It was almost as though it had snowed the night before, but only on Nadine's home. It was a marvel to be seen. I rang the doorbell, and Mrs. Hanson met me at the door.

"Hi, Finn. Nice to see you. Why don't you come in for some hot chocolate?" she offered.

I sat in the kitchen and sipped from the warm cup. "Is Nadine around?"

"No, she ran out with her friends this morning. You know Nadine."

"Not really. My mom told me about you getting TP'd and I was curious to see how it looked," I replied.

"It's a mess, Finn. But I gotta' tell ya, I almost got one of those little jerks."

"They got you pretty good," I assessed. "I told my mom that I would try to find out who it was that rolled you."

"Thanks, Finn. You're a good boy. Imagine if I didn't catch them when I did."

"What do you mean?"

"They were in such a rush that they left a lot of rolls behind."

"Tell you what, I'll take those rolls, and when I find out who did it, I'll get some of my friends and pay them back."

"Are you sure? I wouldn't want you to get caught doing something like that."

I smiled and said, "I'll be careful. I'm pretty sure that if I ever tried to TP a house, I could do it without getting caught."

"Okay, Finn. Come with me." Mrs. Hanson led me to a pile of rolled tissue.

I felt pretty proud of myself as I loaded what amounted to four shopping bags full of toilet paper. Our mission had been a success, and I had secured ammunition for our next raid. I never did find out who assailed Nadine's house. My friends and I had a storied career in the midnight landscaping profession.

Chapter 16
Hello Ladies

"Finn! Is that you?" I was greeted by Debbie Thompson as I entered the school.

It was the first day after Labor Day, the traditional first day of school in Virginia. I hadn't seen Debbie since the end of sophomore year and the span of summer days saw me continue to grow. I was approaching the height genetically passed to me from my parents. Dad was six feet three inches tall, and Mom stood at five feet nine inches. As I started my junior year, my six-foot frame was quite different than just several months before. I was no longer the diminutive adolescent that started high school with the appearance of a grade schooler.

"It is you. I hardly recognized you. You're so tall now," Debbie continued.

"Yeah, it's me."

"You look really good - so much older."

"Thanks. I guess. How was your summer?" I inquired.

"Oh, it was good. I spent a lot of time at Ocean City with my family.

I looked Debbie up and down and said, "So, that's why you are so tan."

Debbie had always been nice to me. I was that cute little brother that she never had. Now, however, something appeared different between us. Her mannerisms and smile were more inviting. She pressed to stay engaged in conversation with me, and I wasn't immediately sure what to make of it. As we spoke, one of her closest friends, Sally McBride joined us.

"Finn, I didn't know who Debbie was talking to until I got next to you. You really have grown," remarked Sally.

I was a little embarrassed by the attention and sheepishly said, "Yeah, that's what Debbie just told me."

As we walked towards our classes, Sally, Debbie, and I continued to talk about the summer and how we were looking forward to the school year. I felt the same emotions directed to me by Sally, and it finally dawned on me: I was of interest to them. As a short, yet undeveloped male at the start of my freshman year, I was easily overlooked. The result

MILITARY BRAT   Pete Masalin

of my invisibility was a shy awkwardness in talking with girls. It wasn't long before my bashfulness receded, and my confidence grew as more of the girls took notice of me. Finally, the day came when I had enough self-assurance to ask a young lady out for my first date. Bethany Wilson was in many of my classes, and we shared the same circle of friends.

As the day approached, nervousness, unease and uncertainty filled my soul. While I was gaining poise, dating was a new experience for me. My favorite elixir, adrenaline, overcame any anxiety I was suffering. Dating at this age was made easier by group association. I remember picking up Bethany in the family station wagon and immediately driving to the bowling alley to meet with our friends. Having my squad mates nearby, and she with hers, made for a more comfortable setting. We bowled a couple of frames, finished with a pepperoni pizza at Pizza Hut, and I returned her home. Escorting her to her front doorstep, my mind was in chaos regarding my parting sentiment. Do I merely hug her? Should I kiss her good night?

The doorway was dark. I exited the driver's seat and moved around the front of the car to open her door. As we walked towards Bethany's house, one of her parents flipped the porch light switch on, illuminating our approach. I became more reticent with the realization that her parents were certain to watch my every move. Stopping at her front door, I looked into her brown eyes and she into mine.

"I had a great time tonight," I said. "Thanks for coming."

"Me too, Finn."

I placed my arms around Bethany and hugged her gently. I was certain in my determination to kiss her as I bent my head forward. At the last minute, my resolve weakened, and I softly kissed her on the cheek. I thought to myself, "That's it, you idiot. You had a chance and that's all you got."

"See you on Monday, Finn," Bethany said as she turned away.

"Yeah, I'll see you then."

When I got home, my mom was still up, waiting for me. "How was your date, Finn?"

MILITARY BRAT   Pete Masalin

She was excited to hear the details. I offered none except to say, "It was good."

Too many questions followed. "What is her name? Where does she live? What is she like? What did you do? Where did you go?"

"We went bowling and had pizza, Mom. I'm really tired, and I'm going to bed."

"Well, will you see her again?"

"I don't know Mom. I'll see her in school for sure."

"You know that's not what I meant," my mother insisted.

"Mom, I'm really tired, good night." I quickly retired to my bunk.

My parents never met anyone I dated, except years later while living in Virginia, I flew a girlfriend in from Atlanta. Lori Lowell and I met on a blind date while I was in college. Over a span of three years we stayed in touch, seeing each other when our schedules aligned. I asked her to accompany me as my date for a Marine Corps formal event, and she stayed at my parent's Reston home for the weekend.

My relationships in high school were typically brief. Initially, it may have been the awkwardness that I associated with an introduction and pursuit, or perhaps it was the drama involved with the young ladies to whom I was attracted. Either way, I suppose this is the primary reason I never saw the purpose of an introduction to my parents or family. Quickly, I grew more comfortable with the chase and confident in my presentation. The drama, however, never seemed to wane. I found that girls could be so pleasing and pleasant on the outside, but nefarious and calculating within, more so with women peers than with men. Men could get in a fight, smash each other's heads, blacken eyes, or bloody lips, and, for the most part, leave any malice in the arena and be friends the next day. My observation with ladies was the opposite. Girls could smile brilliantly, deceiving their adversary of any ill intent while holding a dark and conniving heart against them. Polite conversation masked future venomous innuendo and rumors spread by girls in conflict with one another.

I witnessed such behavior on my first date with a beautiful girl I had sought so hard to win. Deanna was my age and had two sisters: Samantha who was a year younger than me and Olivia who was the same age as my sister Leigh. Deanna and I went to dinner and spent the quiet time getting better acquainted. We spoke of our families and where we had lived. When my sister's name entered the conversation, Deanna became visibly irritated. She didn't wait for me to inquire as to her discomfort. Instead, she went on a rant about Leigh being an awful person.

"Your sister is a bitch," Deanna blurted out.

I about choked on my Coke. "What did you just say?"

"I said your sister is a bitch. Olivia can't stand her."

"Wow. That's pretty brutal. Why would you say that?" I wondered.

I had no idea they knew one another. Olivia and Leigh attended the newly opened high school, South Lakes, whose highest-ranking class was the tenth grade. Deanna and I were too old to attend, as the school slowly filled its ranks by introducing a new class for the next two years.

Deanna continued, "Do you know what?"

"What?"

"Leigh thinks she's a hot shit dancer. And she thinks she's better than everyone else."

I thought to myself, "Well yeah, she's only been dancing since she was about three. She's pretty good."

But I contained those thoughts and instead asked, "What makes you think that?"

"Olivia and she tried out for the same dance lead in the school play, and they gave it to Leigh because all she did was brown nose everyone," Deanna complained.

Trying to diffuse the tension, I offered, "Let's just finish our meal and head to the movie."

Quietly we completed the dinner and walked to the theatre next door. I paid for the tickets, and we entered to take our seats. All was well as we watched the previews, even commenting to each

MILITARY BRAT — Pete Masalin

other about which of the movies we would like to see. The feature presentation hadn't been on screen ten minutes before Deanna leaned over and whispered in my ear, "Your sister really is a bitch, you know."

"What are you talking about? Can we just watch this?"

"You just don't know what she's like."

"She's my sister! I think I know," I said as quietly as I could so as not to disturb those around us.

"You haven't seen her at school. Olivia told me everyone hates her and that she really can't dance. She's just a brownnoser."

I was past my burning point, and I contemplated my escape. "I think your sister might just be a little upset that she lost the part to Leigh."

Deanna became more incensed, took a deep breath, and said, "You're an idiot! You don't know what you're talking about."

By now I knew what I would do. "Deanna let's just calm down a little bit and enjoy the movie. We can talk about this later."

"Fine," was her response. We didn't speak for the remainder of the film.

Still mute, I broke the silence between us and offered to go retrieve the car and pick her up curbside in front of the ticket counter. Previously, as I sat in my theatre seat, I contemplated and planned my counterattack of Deanna's verbal assault. It would be a one-man mission with a high probability of success. I arrived at my car, unlocked the driver's side door while looking back at Deanna waiting for her chariot. It would not arrive, at least not by my hand. I slipped into the driver's seat and slowly drove away. As I exited the parking lot, I could see Deanna still waiting alone for my arrival. "Yeah, who's the bitch now?" I cogitated. No one talks about my sister, Leigh, like that except me and her brothers. That was the last time Deanna complained to me about my sister. In fact, over the next two years following our date, we saw one another many times and she never uttered one word to me.

Even for the most celebrated occasions, two proms - one junior year

MILITARY BRAT   Pete Masalin

and one senior year - my mother was never able to attain a picture of her son dressed in formal attire with his elegant lady by his side. My junior year prom date, Penny Kiser, was the oldest of four sisters, three of which I dated. She was a year older than me. It was to be my first prom and her last before she graduated and advanced to college. She was considered to be very popular, and I felt it to be a great coup for me to be her escort. It was a most memorable event. We were part of a small group that dined at Trader Vic's in Georgetown before joining the other revelers at the Watergate Hotel where the dance was hosted.

I, as a member of the prom committee, was afforded free entrance to the celebration with my date, Penny. The band was particularly exceptional and how could they not be? My reputation was at stake. I had been designated with a few other committee members to select a band for the occasion.

As luck would have it, the first band we auditioned proved to be worthy of consideration. We all sat and listened as they covered songs from artists such as Fleetwood Mac, Heart, and some softer fare. As we listened, they provided us with refreshment in the form of beer. The drinking age at the time was eighteen and juniors in high school we were seventeen; close enough we all agreed. They concluded with a cover of our theme song "Come Sail Away" by Styx. Six songs and three beers later, the choice was unanimous. This was the best band ever!

"You guys are awesome!" I yelled.

Michelle Gleason agreed. "Yeah, that was great."

We committed to the band, and they offered us another beer. Fortunately, at the prom, the band was well received by all the attendees. They did prove themselves to be a worthy choice after all and our judgment had not been clouded by our consumption of ale.

Penny and I had a wonderful time at prom and our relationship continued through mid-summer. As autumn approached, the practical realization of our circumstances parted our romance. She was heading away to school, and I would remain mired in another year of adolescent education. No self-respecting college coed would consider a high school sweetheart a worthy beau. There were no hard feelings between us as we both agreed and understood that life advances in new directions, and sometimes people cannot journey together on the same passage.

Today, I remain friends with Penny and two of her sisters, Cathy and Jill. Years later, while I was back one summer from college, I dated Cathy who was my classmate and a close friend while we were in high school. When I graduated from college, I returned to live in Virginia and started my career. Jill, the youngest Kiser sister, and I often spent time together until I was transferred.

"Hey, Finn!" a voice laughed on my phone line. "I'm putting you on speaker."

More laughter ensued "It's Penny, Cathy, and Jill! We are on a sister trip at the beach, and we are all talking about you."

"All lies. Y'all can't believe each other," I stated with a smile.

"Oh no, Finn, it's all true," I could hear Cathy say while hilarity erupted over the line.

"You girls used me. I was just the Kiser sisters' boy toy," I joked. "It took me years of therapy to recover from the damage y'all did to me."

I was fortunate that, excluding Deanna, I remained friends with the girls that I dated no matter how long the pairing. I believe that I was always a gentleman, a trait I witnessed in my father and demanded by my mother. Still, the end of a relationship is not without emotions and some hurtfulness, but in my case, the feelings of discomfort ceded quickly. The truth is I was never tremendously vested beyond friendship with any of my high school flames.

Chapter 17
A Time of Testing

Beyond my extracurricular activities, my parents demanded I pay attention to the serious proposition of academics and work. Although Levi now resided at the Naval Academy, his example remained ever present in our home. His scholarly prowess hovered above me, tormenting me as a lofty goal. The formula was simple: The more effort one dedicates to his studies, the more likely he will achieve higher grades.

The direct correlation was an undeniable truth; however, I thought it necessary to schedule and prioritize my time supportive of a much broader grouping of activities than just schoolwork. The fact that I was not my class valedictorian can only be attributed to multi-tasking. Mine was a well-rounded education, focused on the whole man, not just the scholarly attributes. My father never fully concurred with my logic. It was my misfortune that I followed Levi in the family lineage, and he had demonstrated the capability of Makinen children when properly focused.

Levi attained knowledge easily and achieved many accolades to include the highest honors upon graduation from high school. I scarcely saw him study. His mind was a skillful trap, easily snatching key information from his lectures and retaining the information within his brain housing group. Levi took the much-dreaded SAT at the age of fifteen and attained a perfect math score of 800 for the math section and a notch below at 750 for his verbal portion. Combined, it was a total of 1550, a remarkable score. Levi would never take the test again. His great achievement became my curse. He set my parents' expectation that all their children would accomplish similar results. Fortunately for Leigh and Ash, Finn would be the thoughtful older brother able to reset expectations for his younger siblings. Without intention and without my sister and little brother knowing, I labored to ease our parents' expectations for them. I quickly detested the SAT. One was bad enough and the second was even worse, but I took it seven times!

Mail deliveries were never anticipated by our family. It was just something that occurred each weekday. The postman would slip our intended envelopes into our mailbox. Mom would collect them each afternoon and wait to review the mail that evening with my father when he returned home from work. I remember one fall day, Dad came home

MILITARY BRAT Pete Masalin

and as was the evening ritual, fixed himself a Manhattan and a Whiskey Sour for my mom. The first hour he was home, the kitchen became off limits for the kids. We were instructed to find something to do, and our mother would call us when supper was ready. At the risk of banishment, their time together was never to be disrupted by any of us, for any reason.

"Finn, get in here," my father bellowed.

I was shocked. I had never been instructed to join my parents' quiet time. None of us had. I quickly joined them as commanded. "Yes, sir?"

In my father's one hand was an open envelope. In the other was an unfolded report. "1,030. You got a 1,030." Dad's words conveyed partial disgust.

"What are you talking about?" I responded. "What does 1,030 mean?"

"It means you're not as bright as you think you are."

"Huh?"

"Don't 'huh' me. You only scored 1,030 on your SAT."

"John, it's okay. Finn can sign up for the next one," my mother interceded.

"You're damn straight, he's taking it again."

I could see Leigh and Ash peeking around the corner. The tone coming from my father led them to believe I had done something wrong and that I was being punished. They had no idea what an SAT was but there was no doubt I would be punished. The disparity of scores between his first two sons was hard for the nuclear engineer to reconcile. John Makinen was a brilliant mathematician. His oldest son took the test only one time and nearly achieved perfection. I looked normal. I even favored my father's appearance. How could it be that his second son could be so average. He wasn't mad. He was just sure that enough of his intellect had genetically been mapped to my DNA such that I might score higher on the next test. My punishment would be another test and another and another until I reached a total of seven.

During the summer between my junior and senior year, my sentence was stiffened based upon my nonperformance as recorded by follow up

MILITARY BRAT   Pete Masalin

aptitude tests. I was enrolled in a boarding school in Maryland where they focused on raising the SAT scores of underachievers such as me. Rear Admiral Trainer, a good friend of my father, had a son with a similar disability to mine. In conference and in concert with each other, Admiral Trainer and my father decided that it would be beneficial for Jake Trainer and me to both attend the boarding school boot camp. I fault Levi for the near tragedy that would happen in the dorm that summer. Had Levi not set expectations so high, I may have never been assigned to a score enhancing program and mortal combat would not have resulted.

On arrival at Bullis School, Jake and I were assigned a room as bunkmates. The barracks configuration was an assembly of Jack and Jill suites affording each camper a two-man room adjoined to a bathroom. Fellow attendees came from a wide array of backgrounds. Most notably were several Iranians who were sent by their elite families in Iran to receive a high-end education in the States. My companions joining me from the US were generally from the Mid-Atlantic and a couple from Texas. It was a dysfunctional group, hardly adequate to make a harmonious unit. In fact, turmoil often erupted in the dorm. As is often the case with young men, the natural course of integration between them involves a series of challenges to vie for heightened status.

Jack and I played football, enjoyed muscle cars, and dipped Copenhagen. We were well-suited as roommates. Meeting our suitemates, we knew that all would not be well between us. Bradford Wellington was an elitist; born of wealth, he was never hesitant to remind us of his privilege. His assigned partner, Travis Snider, was of more meager roots; however, he quickly became Bradford's sycophant. Jake and I did not like them, but tolerated their behavior as long as it didn't interfere with us.

"Is this yours?" Bradford asked while exiting the bathroom into our room. "It doesn't belong hanging on the shower curtain rod."

"Yeah. You keep it out of here," added Travis.

"That's my towel," Jack responded.

"Well, you keep your shit in your room," demanded Travis as he threw the towel to the floor.

MILITARY BRAT   Pete Masalin

"I'll kick your ass!" Jack yelled as he rose from his chair.

"Bring it!" Bradford said.

"Yeah, bring it," echoed his little toad, Travis.

I grabbed Jack. "Hold up, buddy. We'll take care of this later." I then looked at our suitemates. "If that's how you want to play, you better be ready to play by the same rules."

"What do you mean?"

"You just make sure you keep your own shit in your room."

Two days later I was using the restroom when I noticed one of them left his conditioner in the shower. Neither Travis nor Bradford was in his room. The doors did not have locks, allowing Jake and I easy access to their bunks. We smiled at each other and silently slipped in and lathered their pillowcases with the conditioner. At taps, a surprise awaited our two adversaries. The ensuring profanity laced dialog marked the onset of a series of skirmishes between us. Each time the retribution escalated beyond the previous attack. Neither party thought to alert the staff for fear of dismissal.

One day, I sought to rectify our defensive shortcomings by installing a latch on our bathroom door. I had just made a successful assault of Bradford and Travis's position and they were retaliating. I was successful in denying them access through the adjoining bathroom and laughed as they banged upon the door. They regrouped and considered an alternative plan of attack. Within minutes, they rushed in through the hallway door. I was alone in the room still holding the hunting knife that assisted me in installing the lock. Bradford in the lead with Travis close, they approached cautiously with tubes of toothpaste that they planned as a weapon.

"You better back off!" I cautioned while brandishing my knife.

Bradford stalled for a moment and contemplated his position before expressing his intent. "Finn, you son of a bitch! You are going to pay."

"I'm telling you. You better get out of here."

Jack was out of the room, and I was outnumbered. "It's just you, Finn," Travis uttered.

MILITARY BRAT Pete Masalin

    I could see Bradford's eyes focus, determined to attack, he lunged towards me with his toothpaste tube at the ready. I met his ambush with equal intent, but with better weaponry. My blade pierced deep through the back of his hand between the two middle bones and exited through the palm. The assault was over. The assailants retreated to their headquarters and assessed the wound. I soon followed, quickly structuring a truce. The war was over.

    Together, we worked to stop the bleeding by applying pressure to the gaping wound. United in our concern about the school's possible reaction to our conflict, we tried to keep Bradford's injury secret. We made it through the night, but the morning sun cast light on the seriousness of the damage to my foe's mitt. Plasma oozed from the opening and no amount of pressure would stop it. Prior to alerting the administration, we manufactured a story stipulating that it was an accident caused by carelessness, a loose carpet, and an unsheathed knife. The school became more concerned with their liability than a thorough investigation of the circumstance. Bradford was quickly delivered to the emergency room for suturing and when he returned the peace between us was never broken or tested.

    At the first offering of the SAT my senior year, I arrived ready to excel with the expanded knowledge I attained at Bullis. A few weeks later, my scores arrived, and they were improved. Weeks of summer study did provide for an uptick in my tally. Previously, my best score for my four attempts was 1,050: 490 verbal, 560 math. I anxiously opened the envelope and discovered my combined score; 1,090. All that time away and I only increased my marking by 40 points! Disappointment was shared by my parents and me. They were discouraged having spent so much money for a boarding school and I was frustrated by the prospect of another test. Damn that Levi.

    On a chilled autumn Friday night, the last football game of the season arrived, and I was scheduled to sit for yet another SAT the following morning. Towards the end of the game, I came across the middle of the field to meet my play assignment and perform a crackback block on a middle linebacker. However, on this play, the linebacker was absent from where I expected him to be. I stopped, stood motionless looking

MILITARY BRAT　　　　　　　　　　　　　　　　　　　Pete Masalin

for someone to block, and was drilled to the ground by an opponent. The force that was delivered upon my head resulted in my concussion.

Entering the school cafeteria with two, number 2 pencils, I presented my identification and sat down for another multi-hour test. The residual effects of my head smashing of the previous night left my skull throbbing with pain. I was in no mood to read and answer multiple choice questions. This was SAT number seven, and I had all but given up on any improvement. It was only at the urging of my father that I continued. I raced through the test, desperate for it to be over so that I could tend to my suffering. I finished it in record time.

A few weeks later, I was stopped in my tracks by the echoing words of my father reminiscent of my first SAT conversation with Dad.

"Finn, get over here!" My father commanded while engaged with my mom in their evening private time.

"Yes, sir," I quickly reported.

"1,190, Finn. You scored 1,190!"

Mom was smiling and added; "I knew you had it in you. Your father and I are very proud of you."

I thought to myself finally, no more tests. I confirmed this with my father, "Does this mean I'm done?"

"Yes, Finn. You're done. Now let your mother and I go back to our conversation. You're dismissed."

As I left, he added, "Good job, son."

I smiled and reflected on my last test as I left them in the kitchen. Who knew that receiving a hammer like hit to the head could improve a score so greatly?

Chapter 18
Dam Summer

It is a remarkable transition from birth to manhood. First, all is provided, and the young worry not about the future. As we age, the burden of self-reliance and the release of the parents weigh on our calculation. At five, I worried nothing of material matters. As far as I knew, everything I needed was readily available. My limits of understanding for things required rested in the environment of my family.

However, as I matured, there was an innate understanding that grew within me directing an assumption of accountability for my own actions. This, coupled with the parenting skills of John and Susan Makinen, appropriately transitioned acceptance of my obligations and helped me to develop ownership of my individuality. I soon learned that independence demanded responsibility. If I didn't do my chores, my allowance would be docked. There was no debate. My duties were clearly defined by my parents and falling short resulted in reductions to my pay. It was a valuable lesson towards my development as a contributing member of society. Moreover, I learned that my successes were directly attributed to my effort.

I witnessed Levi toil as a fry cook at the recently opened McDonald's. It was the first McDonald's in our hometown and vastly popular with the residents. Each night, he returned home smelling of stale French fries and griddle smoke. Seeing him arrive home with a hair net upon his crown, I knew that better jobs existed for me when I entered the work force. When I became of working age, my father encouraged me to find a job. Fortunately, a friend of mine's family owned a pet store, and I was offered a job. Simple - feed the fish and vacuum the shop before leaving. Comparatively to Levi's job, the worst smelling task was cleaning the guinea pigs' pen. Two of the most exciting responsibilities were feeding the caiman alligator and constrictors. The chore was short lived as both species quickly consumed their live prey.

One advantage of my employment was the discount they provided on products. Of particular interest to me and my squad mates was the Siamese fighting fish. The males of this breed required independent holdings as they are fiercely territorial and would battle to exhaustion to

MILITARY BRAT   Pete Masalin

maintain their domain. Consistent with peers, we were close friends, but also very competitive. On many weekends, we played poker, hosted at the homes of Rob Yaeger or Tommy Attaway. Our card games had a limit of nickel, dime, quarter, but the prospects of unpredictable battle intrigued us all. Once a month, we would schedule "fish fights" as a substitute for card games. My advantage was that I saw the potential contestants as they arrived. In the week prior to our scheduled matches, my challengers would visit the pet store to select their champion.

Friday nights we would arrive at the arena with our individual warriors prepared for battle. In the center of a card table, a fishbowl stood still awaiting conflict. Numbers were drawn and the multi-colored scaled gladiators awaited their entrance. Before the bowl, small containers held the fighters on display awaiting their call to duty.

Rob drew numbers from the hat. "3 and 7."

We measured the competition and placed bets. Wages finalized; the fish were quickly paired into the water-filled container before us. Immediately, the two adversaries ripped at each other, tearing beautiful fins apart. Finally, one would acquiesce, ending the match. Monies exchanged hands to the victors and the next pairing proceeded. I was more often the champion in these duals. At the pet store, I privately held pre-tournament trials as the fish arrived.

Knowing that competition was eminent, I conducted tests before my friends could view the combatants. My position allowed me the first choice of incoming stock. I had already segregated my participant for the games. While they would assess their choices on size, I learned that the plainer, less flamboyant fish were hardier. I won many more times than I lost. Soon, my means were discovered, and we returned to cards as the only choice of gaming amongst friends.

During the summer, I opted for physical pursuits of employ. The hourly pay was much more beneficial than that of a pet store cash register attendant. $2.15 per hour was my wage at the pet store. As a plumber's apprentice I received $3.50. I enjoyed the physical labor associated in the construction industry. The plumber with whom I worked was a simple but honest and hardworking man. Rhett Walker reminded me of Boots. He was not distracted by the culture and haughtiness of the homeowners for whom he was contracted.

Reston was a community built in the humble rural scenery of Virginia. It was being swallowed by the metropolitan growth of Washington, DC. He didn't realize it, but Northern Virginia was soon to leave the simple country lifestyle that was his roots. He hated the intrusion, but he was an unwitting contributor to its growth. It would become the antithesis of everything he believed. He had a family to provide for and that was all that mattered.

In the hot sun and humid air, I would sweat as I shoveled pipelines before foundations were poured. In the distance, I could hear Rhett's radio playing his favorite country tunes. Conway Twitty, Moe Bandy and Joe Stampley, Hoyt Axton - I knew them all. Often, I would find his radio near my workstation and when his back was turned, I switched stations to listen to hard driving guitar refrains.

"What the hell is that, Finn?" was Rhett's common refrain.

I would act as though innocent and shrug my shoulders. "What do you mean?"

"You know what I'm talking about. That shit on my radio."

"I think it's something new from George Jones."

"That ain't no George Jones. He don't sing that crap." George Jones was his favorite artist and Rhett knew all his songs.

"I think he's just trying something different, boss," I said with a grin.

"Shut up, Finn. You change that station back and get your ass to work. Don't you never change it again."

"No, sir. I won't." Rhett and I laughed because we both knew I would. I had done it many times before, and it was always George Jones.

Early summer after my graduation, work slowed for Rhett, and he had to let me go. We both were disappointed by the unfortunate circumstances. He apologized though I assured him it was not necessary. I was astute enough to know that it was his livelihood that was in jeopardy. He needed to hold on to as much of his earnings as possible. I bounced around to a couple of general labor jobs at construction sites before landing a job that nearly derailed my entrance to college.

Not far from my house, the dam to the lake where I resided was failing. An engineering firm was hired to penetrate the earthen structure and permeate any cavities and crevices with cement. I happened by after an early day of work one day and asked the superintendent if they needed any help.

"When can you start?"

"When do you need me?" I asked.

"Tomorrow," he said.

"Okay. What time?"

The superintendent replied, "We start at 6:30 in the morning and work for ten hours, four days a week, Monday through Thursday."

"Really? I can start tomorrow."

"Yup, pays six bucks an hour."

"My name is Finn Makinen, and I will see you in the morning."

"It's hard work son. You better be able to keep up, or you'll be gone," he said.

Six dollars an hour was a high wage, and I would have Friday, Saturday, and Sunday off. I couldn't believe my new opportunity was real. $240 a week was more than any of my friends were earning. I arrived 15 minutes early the next morning eager to show that I was worthy of their consideration. I soon learned that my role on the team was not very complex, but the physical requirements were grueling. My tan would also suffer. As a laborer on other jobs, the only attire I required was boots and shorts. Here, it was mandatory that long pants and shirts always be worn.

My position was as chuck tender for a drill rig as it bore through the ground deep into the depths of the dam. I was the mule employed to carry ten-foot steel casing segments and bit extensions to the rig, hoist them vertically into position, and ratchet them together with a pipe wrench.

MILITARY BRAT   Pete Masalin

After the first day, I pondered my decision to accept the job as I lay on the sofa recovering from the toils of the day. Seeing my first paycheck, I never gave it a second thought. I cashed it, joined my friends at the bowling alley and bought them the first round of beer. I couldn't believe the amount of money I was collecting, and I felt like flaunting it in front of my squad mates. They were both surprised and envious, and that was just the beginning.

I knew nothing of labor unions; however, I soon discovered the strength of their bargaining power. Although not required to become a union member, I was the recipient of their leverage. According to established employee protocol, after three weeks, I was due a raise provided that I had abided by all my employer's rules and met their performance criteria. I exceeded at both and benefited from a $3 raise. My hourly rate was now $9. Three weeks later, another benchmark was reached, and another $3 raise extended - $12 per hour! The project was fast approaching its deadline for project completion. Management worried we might be behind schedule. They conferred and decided that our Friday's off would be forfeited so that we could meet mission accomplishment.

We would now work five days a week, ten hours a day. I could not have been more overjoyed. The union was mightier than I had imagined. The firm was required to pay its non-salaried employees double-time for any overtime hours performed during the week. For me, each Friday represented $240. I was pulling in $720 per week. I seriously contemplated my college aspirations. I didn't see or concern myself about the transient nature of the industry. I was blinded by the green of money, and it clouded any reasonable thought.

My consciousness was restored by tragedy at my rig. Dave Adams was the operator of my drill rig. Each day we would team together to plug the holes we created. As the operator, Dave manned the controls as I hurled steel into position before watching it plummet into the soil. Above the din of the machinery, he and I would talk about aimless subjects, and we developed a good rapport. He was a huge man who played football at the University of Maryland. On weekends he played linebacker on a semi-pro team in Baltimore. He had just gotten engaged to his high school sweetheart, and they planned to get married in the fall - partly out of

MILITARY BRAT　　　　　　　　　　　　　　　　　　　Pete Masalin

necessity, but mostly for love. The necessity part entered the equation when his fiancé became pregnant.

　　The drill rig not only rotated the bit, but it also included a hammer apparatus that violently struck steel upon steel when the ground became resistant. When Dave engaged the hammer, the noise was considerable, but we still managed our conversation.

　　"Finn, you're making good money. You still want to go to college?" Dave asked.

　　"Yeah, I think so," I responded.

　　"Why? You're a good kid. Everyone here likes you. You work hard. I think you would make a ton of money with us. I went to college and looking back, looking at what I'm doing now, I really didn't need to."

　　"You think so?"

　　"I know so, Finn. You should think about it."

　　"Yeah, but my mom and dad really want me to go."

　　"Hey, it's your life not theirs." Those were the last words I heard from Dave.

　　The drill stopped. I looked back to see what was happening and saw Dave crumble to his knees.

　　"Dave! What's wrong?!" I shouted.

　　He looked up at me, closed his eyes and fell back to the muddy surface by the controls.

　　"Help! Help!" I pleaded.

　　"What is it, Finn?" a coworker asked.

　　"It's Dave. He's out. I don't know what happened."

　　Everyone rushed to aid my friend. He wasn't breathing. The only noticeable mark was a small crescent shaped cut through Dave's shirt left of center upon his chest. The superintendent rushed to the jobsite trailer to call the paramedics. Kevin Shelton, Dave's best friend, wept as he performed CPR on Dave's lifeless body. The ambulance finally arrived, and they worked feverously to revive Dave.

MILITARY BRAT   Pete Masalin

They continued as Dave was strapped to the gurney and loaded into the ambulance.

Dave never recovered and was pronounced dead at the hospital. The small incision to his chest was caused by shrapnel separating from the drill's hammer and propelled by great force into Dave's heart. We took the rest of the week off to mourn the loss of our comrade, returning to a somber worksite on Monday. The mission needed to be completed, but it wasn't without heartache. I was teamed with Kevin, who replaced Dave on the rig we shared.

"So, Finn. What are you doing after this job's done? Are you going to college?" Kevin inquired.

"Yeah. I leave in August." I no longer struggled with my decision.

In my teenage years, I was fortunate to have employment that taught me the value of hard work, the importance of teamwork and the responsibility one has not only for himself, but to those around him and the goals and objectives of one's employer. My free time was mine, and I was never deficient when seeking rest, relaxation, and merriment. However, my time as an employee developed in me the understanding of an appropriate work ethic when work is required. There is a time for fun and there is a time for seriousness. I understand where that line is delineated.

The marker of one's character resides within his soul. The unfortunate reality is that, for many of us, we choose to allow our pride and arrogance to be the governor of our soul. I was no different. I let my popularity and successes fill my ego, and I felt accountable only to myself. It was a false sense of security because I didn't recognize my own limitations and imperfections. A relationship with the Lord revealed my sinful nature and pointed me to the proper focal point for my conduct. My parents valued family church attendance.

Towards the end of my junior year, we moved our church membership from one whose message became stale and hollow. Our destination was a new non-denominational church with a vibrant message of hope. The pastor had been raised Catholic, attended the Naval Academy, and later became a preacher focused on faith rather than ritual. His message was clear: The soul within us is fallible. Only through the surrender to God's authority could we find direction and salvation. I recognized my failings and accepted Christ's authority over me. It was and still is the most important decision of my life. I would never be perfect, but I was forgiven.

Chapter 19
Cap and Gown

As it was for Levi, it would be for me also. Having navigated my existence through the pitfalls and triumphs that accompanied my evolution, I was soon to deploy far from home, chasing pursuits of my own. On an early June day, a stage stood mid field of the high school stadium, awaiting the procession of graduates to receive their diplomas. The sky was blue but hazy as humidity common to Virginia thickened the air. Within the alphabetically seated crowd of cap and gown robed participants, I waited to cross the platform, shake the principal's hand as I received my diploma, and return to my seat as a newly assigned member of Herndon High School Alumni.

While I was eager for the ceremony to conclude, it was a prolonged wait. In addition to the obligatory speeches by the most scholarly gifted and the concluding comments of the administration, my class was comprised of more than 800 students receiving diplomas this day. Every graduate's first, middle and last name had to be read. As I waited, the bright morning sun beat down upon us as we sat unshaded and without relief on the football field. Mary Angela Matson sat to my right while Edward Jonathan Makers sat to my left. Both were sweating profusely. It was obvious that Mary had spent considerable time preparing her hair just right so as to properly display her cap and tassel adornment. It was a battle lost. By the time the role reached "Tonya Sheila Jackson", Mary's hair more properly represented a carriage horse's tail drooping below a diaper bag. I, on the other hand, remained reasonably comfortable. One could look at me and see my shoes and pants, but above the knees I wore nothing.

"Finn. How come you're not sweating?" Mary inquired.

"I'm just not hot," I returned.

"But it's so hot right now, and the sun is brutal," Eddie said.

I leaned over to Mary and whispered in her ear. As I spoke, her eyes widened. "Shut up, Finn! You did not."

I looked at her and smiled, nodded slightly and just said, "Yup."

"You're an idiot!" Mary laughed.

MILITARY BRAT — Pete Masalin

"Yup."

Finally, the row to which I was assigned was ushered to stand and advance towards the stage. Before I stood, I tapped on Mary's shoulder, pointed to my right knee, and raised my gown above the knee, offering proof of my deception. My pant legs only rose as high as each knee. Above the knees to my neck, I was naked under the gown. We both laughed as we made our way to the steps before the platform. Announced over the stadium's PA system, I heard, "Finn Welding Makinen." I responded by walking across the stage; it was complete. I was now a high school graduate, soon on my way to my own path.

Three summers before, Levi separated from the ranks of life as a military brat by entering the Naval Academy, marching the route preceded by our father. While I would be discharged as well, my journey would take a more southerly route. I would enter the historic white walls of The Citadel in Charleston, South Carolina.

My friends and I would all be assigned to new units, separated not only by distance, but a culture and lifestyle opposite in most all aspects of academic pursuits. Most would attend universities in the heart of the Virginia countryside: University of Virginia and Virginia Tech. Others chose to venture out of state, and some chose to enter the workforce. However, I alone traded my long blonde locks and Levi's jeans for a shaved head and a grey uniform worn by the cadets of The Military College of South Carolina. It was an easy decision.

Years ago, as a kindergartener attending Maunawili Elementary School, we were asked to complete an assessment form to help our teacher better measure our temperaments and goals. One section queried our individual desires for future employ. Our choices were provided to us listed on a form with a box next to each profession from which we could indicate our preference with a checkmark. We could only select one from a limited offering, and they were simple. The boys could choose from policeman, fireman, businessman, doctor, or soldier. The girls were even more restricted: nurse, secretary, teacher, mommy. I chose soldier and that proclamation remained constant as I grew. It was further reinforced by seeing my father in uniform, visiting the many bases and post to

MILITARY BRAT   Pete Masalin

which he was assigned and interacting with other military families where we lived.

It wasn't until after Christmas break my senior year in high school that I even knew of The Citadel. Coming in from retrieving the mail, my dad pulled out a post card addressed to me from the Charleston based school and handed it to me.

"You still want to go in the military?" he inquired.

"Yes. Why?"

"Finn, I've served with graduates from this school, The Citadel, and they're pretty good guys."

"Really?" I asked as I evaluated the mailer, paying particular attention to what I believed were palm trees pictured. I would later learn that they were actually palmetto trees while doing pushups for misidentifying the hallowed tree that prominently adorned the face of each Citadel class ring.

Dad said, "You know son, I have to visit the navy base in Charleston in a couple of weeks. Why don't you come with me, and we will go check it out."

"That sounds great. Look they have palm trees on their campus."

We arrived in Charleston to an unfamiliar and uninviting smell. Depending on wind conditions, a pungent aroma would drift east from the pulp mills inland along the Cooper River. The unpleasantness quickly faded as the charm of the historic city easily masked the surrounding odor. Once on campus, I was inspired by its presence. The large castle-like buildings were neatly aligned mostly surrounding an expansive parade ground. I had visited the Naval Academy with my father, but this was different. The well-manicured parade ground was encompassed by massive live oaks. Military equipment: an F4 fighter jet, an LVTP 5 Marine amphibious vehicle, a Cobra and Huey helicopter, a huge missile all guarded the parade ground corners. Before meeting with admissions, my mind's decision was secure. My father could see it on my face.

"What do you think, Finn?" he asked, knowing my answer in advance.

MILITARY BRAT   Pete Masalin

"It's great Dad. I really like it."

"Well, don't get too excited. We haven't even spoken to anyone yet," he counselled.

Our meeting with admissions was brief. A review of my grades and SAT score, and it was determined that I would be accepted. All that was required was validation of my transcript and scores. My father thanked the staff for their time, and we exited Bond Hall excited about my future. I hadn't been in the barracks or spoken to any of the cadets, but I was certain. My decision was final. I would join the ranks of The Citadel. I knew nothing more of the school; however, I was certain based upon three very important factors: a multiple-choice selection made when I was five, a post card, and "palm trees."

Returning to Virginia, Mom was very happy that I had determined a direction for my life. She was comforted that I would be entering college in pursuit of higher education, but I think she was even more excited that I would be in an environment requiring structure and offering close supervision. I needed the encouragement The Citadel would later provide me, and she knew it. The next day my required application and supporting documentation was on its way to the admissions office.

In the summer before I left, I readied myself for enrollment. Dad took me to the PX to purchase my required shoes. The Citadel provided me with *Knob Knowledge* information. I was expected to assimilate and be able to recite all the information upon my arrival - school history, alma mater, chain of command, phonetic alphabet, Citadel Prayer. The list was endless and impossible to master. I never gave it much consideration and figured I would have time to learn it once I reported for duty. After all, a man has his priorities to consider. I needed to spend time with my squad mates before our unit was decommissioned. I would later discover that I had used poor logic and miscalculated the importance of *Knob Knowledge*. Fortunately, I did arrive with a pair of fairly decently spit-shined shoes, pardoning me from some punishment of my ignorance.

Summer passed quickly, and on the final night before I departed for college, many of my friends assembled at the bowling alley to bid our farewells. It was a short visit as my father and I synchronized watches to ensure for an early morning departure. Leaving the lanes, I had one more stop. I knew it to be likely that my mealtimes at The Citadel were not to be leisurely or overly filling. Pizza Hut presented me with both. I sat alone in a booth and order two large pepperoni pizzas and two cartons of milk.

"Do you want me to wait for the others joining you?" the waitress asked me.

"Oh, there's no one else coming," I replied.

Incredulous she responded, "You are going to eat both these by yourself?"

"Sure. Why not? I am heading to college tomorrow."

There was a family of four seated next to me. The mother was astonished by the conversation and the prospect of me eating two large pizzas by myself. They had a large cheese pizza on their table intended to feed the entire family, and she just witnessed me order two. Within minutes, my pies arrived. I easily devoured the first and went full attack on the second. Throughout my binge, I continued to order more milk. Halfway through pizza number two, fatigue set in. I could go no further, or so I thought. I was never one to back away from a challenge and unbeknownst to the challenger, one had been proffered. The father of the adjacent family, looked at his wife and stated, "See, I told you he would never eat all that."

Overhearing his comment, I resented his tone. I felt he was being condescending towards me. I regrouped and launched a final assault. My mess hall valor had been questioned, and I would not retreat or surrender. I ordered another milk carton, folded the final two slices together, and consumed every last morsel. As I ate, occasionally I glanced towards the family as they sat quietly watching me in disbelief. Mission complete, I hailed the waitress to request my check. Leaving my money on the table, I rose and began to exit when the father grabbed my arm and said, "I can't believe you just ate two large pizzas by yourself. And half a dozen milks too."

"Mister, it was two large pizzas and ELEVEN milks," I replied proudly

MILITARY BRAT   Pete Masalin

and left the restaurant.

    I was never more stuffed in my life. It was obscene and sickening at the same time. I wanted to relieve myself by vomiting. I could not and limped home, crawled under my covers as a food coma overtook me.

Chapter 20
Hello Low Country

Driving down Interstate 95, I had plenty of time to contemplate my future and reflect on my past. It was my great blessing to be born the son of John and Susan Makinen. It was a life filled with events, places, and people that more than adequately prepared me for the requirements of The Citadel and my follow-up career.

Dad and Levi shared matching journeys. Both were midshipmen at the Academy. While similar, my passage was slightly separated from theirs. I headed south to a civilian institution with a high regard for instilling discipline in its pupils by means of a Spartan military lifestyle. At the Naval Academy, the alliance was to the Navy. Even though The Citadel fostered a military lifestyle and commissioned many officers into each of the four service branches, the cadets' loyalty was to the school.

Another slight modification between us was that they chose the Navy and I the Marines. I received a full ROTC scholarship resulting in my commissioning. For some who knew me at various stages in my youth, this would be hard to envision. It was a far separation from my first appearance in high school as an undersized freshman. Years in the future, I appeared as a square-jawed, muscular Marine Corps infantry platoon commander, standing six feet four inches at 220 pounds. However, others knew me as a solid young man with a touch of recklessness, and the Marines seemed a natural fit.

The hours passed slowly as we traveled along I-95. I sat in in the back seat as Mom and Dad chatted, occasionally including me in the dialog. Mostly, I considered my life. Seeing my parents in front of me, I was thankful of the devotion and love they had for each other and demonstrated before their offspring. It was a lesson well-taught and well-received by the Makinen children. I thought of my brother Levi, preparing for his last year at the Naval academy, and what a great brother and friend he had been. He had only failed me once by setting the SAT benchmark so high. Fortunately, it was an action repairable for the two who would follow me; however, not without considerable effort on my part. Leigh and Ash were safe from such elevated heights.

Challenges associated with moving multiple times, weren't really challenges at all. They were adventures fostering character building

MILITARY BRAT   Pete Masalin

qualities that would prepare me for many of life's trials. I had to learn to adapt to new cultures, make new friends, and endure the hardships of forbidding climates such as Hawaii, but along the way I was made stronger. Discernment from friend and foe became a requirement with each new duty station or school. I thought of the misfortune for those who were confined to the limits of their hometown. Never were they stretched beyond the same environment of yesterday. They lived in the same house, rarely made new friends or enemies for that matter. I suppose there was great security and comfort in the known, but they missed the excitement of the unfamiliar, the tests of new offerings, the fear of uncertainty, and the triumph over all of it. How boring life could have been for me.

I was thankful to be the son of a devoted naval officer. He may have thought it hard for his family, but in truth, it was more likely rougher on him. He was the one separated from us. I remember times when Dad would deploy for several months at a time, often penetrating the dangerous territorial waters of the Soviet Union. When he returned, he was thankful to be home, but sorrowful to have missed so much. To us, he looked the same. To him we had grown taller, began to walk, or learned to read. As toddlers, reuniting could even be upsetting as we were reintroduced to a man forgotten who was our father. Still, in all his sacrifices, there was great reward. John and Susan Makinen provided their children with intrigue, curiosity and a foundation of self-reliance that served as an anchor holding fast our direction. Levi, Leigh, Ash, and I were all provided with enough line to sway in the current, but not enough to crash upon the rocks.

Crossing the South Carolina border, my father was pulled over for speeding. As the officer approached our car stopped on the highway shoulder, Dad rifled through his wallet.

"License and registration please," the state trooper demanded.

Pulling a tattered, worn, and faded document from his wallet, my dad presented his license.

"What's this?" the trooper asked as he unfolded it.

"It's my license."

MILITARY BRAT   Pete Masalin

There was no picture on the hand drafted record issued from the state of Maine. As a military member, one was never required to renew his license and my father hadn't. It was originally issued in 1949 and referenced an address on Mill Street, Camden, Maine. Long ago, my father left his home on Mill Street to report to the Naval Academy. When he left his home for Annapolis, Maine remained his home of record. It would remain so for thirty years until his retirement. A benefit for all service members was that as long as they were on active duty, renewing a driver's license was never required. Dad explained this to the officer in great detail.

"Are you serious?" the officer asked.

"That's the regulation. It's the law," my father explained.

"I've never seen a license this old."

My dad thought the cordiality of the dialog an indication of forgiveness and that he would not receive a summons. He smiled at the trooper, and the trooper smiled back.

"So, do I use Mill Street as your address?" he queried.

"Oh no. I live in Virginia."

"What is that address?"

"Why do you need my Virginia address?"

"I need it for the citation," the officer explained.

Quickly, we continued our march through South Carolina. Exiting Interstate 95 onto Interstate 26, I had a little more than an hour before I would reach my new home of Charleston. Thoughts of my other siblings, Leigh and Ash, entered my head. I had my occasional altercations with them both, but I would miss my time with them. For the most part, our family was a cohesive unit; however, it suffered another casualty by my departure. With Levi and me gone, the family squad dwindled to two thirds of its original strength. Ash would now be the sole heir to a mower stowed neatly in the garage and would have the opportunity to use it frequently. Leigh was promoted from princess to queen bee. She was now the eldest Makinen child remaining at home.

MILITARY BRAT   Pete Masalin

    Looking out the window as we traveled towards the coast, I remembered the hills and red clay of my youth in Virginia replaced by live oaks and the sandy loam of the Low Country. As we closed in on our objective, I wasn't certain of what adventures lay in wait for me at The Citadel. I was ready for my new assignment, but the uncertainty of the unknown caused me to be slightly anxious. I was never one to share my discomfort or concern with my parents. Naturally, we were always shadowed and directed by my mother in our home. She was raised with the Ofstad determination that required a stiff upper lip and durability. From her, we all received common doses of stoicism that required muted responses to our perceived inadequacies or worries. Susan Makinen's intent was that her children would be tough and self-reliant. Perhaps, it wasn't always the most nurturing quality in my development, but it served me well. I stayed quiet and mentally prepared myself for the oncoming mission.

    A road sign indicated that Charleston was only 40 miles away. My life passed before me. Reflecting on my past, I remembered so many people and so many events that formed me into the young man I had become. There was Smelly Shelly whom I disliked yet had to submit to her authority. I learned compassion in spending time with Bill as he shook uncontrollably in his chair while imparting the wisdom of a life well lived. The importance of teamwork was a repeated lesson played over and over with family, ever changing squad mates, sports teams, and fellow pranksters. I pushed the envelope of practical limitations beyond common sense and only learned restraint by witnessing the tragedy of others. I was fortunate to have survived such foolishness. Always active, I was fit from a life of physical challenge and competition. Teachers, coworkers, bosses, and girlfriends all contributed to a well-rounded education that defined who I was. A cadre of well-appointed overseers awaited my arrival for further development. I was ready.

    Pulling into Charleston, we arrived at the Mill Street Inn. It would be the last evening when I would maintain the freedom to decide for myself the activities I would pursue. Tomorrow, I would report to the Citadel, and everything would be directed for me: what to wear, what to eat, where to be. I would be part of the collective and the unit was more important

MILITARY BRAT   Pete Masalin

than the individual. It was a philosophy I understood but had never been required to live 24 hours a day. I had only done it when necessary for the missions required of the teams or units I assembled with for specific events or games.

"It's your last night Finn. Where would you like to eat?" my father asked.

"I don't know. I have no idea where to go in this town," I replied.

"I think you should have a nice meal this evening." Mom suggested. "I saw this nice place around the corner called Magnolia's."

"Yeah, that sounds great Susan. What do you think, Finn?"

"That's fine with me," I concurred.

The dinner provided us by Magnolia's was beyond any expectation I could have imagined. I never had shrimp and grits before, nor had I ever tasted anything as pleasant as she crab soup. We lingered at the table for at least two hours. My father mentioned to the waiter that I was to report to The Citadel the next day, and the maître de returned offering wine for a toast. Walking back to the hotel, I thanked my parents for the dinner and told them I was going to make one last stop before I joined them at the hotel.

"Where you headed?" Dad asked me.

"I thought I stop at the bar we passed on the way to Magnolia's for a beer."

"You want some company?"

"No. I won't be long. Just one beer and I'll see you at the Mills House Inn. You and Mom go ahead."

I entered the establishment and joined other guests at the bar. Ordering a beer, I was asked to present my ID. Satisfied, the bartender poured me a draft and I slowly sipped it while contemplating my future. Dinner was great and the city was charming. I thought Charleston to be grand and pondered my decision to attend The Citadel. I was quite satisfied and certain that my first year away at school would be the most memorable year of my life. It was, but not for the reason I thought.

MILITARY BRAT   Pete Masalin

    We arrived on campus and the traffic control detail directed my father to my appointed place to report my arrival and join the corps. I exited the car along with my parents, hugged them both before picking up my luggage. As I approached the sally port gates of the battalion to which I was assigned, I looked back at my parents one last time. My father, John Makinen watched me with a smile upon his face. I imagined that he was reminiscing of a similar event. A few decades before, his parents delivered him to Annapolis and watched him report to the Naval Academy. His expression displayed his confidence. His son Finn was ready for the challenge. Looking at Mom, one small tear from her eye displayed her uncertainty and fear of my welfare.

    "Be careful, Finn!" My mom cautioned.

    "We love you, son," Dad added.

    "I love y'all too!" I replied immediately disappearing into the unknown.

Chapter 21
"Get Your Hand Off My Desk!"

"Get your hand off my desk."

"Are you looking at me?"

"Do you miss your mommy?"

"Get...your...hand...off my desk!"

So was my introduction and helpful welcome to The Citadel. Confusion was common, and the destruction of ego was purposeful. No incoming freshman, commonly referred to as *Knobs*, was above the lowest insult. The state bird of South Carolina, the palmetto bug, was held in higher esteem than any plebe on the day of matriculation.

Before this moment, my day started quite comfortably while relaxing in the Mills House hotel restaurant leisurely with my parents, dining on crab cake eggs benedict and home fries. Two hours later, it would all seem so distant. Comfort and leisure would abandon me for the remainder of summer and well into the fall. Mom and Dad helped load the family station wagon with my limited wardrobe. After all, how fortunate was I that my clothing would be provided and my attire each day regulated.

Passing through Lesesne Gate, the main entrance of The Citadel, I was silent while observing my new surroundings. Discipline was defined in all that I observed. The white castle like buildings stood firmly on the banks of the Ashely River. The vast parade ground centered the campus as military relics adorned its perimeter. A missile aimed towards the sky anchored one corner; an F-4 fighter jet sat on another; a cobra helicopter neatly claimed a corner among live oaks. Along Lee Street, on the eastern edge of the parade ground, two howitzers held a center position. For years on Fridays, I would hear the roar of these cannons and feel their power as the concussion from explosions rattled the air and reverberated through the bones of cadets standing rigid at attention during each ceremonial parade. In the stands, the observants saw pageantry and glory. To those aligned in display, we only saw the end. "Pass...In...Review" was a command of relief indicating the finale of each parade and the beginning of weekend revelry. It was the same sentiment for each cadet, be it a

MILITARY BRAT   Pete Masalin

Knob or senior private. In this, we agreed.

"Finn, here we are," Mom plainly stated.

"It's a big day, son. You're going to do great. Let's get you checked in," my father encouraged.

There was nothing remarkable in our departure from each other. Perhaps it was the distraction of screams echoing within the barracks. Maybe it was pungent odor emitted from the smokestacks of the distant paper mills that held my attention. Lastly, the humidity and heat of a Charleston August could not go without notice.

I exited the car, hugged my mother, shook my father's hand, and thanked them both for everything. It was a pleasant although brief farewell. I turned from them and crossed the threshold of the Stevens Barracks sally port and into the belly of military rigor. In an instant, the pleasantness of my day and my relaxed demeanor changed to chaos and intensity.

"What are you looking at?!"

"Hey numb nuts! Are you lost?"

"Get your ass over here!"

"Who me?" I asked. That was the wrong question. In fact, I learned immediately that that these very nice gentlemen only had my best welfare as their highest priority and wanted me to preserve my voice.

Three cadre NCOs rushed to greet me and ensure my comfort. So concerned that I understood and could clearly hear their instruction, one of my escorts stood nearly nose to nose with me and shouted instruction, "You don't speak unless spoken to!"

"What are you looking at! Get your eyes off me."

I responded, "Man, your face is right in front of me. I can't help it unless you get out of my face." Wrong again.

"Man! Man. Maaan! You will never address me as MAN. Do you understand me? You will only refer to me as sir or Mr. Wilson."

The good news was that I now knew one of my overseer's names

MILITARY BRAT   Pete Masalin

with the added benefit of also knowing what he had for breakfast. As he shouted, spittle projected upon my face. His eyes grew wide. The veins of his throat and forehead expanded. Sweat dripped from his brow. It was at this moment that I came to the realization that he was not my friend. In fact, I believed that he kind of didn't like me – no, he despised me. What had I done to deserve such treatment?

"Get your eyes off me!" repeated Mr. Wilson. "Move it! Move your ass to that line over there and report to the Company First Sergeant."

As a walked to the end of the line Mr. Wilson had designated, I noticed a similar scene, of which I just endured, being replicated at several locations of the open aired quadrangle in the center of the barracks. Four companies were housed in each barrack. Each barrack represented one battalion. Of The Citadel's four battalions, there was one exception. Second Battalion housed five companies with Band Company as the exception to the 16 "letter" companies comprising the Corps. E, F, G and H companies were housed with Band in Padgett-Thomas Barracks. I was in Fourth Battalion and while I could only see the antics within my barracks, I could hear the shouts of the unsuspecting cadet recruits, reacting to vocal assaults. Their voices audible but slightly muffled amidst dense, hot air that was inescapable.

I stood silently in line behind a classmate I had yet to meet. Greetings were not allowed. Isolation added to the method of breaking the individual down to near worthlessness so that the team could be built. None of that mattered, and I couldn't see the team building logic. I only saw the head of a kid one pace ahead of me whose long brown hair would soon fall unceremoniously to a barbershop floor. You were offered no peace. Even in line, the cadre tormented the newly arrived. As I awaited my turn to officially sign the logbook, I smiled. I thought to myself, "They don't hate me. They hate all of us."

"What the hell is so funny?" a yet unknown Sergeant yelled at me. "What's your name?"

"Finn."

"Finn. What kind of name is Finn? Are you a fish?"

I laughed and replied with sarcasm, "That's funny. I've never heard that before."

"I'll beat the shit out of you! This is no joke. Do you think you're cute? Is your last name Finn?"

"No," I said.

"Sir, no sir. That is how you will respond to me. You will always address me as sir. Do you understand?"

"Yes," was my response. It would take me a while to learn the standard "Sir, yes sir.", "Sir, no sir.", "Sir, no excuse sir." Three basic statements required of Knobs.

With modest hostility, I was removed from the line, introduced to my new Squad Sergeant, Sgt. John Banner. Sgt. Banner's stature was smaller in scale than mine by about eight inches. He had a slight lisp, and it was required that he look up to me to yell at my chest. He could not reach my face. I smiled - another mistake.

"Wipe that smile from your face. Do you have something you want to share with me, a joke or something?"

"Sir, no excuse sir." Became my common phrase for the day and weeks to come and my smiles became less frequent in the open.

Just before instructing me to return to the First Sergeant's line, Sgt. Banner whispered an ominous warning in my ear. "I can't do anything to you yet, but you're going to pay you little shit. Once this day is over and the fourth-class system is in effect, you are going to pay. Now get over there!"

What just happened? I wondered about my decision to come to The Citadel. It had been less than 30 minutes since I crossed the threshold of Stevens Barracks, and this was not the welcome I had anticipated. Standing in line, I held fast to my position of not moving without instruction. Without moving my head, I assessed my surroundings as best I could.

My circumstance was no different than other Knobs enlisting into The Military College of South Carolina. I caught a glimpse of a mother crying

MILITARY BRAT   Pete Masalin

as she stood outside the white walls of her son's entrapment. No doubt she was concerned about her baby boy's very life as she witnessed what was being done to him. Her husband came to her aid, encouraged her to leave with him, and they departed. As they left, her husband looked back into the barracks, smiled, and gave a big thumbs up to his son left behind. It is now my assumption that the father was an alum and could find humor in his son's turmoil. All Citadel grads can.

Across the quad from me was another company's First Sergeant checking in on his little lambs. He was massive with biceps that stretched his duty shirt beyond capacity. To approach this man must have been more intimidating than the new recruits could have imagined. Then in an instant it went from intimidation to absolute horror and fear. I feared for them.

"Get your filthy hands off my table!" I heard as the First Sergeant arose sending his chair back at least 15 feet. Enraged, the senior staff NCO slammed his fist on his table causing it to break in half and crumble to the ground. Other staff members rushed to the scene grabbed him, calmed him down and walked him out of sight. The incoming freshmen, witnesses to this rage, were left to ponder what laid in store for them and surely wondered if they were going to live.

A year later, I learned that the table crash was a brilliantly and effectively executed stunt that forever instilled fear of First Sergeant Trask. His Knobs trembled whenever he was near. On campus, they avoided walking in his direction instead choosing a longer pathway to class or barracks. It was told to me by one of my classmates in his care that a Knob once peed himself when he heard his voice. What wasn't known to us at the time was that Cadet Trask had scored the underside of the table, leaving just enough veneer to hold it together.

Witnessing those across from me and my interaction with Bannon correctly guided my actions as I reported in.

"Next!" my company First Sergeant, Cadet Gutierrez requested.

I took one pace forward and reported to the First Sergeant.

"Name?"

MILITARY BRAT   Pete Masalin

"Finn Makinen, sir," I responded.

First Sergeant Gutierrez was a native of Puerto Rico and his accent was noticeable. He spoke English well; however, he maintained a compromising stutter when trying to enforce discipline. Thankfully, his impediment was barely noticeable on this day, and I survived my own stupidity by not noticing it at first and reacting in a manner certain to cause me pain.

"I...I...I don't care what your first name is!" he tore into me. "Shut up! Get your eye...eyes off me! Sign next to your name and get away from me. I can't stand looking at you."

Remembering what I had learned, I bent over, found my name in the log, and signed in without looking at the First Sergeant or touching his desk.

"What are you waiting on! Get away from me!" was his final command, whereupon the cadre descended upon me hurling insults and commands.

Quickly, I was ushered away to receive my PT (Physical Training) gear of a white T-shirt with blue trimmed collar and sleeves and blue shorts. The words "The Citadel" were lithographed on the left breast, and we were handed and "idiot bag" to wear around our necks. The idiot bag contained key information and computer cards we would use at each stop to help us through the check-in procedure. I was ordered to my room to change, pack my belongings for storage, and report to formation next to the company letter. Without wasting a moment, I did as commanded and joined my Knob company mates immediately. As soon as enough of us assembled to form a squad, we were introduced to a corporal and sergeant, members of our Cadre who were to escort us in our transition from civilian to military men. First stop – the barber shop!

I was lucky enough to have my new best friend, Sgt. Banner in charge of my detail. He reintroduced himself to us. "Men, we are going to march to Mark Clark Hall to get your hippy asses a proper haircut. If you have a mole, a wart or part of a Siamese twin anywhere on your scalp, you best point it out to the barber, or you will be bleeding for the rest of the day."

Marching was not what we accomplished. Close order drill was a

MILITARY BRAT   Pete Masalin

foreign concept to us and walking in step was an impossibility resulting in frustration clearly visible on the faces of Sergeant Banner and Corporal Simonson. Corporal Simonson was from Anderson, South Carolina, whose hill country accent sometimes made him less understandable than our Puerto Rican First Sergeant.

"Oh hell! Who'n the hell taught y'all how to march like dat!" Simonson screamed at us.

I thought to myself, "Well, no one you moron. We just got here." At least I was smart enough to hold on to my earlier lesson of the day that sarcasm isn't often appreciated by these folks no matter how funny it might be.

"Damn it! Y'all march like a pack of monkeys. We ain't never gonna get you straight," the corporal bemoaned.

Nobody dared respond or say a word. We wandered to Mark Clark Hall and took our place in line at the barber shop.

Standing in line, we were instructed not to speak and study our Guidons. We obeyed. Each of us with our attention in the Guidon, a book detailing fact, history of the school, chain of command, The Citadel Alma Mater and Prayer, and much more. This information in its entirety was required of us to memorize and quote on command and at any given time. The information was simply referred to as *Knob Knowledge* and it could save you or cause you punishment by command of it or absence of it.

Approaching the barber shop passageway, I spied young men who entered with free-flowing locks of considerable length, sit in elevated leather upholstered chairs, and exit absent any hair. I expected the dramatic change, but I was unprepared by the speed with which the change occurred. In less than five minutes, a healthy mane of hair was dispatched, and a cadet recruit was created. The lasting result and tradition of this shaving is responsible for the name long associated with The Citadel freshman, *Knob*.

Peering inside, I marveled at the efficiency. Eight barbers manned eight chairs. There were no pictures of hairstyles available to direct the barber to a fashion choice of one's choosing. The floor tile was barely apparent, having been matted with the woolly remnants of those who visited before me. There was no conversation with the barber as so often depicted in Floyd's of Mayberry on the television sets of our youth. As I took my position, I looked across the room and noticed two matriculants with index fingers maneuvering among their scalp as their barbers looked on. Five minutes later, I rejoined my detail led by Sgt. Banner. "Well, well, well. Look at you all now. You'll be a big hit downtown with all those sorority girls."

"Git your ass in formation," Cpl. Simonson demanded. "Next stop, we gonna turn in all your civilian clothes. Y'all ain't gonna see them for a long time."

The rest of the day was a flurry of activity: measurements at the tailor shop for our new uniforms, receiving spartan supplies to accommodate our rooms, a trip to the armory to receive our M-1 rifles, and mealtime at the dining facility. Conversations were typically one way. Our cadre directed our activities with tireless rigidity and discipline. Our responses were limited to three phrases. "Sir, yes sir. Sir, no sir. Sir, no excuse sir." Other replies were rarely tolerated.

At the day's end, we were instructed to go to our rooms, change into our robes and proceed to the showers. To add ridiculousness to our bathroom attire, we were instructed to wear our soft cloth military cap as we rushed to the latrine. Flip flops, a robe, and a cap. I had to laugh as I prepared for a relaxing hot shower.

We all arrived simultaneously. There would be no leisure even in our bathing. As it was at the barber shop, we were herded in like cattle. The shower was an open bay with four shower heads. Each of the showers was turned on and flowing. There were no doors or means of privacy. We stood in line. One by one, we were ordered in.

"Get in the shower! Move it! Move it!" All did as commanded and entered streams of water - cold water. I tried to turn on the hot water.

"What the hell are you doing, Makinen? Did anyone say you could touch my shower handle?" resonated from the cavernous latrine.

"Sir, no excuse sir," was my only response as I resided beneath the shower head.

Further instruction came from the shadows. "Lather up. Now. I said lather up. You Knobs worked up a sweat today and your mommies want you clean. That's it. We want to see soap all over your bodies." Complying with directions, we were covered with the foam of our soap, no shampoo was required, and then, with preplanned intent, the order came.

"Get out now!" There was no rinsing, no prolonged ability to rid our bodies of our combined sweat, dirt, and soap residue. "I said get out Knobs!"

We were assigned roommates earlier in the day. Mine was John O'Malley, a chain-smoking New Yorker from Brooklyn. As we all settled into our new surroundings, the activity, and the care our cadre had provided throughout the day denied us the ability to meet our Knob company mates. From the shower, I immediately returned to my room, placed my head in the sink and rinsed the soap from my eyes, face and scalp. John was in the room when I arrived noticeably shell-shocked from the day. We all were.

"Damn! What the hell was that?" he asked me. "I hate this place already."

"You and me both, John. You and me both," I replied.

"Do you think we are done for today?" John pondered.

I looked at John, hung up my towel and offered, "I hope so. They said they would see us at formation in the morning. I am ready for bed. It's been a long day."

John and I spoke for a short while, catching up on each other's background and family. We closed our conversation in agreement of our stupidity by subjecting ourselves to what we had just endured. We flipped a coin to decide who got the top bunk and who would rest in the bottom. I lost and climbed onto the top rack. Sleep came easily even while covered in soap, the smell of the paper mill and the unrelenting swelter of Charleston in August.

Chapter 22
I'm Not Dreaming

Reveille! The morning bugler blasted the alert over the campus P.A. system stirring us from our slumber. Summoned by the tune, our cadre charged into action and the screaming began. Heavy fists beat on our doors. "Rise and shine! Get your assess out of bed and into muster formation!"

"Finn, what is mustard formation?" John asked.

"I have no idea. I am just..." my door flew open to reveal Sgt. Banner looming between the door jambs. He promised to make me pay the previous day, and he came to exact his toll.

"Makinen, O'Malley! Let's move it. Get your asses down to muster now!" my squad leader screamed.

All Knobs were assigned two-man rooms on either the third or fourth division. A division indicated floor or level. Quickly, I was learning unfamiliar jargon that would reside within my brain and alter my manner of speech. The floor would be replaced by division and muster would replace "get together". I was on the fourth division. Rushing out of my passageway, Sgt. Banner matched each step by my side yelling in my ear. My first morning at The Citadel was surreal. My mind was in a fog and the screeching of Sgt. Banner seemed muffled. Clearly the circumstances and shock of my awakening left me off balanced. With each step down the stairwell, I became more cognizant and alert. Was this a dream? The lisp laden commands of my cadre sergeant indicated that I was not dreaming. Any word with a letter "s" was especially challenging for Banner. Further confirming the reality of my situation was the showering of saliva accompanying shouts into my ear. Yes, s's were challenging for my escort, but it was especially soaking and comical when he included "asses" in his verbal directives. I did not laugh. By now, I knew better.

"Get your eyes off me! Stop moving. What are you looking at? Get over here! Oh, do you miss your mommy?" The barks of insult and command echoed in the dark early morning. They came from not one cadet leader, but from all of them and from every corner and company in the barracks. Muster complete, our cadre platoon leader, Cadet Second Lieutenant Tom Dorman, took command and attempted to march us to Coward Hall Dining

MILITARY BRAT   Pete Masalin

Facility for an early morning breakfast of powdered eggs and grits. To the outside world, we must have looked hopeless. The wide eyes of unnerved plebes, uneasy in their surroundings and uncertain in their steps, failed to display any sign of a well-disciplined and cohesive unit. We were the exact opposite. We were pitiful. As we marched, Lt. Dorman called a cadence which few could perform. We tripped each other and clashed limbs as the remaining cadre traveled alongside our formation shouting corrective commands, "Get in step! What are you looking at!" It was a scene that was replicated in every new platoon of Knobs marching to their first Citadel breakfast.

While academics were not scheduled to commence until two weeks after our arrival, the education of my military mind started the moment I recorded my signature in the Company First Sergeant's logbook. The full rigor of our cadre training was not immediately implemented. We were allowed to acclimate to our surroundings and coastal South Carolina's often overwhelming warmth and stifling thick air.

In our rooms, we were generally left to our own recovery and break from the staff. If they did enter our room, it was demanded that we stand to attention. After a few responses of "Sir, no sir" or "Sir, no excuse sir," they would leave us to our thoughts. I'm pretty sure these visits were just to ensure that they were always present in our consciousness.

"I hate this place," John expressed. "I hate Lt. Dorman. I hate Gutierrez, Banner, Simonson, Johnson, Ward....." He continued to name the entire cadre.

"I know John." I tried to console him, but I had to admit they were not my favorite people. "Let's just get through each day one at a time." I turned my attention to the shining of my shoes. The best way to minimize the pain offered by my tormentors was to work on my military bearing. It wouldn't stop the harassment; however, it did abate it. I didn't need to have the best-shined shoes and brass. I just needed to look better than the man standing next to me.

"John, did you get spit on by Banner today?"

Erupting in laughter for at least 30 seconds, John finally replied, "Man, he slobbered all over my brass buckle while inspecting it and

MILITARY BRAT   Pete Masalin

yelling about how it was all tarnished. I wanted to tell him that he's the reason it's tarnished."

We both started laughing probably harder than we should have, but truthfully there was rarely much to laugh about.

"What do you think about Hell Night they keep mentioning to us?" I inquired.

"I don't know. I think I'm in hell right now." We both chuckled nervously.

We would learn about Hell Night soon enough. These few days were pleasant when compared to what we would soon face. They were instructional days to break us from our lazy civilian habits and clarify our military requirements. How to march, wear the uniform, clean the latrine and all manner of things associated with cadet life. Even so, the days were not without casualties.

"John! Come here. Look out the window," I requested.

"What's going on, Finn?"

"Kincaid is leaving," I responded.

John couldn't believe it. "Yesterday, he was bragging about how his dad and grandfather were grads."

"I know. He was bragging to me about how his whole life he wanted to go to The Citadel. Is that his mom? She's crying."

Charles Kincaid, CK as he asked to be called was a lanky and lean young man standing about six feet tall. The Citadel wasn't just a school. It was a family tradition. With my window open, I could hear the sobbing of Mrs. Kincaid. Only two days before she and her husband had proudly delivered her son to the alma mater of her husband and father. It was hard for me to imagine the thoughts racing through her head. Had she bragged to her friends and family about CK's decision to continue the family's legacy of The Citadel through three generations? Was she concerned about the opinion others might form of her son? Mr. Kincaid's opinion was easily discerned as I heard his one-way conversation with CK.

"It's too bad your sister can't go to The Citadel. She's tougher than you. We haven't even left Charleston, and I have to bring you back home with me. I can't believe you couldn't last two days."

CK said nothing. He dropped his head, hugged his mother, and climbed into the car. As I looked toward the sally port of Stevens Barracks, I saw members of cadre smiling and joking. I don't know if it was directly in response to Cadet Recruit Kincaid's attrition or not, but I thought it in bad taste to do so in front of the Kincaid family. In CK's defense, The Citadel is not for everyone nor every alumni's child.

"Wow," John mumbled walking back to his desk. "Maybe he's the lucky one."

We both laughed and turned our attention to our shoes and brass. There would be little more thought or conversation given to Charles Kincaid. We had our own battles to fight, and our own survival was in the balance.

Chapter 23
The Fourth-Class System is Now in Effect

Just as routine began to set in, the day we dreaded had arrived. This was the time of Hell Night, our official recognition that the full Fourth-Class system was in effect. Anxiety and anticipation possessed every thought of my classmates and me as the hours and minutes advanced to 2100. From the moment we arrived, all cadre members took pleasure and every opportunity to remind us that our day of reckoning was fast approaching. The evil glee in their tone conjured fearful thoughts in the minds of all Knobs. I was not immune. It was the unknown, and the cadre was masterful in the manipulation of our uncertainty ensuring and increasing the stress we harbored. Often, people hype and bluster about upcoming events only to observe overexaggerated claims. Hell Night was upon us, and it would not disappoint.

At 2045, we were all in rooms before being summoned to muster. On order, we were rustled to first division and positioned into an extended platoon formation with arms lengths between cadet recruits. The cadre had a slightly softer tone with us when directing our movement and walking between us as we stood motionless at attention. I heard no yells or screaming demands.

Sgt. Banner came to my station and whispered from behind, "You are mine. Hell Night is here."

"Sir, yes sir."

"Shut up! I didn't ask you anything," Banner said.

At 2055, the lights were extinguished, and all staff members disappeared into the shadows of walls that have hidden the torments of Knobs of many years past. We stood rigidly in darkness and silence on a red and grey checkerboard quadrangle. Alone in my thoughts, as were my classmates, I had no expectation for a pleasant evening. The entire campus was eerily still except for the audible nervous panting of victims awaiting their fate. The sky was absent any moon to provide partial illumination. Suddenly, at precisely 2100, the silence was fractured by the sound of a lone bugle over the PA. More manipulation of our minds was compounded by the song choice, a haunting rendition of Home Sweet Home. At the song's conclusion, we were allowed a brief moment of silence before an announcement reverberated across the campus and in every barrack.

"Cadet Recruits. The Fourth-Class System is now in effect!"

Mayhem ensued. Instantly all flood lights bore upon us. The cadre charged from their lairs to attack their prey. Seemingly we each had two members of cadre with eyes aflame and nostrils expanded shattering the calm with unrelenting harassment. I was rewarded by the attendance of my friend Sgt. Banner and due an unexpected shower as he screamed at me while we were facing nose to nose.

"It's payday, Makinen!"

Immediately, I was ordered to start running in place. Knees were expected to be raised waist high as we ran. On the command of "Hit it," we were expected to assume a prone position and pump out pushups until our arms faltered. Collapsing offered no relief as we were instructed to return to running in place. This form of discipline used for instructional purposes was known as "racking" or "getting racked." No Knob was immune to it as it was used as a motivational tool for us often throughout the year, but only in the barracks and out of public eye.

"Hit it!" I was ordered.

It is impossible for me to remember how many pushups I completed that evening or how long I ran, but it was safe for me to assume that my friends from high school, who chose Virginia Tech or the University of Virginia, were not having as much fun as I was. Considerable time had passed as we continued our calisthenics; exhaustion reduced all Knobs to sweat soaked participants. While our energy waned, the exuberance of our masters did not. There was more fun to come, and the highlight of Hell Night was looming.

Sufficiently depleted in the eyes of the training cadre, our physical training session ended. Many among us thought that surely, we would retire for the evening. Sgt. Bannon was in my ear again. "Are you tired? Are you ready to call it a night?"

"Sir, yes sir!" I managed to respond.

"Well, we are just getting started."

MILITARY BRAT   Pete Masalin

    With shouted commands, we were all directed to an alcove room on second division. Alcoves were in each corner of the barracks on every division. They were typically assigned four men and for upperclassmen accommodations. This room belonged to the Company Executive Officer, Cadet First Lieutenant Blake and his roommate and cadre Platoon Leader, Cadet Lt. Dorman. Forty-Four of us were packed into the corner rotunda with a diameter of roughly twelve feet. Space was minimal when considering the accompanying furniture.

    "Assholes to bellybuttons, Knobs. Pack it in!" 1stSgt Gutierrez demanded.

    "Too slow. We can do this all night," Staff Sergeant Kowalski aided. Kowalski was the cadre Platoon Sergeant.

    Compactly shoved in and still reeling from our workout, breathing was labored. Cadre members pushed on our chests to ensure we were mashed together without gaps between us. Satisfied, the re-introduction of our chain of command proceeded. It was a formality of Hell Night to individually recognize our leaders before us. The Company First Sergeant was the emcee for the night and because of his accent and stutter, I enjoyed some comic relief. This was a time of intimidation, but I couldn't help feeling less frightened by First Sergeant Gutierrez's speech.

    From top to bottom, our leadership individually stepped in front of us to be recognized. Each time he introduced the staff member by name he would say, "L...L... Look at him. You will remember him. Get your eyes off h...h... him."

    His introduction was most memorable. Returning to my room at the conclusion of the night, I began impersonating First Sergeant Gutierrez. John couldn't stop laughing and we laughed long into the evening.

    "Gi...Gi...Give your I...I...love to your m...m...mother, y...y...your k...k... kisses to your girlfriend and your soul t...t...to Jesus, be...be...because your ass is...is mine."

    It was clear to me of Gutierrez's position. I knew he had the power to make my life even more uncomfortable. Any disrespect would cause me strife and I knew my boundaries; however, any attempt to terrorize us by his lecture was diminished by its delivery. The fact is, I hung on every word that he was inclined to hang.

As I recovered in my room from the struggle that was Hell Night, I reflected on the thrashing we had just endured. For the first time, I understood. No one could kill us, but it was their job to break us. Break us from our past. Break us of bad habits. Break us to build us. Break us to weed out the weak and maintain the strong. The Citadel is not for everyone and at the next morning's formation, we witnessed another casualty. Cadet Recruit David LeMay was paraded out in front of us escorted by Cpl. Simonson.

"Well, well, well," Simonson bellowed while displaying a wide grin. "Guess y'all will be saying goodbye to LeMay this morning."

I would like to say I was shocked, but I wasn't. It was obvious. Dave struggled with the simplest of military regimen. Even with the encouragement of his roommate Tim Callahan, Dave didn't possess the fortitude and will to survive in an unfriendly environment. Tim helped shine his shoes and attended to other shortcomings, but ultimately it was not enough for anyone who didn't want to make the effort. As Dave was escorted through the sally port, the early morning silence was disrupted.

"Bye, Dave!"

"Who said that?" Demanded SSgt. Kowalski. "I will rack the piss out of all of you. Who the hell said that?!" Nobody moved and a response never came.

Our formation gained greater attention and higher intensity from the available staff members preparing to march us to breakfast.

"None of you numb nuts will be eating this morning until someone tells me who opened their mouth!"

Callahan threw himself on the verbal grenade he had thrown. "Sir, I did sir." In a frenzy as rendered in a sea of sharks upon a wounded fish, Callahan was engulfed by the cadre.

"Hit it! Get up! Start running!" Commands continued. "Who the hell do you think you are?"

MILITARY BRAT   Pete Masalin

"Sir, no excuse sir." Tim repeated over and over as the onslaught continued.

With all the attention focused on our cadre's quarry, we stood unattended. I did not break ranks, but I was able to spy a glimpse of the commotion. Cadet Recruit Callahan was awash with perspiration and met the challenge with full measure. I also glanced at the barracks gateway to witness LeMay stop to look back at his roommate. Cpl. Simonson directed Dave to move. "Let's go." Dave lowered his head and disappeared from view. Punishment delivered, Tim recovered, rejoined the ranks, and we marched to breakfast.

Meals in the mess hall were never easy. One just didn't stroll to Coward Hall, choose a seat of his liking and order from a menu of varied culinary delights. Marched in formation, we arrived and were dismissed to our assigned tables in the dining facility. Each table hosted a mess carver anchoring at the head of the table. He was a senior member of the staff requiring that his assigned Knobs prepare every upperclassmen's plate before attending to our own. Once the freshmen's plates were prepared, we would balance the plate upon our index and middle fingers of both hands while sitting at attention on the front three inches of a wooden cafeteria chair. Before the first bite, permission to eat was required.

"Sir, Mr. Johnson sir. Would you or any other kind, fine, highly refined Citadel stud care for any of the delicacies from my plate, sir!" could be heard throughout Coward Hall.

"Eat," was always the response of the mess carver, but eating was our secondary chore.

Always the conversationalists, the upperclassmen asked us for answers to our Knob Knowledge, chain of command and general topics of nuisance.

"Makinen, who is the Regimental Religious Officer?" What! We have a Regimental Religious Officer? I thought to myself. "Sir, no excuse sir."

"You don't know who the Regimental Religious Officer is?" countered the cadre.

"Sir, yes sir. I mean sir, no sir," I uttered.

MILITARY BRAT — Pete Masalin

"What is it? You do know or you don't know?"

"Sir, no excuse sir?"

Every meal was the same and all my classmates endured them equally. When leaving the table for the sanctuary of our rooms becomes more important than sustenance, bodies suffer. Swallowing bites between questions was hurried as we raced through our meals and dared not ask for seconds. Apparently, my six-foot two-inch frame carrying an approximate 170 pounds when I arrived was considered portly by my caregivers. Four weeks after reporting for duty, I was a gaunt 145 pounds.

"Sir, Mr. Johnson sir. My sufficiencies have been suffonsified to such a degree that any more sustenance would prove to be super sanctimonious to my health. I, therefore, Cadet Recruit Makinen, request permission to get the hell off your mess." I presented this request to my mess carver when desiring to retreat from mealtime. It was required of us all, and once it was initiated by one, it was uttered by all. No one wanted to be the last poor soul among a table of his superiors.

The chow hall was my paradoxical savior. Sunday was a day of rest even on The Citadel campus. Sunday was a day of celebration in the austere environment in which all Knobs resided. We were able to stay in our racks beyond reveille. No formation marching was required as we individually ambled to Coward Hall for brunch. Brunch! I longed for Sunday mornings all week. Once inside, we could pick a table of our own and dine with the people of our choosing. We could eat leisurely, fully chewing our food without fear of interruption. Consuming unlimited amounts of fried chicken, French fries, bread, and more chicken were the attention of all. Desserts were available and unending. Brunch saved us from certain death by famine. It replenished the deficiencies of the past week and fueled us for the next. As bears gorge themselves before hibernation, Sundays provided for our sustainment. Conversation was also welcomed. In the early weeks of our integration into our institution, it was at brunch where we learned the stories, histories, and family lineages of those who would become brothers.

The early days melded into weeks then into months. As time progressed,

MILITARY BRAT — Pete Masalin

the toil attached to the Fourth-Class system became routine. Most days became routine by the accumulation of time and the acclimation to the school and its requirements. I remember the struggle and humor that bonded us forever. We each ran hundreds of miles that year and traveled nowhere while being racked in place. Pushups were too numerous to count. It is easy to reflect on the punishment, perceived wrong or abuse and complain, but it is the value of the discipline that makes the man. My experience at this military school in Charleston was the embodiment of its charter and the symbol of its ring.

Within the walls of Stevens Barracks, Knobs were allowed to gather in each other's rooms with modest autonomy. We still needed to be guarded for the occasional aggravation of an overzealous staff member seeking to reinforce his authority over us, popping into our rooms and administering harassment for no other reason but to pester us. A few "sir, yes sirs," and they were gone. Those who participated in this type of behavior were quickly revealed and their respect among us was weakened. I came to understand in these moments and similar offenses that one could learn more from poor leadership than good leadership. Good leadership often goes unnoticed, especially when it is expected.

Patrick Stanton's and Art Bibbs' room was a favorite gathering spot for the band of Knobs in my company. It was located on the third division next to the stairwell. None of us could reach our room without passing Pat and Art's room.

"What's up?" I asked.

"Hey man," several peers responded.

By now, afternoon classes were over, and we had down time before preparing for evening meal. "I just blew past Gutierrez. I can't deal with getting stopped by him. Every time he stops me, I get racked because I smile when he stutters," I complained.

"G...g...get your ch...chin in!" Pat aped.

Everyone burst into laughter and the amateur hour of First Sergeant Gutierrez impersonations commenced. We had to be careful. While our

| MILITARY BRAT | Pete Masalin |

hideout was a convenient respite locale for us, it was also an easy target for marauding upper classmates. Too much laughter or commotion was sure to bring us unwanted attention.

"Shhh! Keep it down," Art implored.

Tim Callahan chuckled, "G...get y... y...your eyes..."

The door burst open, and we shot to attention. "Are you scumbags making fun of your First Sergeant?"

"Sir, no sir," all said in unison.

"It sounds like it to me," Cadet Corporal Larry Hovis implied.

Cpl. Hovis was a jerk. That is the politest way I can describe him. He was what many referred to as a flaming asshole. He was easily the most despised member of my company staff, perhaps the entire corps. He was of modest build and overstated ego. His joy came in harassing the defenseless. The only thing rendering us incapable of retaliation was the system that provided him power over us.

"I distinctly heard you folks mocking your chain of command."

"Sir, no sir," I offered.

"Makinen, you know that lying is an honor violation," Hovis warned.

"Sir, yes sir."

"Look at you losers. This room is disgusting." Alleged the angry corporal. "This smoke is disgusting. You all are disgusting. Keep it down." He left the room, closing the door behind him.

We all eased, looked at one another, and snickered trying to suppress any audible laugh from transferring through the door to the ears of Hovis who we were certain was loitering just on the other side. The room was clouded with cigarette smoke. Pat and another classmate, D.J. Broome, were chain smokers, and at each gathering they easily consumed a pack between the two of them in one sitting.

Evening Study Period or ESP was compulsory for freshman every weekday night. During this period, Knobs sat at their desks next to the window preparing for our academic pursuits. Beneficial to this arrangement was that upperclassmen and staff members were not allowed disrupt us in our study time. Only the academic officer maintained the authority to check in on us. ESP was three hours long and a visit to the latrine exposed us to danger. The limits of ESP security ended once we exited the protection assured us while in our rooms. I was fortunate that my room was next to the latrine on fourth division. I did not need to run a gauntlet to relieve myself. Pat, Art, and many others were not as privileged. Their distance to relief was significantly greater. To make such a run, one had to be in proper uniform, and the trip left one exposed to impromptu inspections. Getting caught out of uniform meant demerits that could accumulate resulting in lost privileges. Many fashioned a solution to eliminate the prospect of harassment coupled with time savings by avoiding the trek. Each room had a sink that for some doubled as a urinal.

Stanton had an aversion to peeing in a plumbing fixture designated for proper hygiene. It was where he shaved, washed his face, and brushed his teeth. His bladder full of excess coffee, Pat faced a dilemma. Should he don the proper uniform and risk inspection, or should he urinate in the sink. He would do neither. Pat Stanton was a ready, shoot, aim kind of thinker who often acted on impulse, sometimes overlooking the outcome. He stood from his desk, removed the fan from his window, and peed from his perch of a third-floor windowsill. Within minutes, Art and Pat had an unannounced visitor.

"Who threw water out the window!" The door crashed open, and Cpl. Hovis stood looming.

"Sir?" Bibbs questioned.

"Who dumped water out of the window? I want to know right now!"

"Sir, no excuse sir." Responded Stanton. Looking at his furious persecutor, he realized what had occurred. Cpl. Hovis' face was covered in droplets and his hair and shoulders were moistened. Hovis' room was on the second division directly below Art and Pat's room. The moment Pat peed into darkness his waste descended directly into the pathway of an operating window fan placed on a sill intended to direct cool evening air into the room. Without Hovis' realization, urine was sucked through the fan's blades and onto his face.

MILITARY BRAT   Pete Masalin

"Bibbs! Did you throw water out your window?" the corporal insisted.

"Sir, no sir!" Bibbs declared.

"Stanton! Was it you?"

"Sir, no sir!" avowed Stanton

Hovis offered, "You know lying is an honor violation."

"Sir, yes sir," the roommates responded together.

"So, you're telling me that neither of you threw water out of your window."

"Sir, yes sir." Cpl. Hovis paused for a moment knowing that he had no substantial evidence and left.

It wasn't an honor violation and neither Pat nor Art had lied. It wasn't water that exited their window.

Within the limits of discipline imposed upon us, comedy was often observed even in little events. Being "racked" meant running in place and endless pushups. It was a form of punishment that also served as conditioning. None of us appreciated the conditioning, and we hated getting racked. As the days and weeks passed, it became humorous to ridicule friends and classmates who were issued this frequent castigation. In the privacy of our rooms, we mocked each other and poked fun at the most recent rack sessions of us all. One such incident caused a raucous uproar when we returned from evening mess.

Forming for evening meal, Tim Gray arrived at muster with a shine on his shoes judged to be below standard. "Hit it!" Tim was directed by his squad sergeant. When this is ordered, the subject knob is required to fall into push-up position while placing his hat commonly referred to as a cover between his shoulder blades. Once in place, the offender commences push-ups while calling out the count until the disciplinarian commands, "Start running."

As directed, Tim popped up and tried to retrieve his cover. The problem was that as he arose, he did so rapidly that his cover flew from his back and into a large trashcan ten feet away. I witnessed his head gear's flight. Most of us did yet we could not speak. Cadet Gray was frantic. His eyes

MILITARY BRAT   Pete Masalin

were wide, confusion and despair consumed poor Tim. As he desperately sought to recover his lost garment our leadership descended upon him.

"Where is your cover! Where is it Gray! Did you forget it."

"Sir, no excuse sir!" Gray replied.

"You better find it!" his persecutors demanded.

"Sir, yes sir."

Tim kept running in place while his head swiveled left and right looking for his hat to no avail. Finally, we were required to march to Coward Hall for dinner. Tim marched with his head naked as the screams of the upperclassmen harassed him the entire way. At the conclusion of the meal, Cadet Gray tried to avoid anyone on his walk back to the barracks. It was fortunate that knobs always left the mess table first while the upperclassmen stayed behind relaxing and enjoying their meal. Tim arrived unmolested while returning to his room. Once Tim joined us in Bibbs and Stanton's room, we were unrelenting in our laughter while mocking and joking at his circumstances that evening. After a short period, we relented and told him where to find his misplaced cover. Relieved, he quickly went to the quad, returned to our gathering, hat in hand, and began to laugh.

Finding amusement in other classmates' missteps helped us all endure the daily trials we faced. It also developed in most of us a warped sense of humor. The Citadel was not a soft environment. Its history promulgated a pathway of austerity while challenging the physical and mental capacity of young men. Many did not survive indoctrination as the institution maintained no quarter for the weak. Keep up or be cast aside. The way of spartan conditions and authoritarian regulations demanded strength. Compassion was most often demonstrated in ridicule. In the military world, softness is not allowed among men. It is weakness. If you weren't the target of ridicule in your suffering, it was because no one cared or liked you. I remember, as a Lieutenant at Mountain Warfare School years later, my platoon was conducting a nighttime cliff assault. My point man slipped and fell 50 feet. Once everyone knew he did not suffer serious harm, we taunted him for falling. It was at The Citadel, particularly during my knob year where I learned that finding humor in

MILITARY BRAT   Pete Masalin

the challenge is the cure in prevailing over it.

As the year progressed, the rigors of military life seemed to ease. The days became more routine. Perhaps it was a combination of several factors. Academics became important to our education and most of our hours required classroom attendance with study in the evening. We became more proficient at meeting the military standards required of us. The chain of command became more lenient as the year progressed. It wasn't that our duties lessened, or discipline became soft. It was that we were now aware and comfortable in our environment. We were cadets in every regard, just the lowliest. We still walked in gutters leaving the sidewalk for upperclassmen. We braced and squared corners while in the barracks. We still got racked, and we laughed.

Chapter 24
Liberty

"Let's go to Dino's," I stated to my roommate John.

"You kidding? We should already be there," O'Malley responded as he headed for the door.

All of us were headed to Dino's. It was our first opportunity to leave campus and all of us were excited to crowd the streets of Charleston without supervision. Dino's was a pizza joint at the opposite end of Johnson Hagood Avenue, a straight shot from campus. Knobs were not allowed to have cars, and we swarmed on foot to conquer the city just as Sherman marched to the sea many years before. Our first stop was usually Dino's to requisition provisions in the form of pizza and beer before furthering our mission.

It was a memorable night. Our strength was replenished as we gorged ourselves uncontrollably with pizza. Our bravery to attack the town was emboldened by sharing pitchers of beer. Nobody demanded Knob Knowledge or trivial information from us for their own amusement. We were absent a tether and left to our own direction. Some did not handle liberty and their independence well.

Departing Dino's with a group of my classmates, we noticed the first casualty of the evening.

"What the hell is that?" I asked.

"What are you talkin' about, Finn?" John wondered.

"Over there," Bibbs directed.

Shirt undone, cover missing, and uniform in disarray, a Knob from another company lay face down in the parking lot. A station wagon belonging to The Officer of the Day pulled in next to the scene. The stricken Knob's classmates tried desperately to gather their friend and flee; however, it was futile. The OD stepped out of his car to assess the matter. Barely able to stand or speak, the wounded cadet had succumbed to his libations and his night of freedom expired at approximately 1930 as he was poured into the back seat of a blue station wagon.

"Whoa. What do you think will happen to him?" Mike Jeffries, another of my company mates asked.

"I'm sure he's going to be in a ton of shit if the OD had to come get him. Dino's must have called the campus," John noted.

"Nah. They'll probably rack the piss out of him for losing his cover," Tim Gray offered causing us to erupt in laughter when remembering his own recent experience.

As bad as I felt for the poor lad, it was an important moment. It showed me a guiding principle of the institution of which I was now a member. It is a long-standing directive beyond the school and extending into all branches of service: Never leave a man behind. The Citadel was collecting its fallen and ensuring for his welfare. The system was going to mete out an appropriate disciplinary measure, but it was not going to leave one of its own unprotected even from his own misdeeds.

Tragedy averted, we left and headed deeper into the historic rows of shops, bars, and restaurants fronting King Street. More important than food and beer were the inhabitants. In the heart of the city, The College of Charleston loomed, awaiting our arrival. The ratio of women to men at that school was greatly in our favor, and we were interested in finally meeting and talking with charming ladies who resided in sororities. It was a perfect plan. We had no car. Our regimen and dining restrictions caused our malnourished appearance. Regulated haircuts denied us appealing hair styles. As our pace quickened, the late summer climate withdrew sweat from our bodies, soaking our neatly pressed uniforms. Time was of the essence. Just as Cinderella needed to return from her first ball at midnight so was the limitation of our pass. Never mind that we were oblivious to the facts of our disposition. Facts didn't matter. We were determined. What could possibly go wrong?

We meandered along King Street uncertain of where to begin. None of us were familiar with local establishments, crowded with cadets and College of Charleston coeds. The clock advanced, compressing our free time against our requirement to return to the barracks. We were novices. Frustration began to erode our resolve.

"Where do we start?" pondered Bibbs.

"I thought we were looking for the sororities," I responded.

MILITARY BRAT   Pete Masalin

"Do you know where they are Finn?" Tim wondered.

"No, but..."

"Then shut the hell up," Tim cut me off.

O'Malley chimed in, "I heard they are on Coming Street. Jesse Baker's girlfriend is a member of Delta Delta Delta."

"Our classmate... Baker?" Pat Stanton inquired.

"The one and only. I think he's there now."

I suggested a plan. "They should know we're coming. Need a date? Tri Delta!"

Tim understood the pun I had just offered and cackled. Shortly everyone understood. "Need a date? Tri Delta," Bibbs repeated, and we all joined in Tim's amusement.

"Where's Coming Street?" Stanton requested.

"This way," directed Bibbs.

It wasn't too long before we realized Bibbs had no clue where we were headed. The clock hastened our desperation.

"Bibbs! You don't know where we are or where the sororities are, do you?" Mike probed.

"Shut up, Jefferies" Bibbs said.

"Guys, it's almost 2200. We better find this place soon," I added.

One could see the defeat in Bibbs' face as his navigation shortfalls were evident. "Do you know how to get there, Finn?"

"All Finn is saying is that we need to be back to school in a couple hours," Tim offered.

"I know dumb ass. We're almost there," Bibbs barked.

Maybe we were close, but we weren't "almost there." We marched around the streets with purpose, however, aimlessly. We backtracked unintentionally along routes previously traversed as we sought out coeds to visit. We were all too frustrated to speak as we rushed to find our destination. Ever mindful of the time restriction, each cadet continued to glance at our wristwatches monitoring the time.

"Stop," our impromptu squad leader commanded. "Do you hear that?"

Halted, we could hear beach music in the distance. "That's it! That's where we need to be." O'Malley excitedly pointed.

We quickly recalibrated our route and headed in the direction of the music. As we advanced towards our objective, our pace quickened. As we hit the intersection of Wentworth Street and Coming Street, we heard "Sitting on the Dock of the Bay" begin to play, the music was turned up as the revelers joined in singing along with Otis Redding.

"Let's go!" Bibbs yelled, breaking into a full paced gait down Coming Street. We followed.

It was a sight to behold! The girls offered big bouffant hair atop preppie attire. Oversized faux gold earrings and pearl necklaces were common. Madonna wannabes, dressed in pseudo punk clothes, also stood on the front porch. For young men who had been held captive in an austere environment for weeks, Delta Delta Delta offered relief from the drab vision of uniforms, bald heads, and pale white walls. We stood at the curb gawking at the glamour of it all. Stanton's jaw remained wide while the rest of us grinned and stared. The singing stopped, and the partiers turned their attention to us and stared back. Neither group said a word. I assessed the situation and inspected our appearance. Soaked in sweat, uniforms in disarray and panting after our run, we most assuredly would not be making new friends this evening. And we could forget about getting any phone numbers.

"Can we help you?" A sorority member offered.

Knowing not how to respond, we whispered among ourselves.

"Hello...can we help you?" We were asked again.

"Is Jesse here?" Bibbs queried. Good job, I thought to myself. Surely knowing Jesse will be our ticket to the celebration.

"Jesse? Jesse who?" insisted another beauty.

Bibbs tried his best and pleaded, "Jesse Baker. He's a friend of ours, and we think he might be here."

"We don't know a Jesse Baker."

"His girlfriend is a member of your sorority," Bibbs continued.

"I don't think so. Y'all need to run along."

"But he is in there," added Tim.

"Y'all need to leave," demanded another.

Just as we started to depart, a girl emerged from the house and whispered in the ear of another party goer.

"Wait." Our fortunes were about to change. "Jesse is here."

We all were certain that we were steps away from meeting our future date. "He said he'll be right out. Y'all just stay there for a moment."

Within seconds Jesse emerged from the house, descended the front porch staircase, and approached our gathering.

"Thanks for coming by to get me guys." Jesse spoke. "It's a long walk."

"No. it's not. The house is right there," O'Malley countered.

"House? We're not going in Delta," Jesse informed.

"Jesse, we spent all night trying to find this place; we gotta' go in," I begged.

"Finn, look at your watch. It's nearly 2300, and we need to head back to The Citadel."

"No way! We need to go in there," Bibbs appealed.

"Sorry guys. We can't risk not being back on time, and I'm not risking it." Jesse was correct in his direction.

"Son of a bitch! I spent all night with you losers, and I got nothing," O'Malley lamented.

As we turned to start our trek, the ladies upon the porch snickered and giggled at what one could only assume was the pathetic failure in our first off campus mission. As if on cue and ensuring greater damage to our egos, the music was turned up and the revelers sang along with The Temptations' "My Girl" as we walked away. It was a lengthy hike, and time passed too quickly. All of us were aggravated that we had been unsuccessful at achieving our primary goal of meeting co-eds, all of us apart from Jesse Baker. He had a fine first liberty and his smile was proof of his enjoyable evening. Jesse tried to share his night's story with us, but each time he began to speak he was stifled by "Shut up, Jesse," by one or all of us.

Jesse's advice was good advice indeed. We reported back in at approximately 2330. As we maneuvered back to our individual rooms, the upperclassmen started to amass near the sally port. I wasn't certain of the reason for their assembly, but I had enough awareness and sobriety to know that it probably wasn't good. John and I were in our rooms when a different party than earlier witnessed on Coming Street broke out. 10 minutes before midnight, knobs continued to return to their barracks. Screams resounded off the thick wall in the sally port and stairwells. Poor souls requesting permission to pass their oppressors or climb "their" staircase. O'Malley and I laughed but didn't dare look out our doorway for fear of being called into the fun. The yelling escalated as stragglers arrived after liberty's expiration at 2400. Knobs and even upperclassmen received punishment for being late, but of course it was the knobs that suffered the most. "Start running!"

O'Malley lit up a cigarette and settled into his desk chair. "It was great to get off campus even if it didn't go as we planned."

"Planned? We didn't have a plan," I replied.

"Yeah, you're right, but hey, a least we ain't getting racked right now," He chuckled.

"We know more now, John. We'll get 'em next time." As if I knew what "get 'em" meant.

"Damn right, Finn. Damn right."

Chapter 25
A Semester Ends

Sooner or later, first year cadets accept their new reality and acquiesce to the system. Those that don't, quit. We had three in my company who made it to Thanksgiving furlough, left for home and never returned. Two were known not to be coming back after the break. However, we were all surprised by the one that didn't. Vinny Russo was a graduate of a highly prestigious New York military high school and one of our sharpest Knobs. For him not to return shocked me and my classmates. Vinny would be missed as he was well liked by everyone.

Thanksgiving gave me an opportunity to reunite with my partner in childhood adventures, Levi. Levi was in his last year at the Naval Academy and a stellar engineering student. I alternatively offered a pedestrian correction to the academic achievement of brothers. My mid-term grade report reflected a stellar 1.7 Grade Point Average or GPA. It wasn't enough to require my academic probation, but I wasn't setting any records. On the other hand, my personal military appearance was outstanding, and I couldn't get racked for my grades. It was good to see my parents understand that I had my priorities straight. They were speechless when my grade progress report was delivered to my home address.

The house was more crowded when Levi and I returned. Leigh and Ash quickly and comfortably adjusted to our absence. Reluctantly, they accommodated the added population of siblings if only for a brief extended weekend. It was good for us all to be back together. I would not ever discount the value of time with family; but my top priority was food, and Mom did not disappoint. I ravaged the pantry and refrigerator. A year earlier, my mother would have intervened in my pillage. This year, it didn't bother her in the slightest. She saw my withered appearance and was just happy that her two boys were home.

Dad, Levi, and I exchanged stories and comparisons about our two schools, the Naval Academy and The Citadel. Ash sat quietly at the table. His expression plainly revealed that he had no desire to continue his future education with any institution immersed in a military culture. He looked at us as we spoke, waiting for a pause in the conversation.

At an opportune moment Ash interjected, "I gotta go." And he left the table.

MILITARY BRAT   Pete Masalin

"Start running!" I offered. Dad and Levi were amused in my retort and wryly smiled.

Ash wasn't sure how to react and simply said, "Whatever." And walked away.

Reuniting with friends from high school, I was met with great intrigue. Girls that I knew thought I looked sickly. Guys thought I was crazy to attend a military school and subject myself to such a stringent environment. As would be expected, my friends and I never discussed academics. They spoke of parties, fraternities, and sororities. I spoke of getting beaten every day, being denied food and water, and marching for hours. Perhaps, I took a few liberties, but the expressions on many of their faces were worth the exaggeration. I was never denied water.

In too short of time, I returned to the spartan surroundings that The Citadel afforded. It never promised anything more. First stop, Bibbs and Stanton's room where we all assembled to lie about all the dates we had over Thanksgiving and reconnect with what had obviously become a band of brothers forged by the rigors of the military institution's legacy. A tradition and successful process of breaking the soft individual and instilling discipline and toughness.

"What happened to Russo?" Gray asked the group.

"What do you mean?" Bibbs offered in a puff of smoke after an extended drag on his cigarette.

"I heard he's not coming back," Tim commented.

"He shot a guy in the Bronx and is in jail," I exclaimed.

"Shut up, Finn. That's bullshit."

"No. It's true. I heard the upperclassmen talking about it when I was checking back in. He got in a fight with someone hitting on his girlfriend, and he shot him."

"No way!" Jesse Baker shouted. "He never would have done that."

"He did," O'Malley who had just joined the room added. He was my roommate and knew I was telling stories again. Without missing a beat, he continued, "I live in New York, and it was all over the news. Vinny's picture was all over the TV."

I started to snicker, and O'Malley immediately joined me. Everyone soon realized that we were making the story up.

"Assholes!" Someone shouted, and everyone erupted in a roar of laughter.

Stanton asked, "Seriously, does anybody really know what happened to Russo? I guess he just decided this wasn't where he wanted to be."

In the end, Vinny Russo was counted among the casualties of Knobs who matriculated with us, could go no more, and quit. The expectation of a Citadel Diploma expired almost as quickly as it began. Nobody thought any less of Vinny, but our attention quickly turned back to what was required of us to finish the year.

At the morning formation, I noticed something different. It was modest; however, I could feel an ease in the air of discipline. Our chain of command had relaxed during the Thanksgiving furlough and returned slightly less rigorous in the execution of discipline. Cadre was over and the Knobs were integrated into each of the three platoons that formed each company. Each morning, Knobs were the only cadets required to march to morning chow. Upperclassmen either strolled casually to Coward Hall on their own, or they slept in missing breakfast all together. Freshmen formed in the darkness of the early morning and were inspected before being marched to our morning meal.

"There's something just not right," Sgt. Banner wondered aloud while inspecting Mike Jefferies. "Bill, come over here and check out Jefferies. Something's wrong I just can't figure it out."

Bill, known to us as Cadet Corporal Nychek, noticed the problem immediately. "He has no eyebrows, John."

Banner leaned in, "What the fuck, Jefferies!"

"Sir, no excuse sir."

"Did you shave your eyebrows?

"Sir, yes sir."

Many of us couldn't help it, and we lost our composure breaking out in suppressed laughter.'

"Shut the hell up, Knobs!' the sergeant commanded.

"Start running Jefferies!" ordered Nychek.

Nychek and Banner assembled to discuss the offense. We could hear them evaluate the grooming standards for cadets. Neither could recall any regulation governing the maintenance of eyebrows or the removal of said facial feature. In the end, there was no direct stipulation. Not to be deterred, Banner completed Jefferies' rack session and issued him a disciplinary document known as a *White Slip* citing the violation of improper shave.

When we were able to ask Mike what the hell he was thinking, he offered little information. "I just thought it would be funny," Mike said.

"That's it?! You thought it would be funny?" His roommate Rich Dawson was incredulous in his question.

"Yup."

It was no surprise to any of us. Mike was not going to be on the Dean's List for superior academic achievement. More likely, Mike would spend each summer in Charleston attending classes offered at The Citadel to keep up with his class.

The balance of the semester was brief before our welcomed and long Christmas furlough. Final Exams provided an environment of relaxed military requirements allowing all Knobs and all classes to focus on studying. The Military School of the South is, after all, an academic institution.

Traveling on Amtrak from Charleston to Union Station in Washington, DC, I reveled in hours of solitude as I sat back and observed fellow travelers headed home to join families for the holidays. Of particular note, was a young army private who frequently visited the "bar car." With each trip, she returned slightly more intoxicated. By the time we hit the Virginia border she was blasted out of her mind and inciting disruption among the passengers, who then complained to the train's staff. Amtrak officials immediately jumped into action.

MILITARY BRAT   Pete Masalin

Approaching the young combatant, they attempted to calm her down. She responded with increased belligerence, finally launching a retaliatory swing at a conductor. It was a decision she would regret. In short order, we made an unscheduled stop at the Quantico, Virginia train station located in the heart of Marine Corps Base Quantico. I looked out the window to observe an assembly of Military Police Marines awaiting her removal. The private resisted removal vigorously and spat upon anyone in close proximity to her. Uniformed Amtrak personnel delivered her to Devil Dogs, who immediately handcuffed her. And I assumed they delivered her to the brig to sober up. The train cheered and clapped thankful for her dispatchment. I was certain that she was incapable of understanding her dire predicament. A lowly Army private, drunk, thrown off a train into the hands of a service branch not her own. Not just any branch – it was the Marines.

Dad picked me up at Union Station. We grabbed my gear, walked to the car, and traveled home.

"It's great to see you, Finn."

"You too, Dad. Where's everybody?"

"They are waiting for you at home."

"I'm starving. Can we stop for something?"

"Your mother has prepared a big meal for your arrival, Swedish meatballs. How did your grades end up?"

"Um...what's she serving with the meatballs? Potatoes?" I deflected successfully.

Dad said, "Of course. Oh, and Lemon meringue pie for dessert."

Returning home, I dropped my pack and settled into the relaxed atmosphere it offered. Food was abundant and scheduled sustenance breaks were nonexistent. The mornings and nights were not interrupted by bugles bellowing Reveille or Taps. My sleep schedule was my own and a lengthy recharging of my soul was achieved.

Two days after my arrival, the whole family and I packed into the station wagon and headed through the Shenandoah Valley to the Makinen

MILITARY BRAT   Pete Masalin

mountain home. The A-framed lodge had been our family's Christmas destination since my youth. Somethings never changed and this was proven true in our seating assignments for the trip. Levi and I occupied the backseat window positions with Ash between us. Of course, Leigh assumed her usual travel position for car journeys, the rear cargo area where she slept during the entire trip. It was a tradition to spend the holidays through the New Year in the house built by the Makinen men. Dad affixed a sign above the entrance with the nautical moniker, "The Crow's Nest."

"Finn, Finn. Get up. It's time to hit the slopes," Levi said as he shook me from my slumber.

"I'm up."

"Get out of the rack," Levi continued.

Immediately I arose and dressed in my winter gear eager to ski for the day. For years, Levi and I traversed the Blue Ridge mountains on our skis and our skill had greatly improved as young men. Our style could best be described as aggressive as we tore down the mountainside. Novice skiers became our slalom gates as we rushed closely past them. Our velocity and sudden appearance startled many of them, causing some to crumble in the snow.

"Asshole!" was often shouted by the vanquished as we descended an icy path. Aggressive, yes. Courteous, no. We thought ourselves invincible as men of our age often do. My cockiness paired with recklessness was a volatile combination sure to deliver disaster. I lacked the temperament and wisdom to consider safety, ever increasing my dalliance on the edge of the extremes. I travelled too fast, jumping over moguls which lifted me to travel great distances in the air. It's physics. Once in the air, control is lost. The skis aid in navigation no more. One can't turn, slow down, or stop.

Following two weeks at our mountain retreat, it was time to return home. The Makinens had one last day of alpine adventure. We skied every day on our break, and today was our last day. The slopes were crowded with others taking advantage of their holiday vacation. We were fortunate that fresh powder had arrived the previous evening with the morning offering a brightly lit sunny day. It was colder than normal, but still a

MILITARY BRAT   Pete Masalin

beautiful day. All of us finished breakfast, loaded into the family wagon, and hit the slopes.

It was a great day of leisure. Levi and I left the family for our own pursuits and absorbed the surroundings while racing each other throughout each run. The chairlift closed at 1700, and we rushed to pack in as many rides as possible to maximize our number of trips down the hill.

Offloading the chairlift, we stood at the mountains peak. "Finn! It's 4:45. We can get one last run if we hurry."

"Race ya!" I yelled, pointing my skis tips towards the lodge at the bottom of the slopes. I was off with a head start.

"Not going to win, Finn!" Levi followed in pursuit.

We rushed down a slope designated for experts allowing a trail more vacant of skiers. Laden with moguls, the surface offered great challenge, but more fun. I battled to maintain my lead on Levi cutting through and jumping over snow mass bumps on the trail. I launched my body from a huge frozen hill through the air causing my binding to loosen and drop my right ski. I was now nothing more than a human projectile without equipment beneath me to secure a safe landing.

"Are you okay?" Hello, are you hurt? Talk to us. Are you okay?" Voices around me were muffled. I was dazed, face down and uncertain of my surroundings. Slowly I recovered from my concussion, and the voices became clearer.

"Finn! Get up, Finn," Levi implored.

I gathered myself and stood up in the middle of a crowd that gathered.

"Oh, my god!" someone exclaimed.

"He's hurt bad. Someone get Ski Patrol over here!" shouted another.

I looked at the snow and observed a fractured picture of white and yellow. My goggles shattered in their frame leaving a mosaic of jagged pieces obscuring a clear view. People handed me tissues which left me wondering why. Blood covered the immediate perimeter around my boots. I took their offering and placed a makeshift bandage under my scarf, covering my nose and mouth.

"Here's your ski, Finn," Levi said.

I reattached my binding, looked at Levi and said, "Let's go."

"You should wait for Ski Patrol," one gawker advised.

"I'm good. C'mon Levi." I made my way through the crowd and continued my route albeit less aggressively.

My family and friends that we knew had finished their day. When I approached them at the lodge, I was met with audible gasps, drawing more attention from onlookers. My mom, always the nurse, was quick to offer aid.

"That looks pretty bad, Finn. It's an ugly gash sure to require stitches," Mom diagnosed.

"I'll check it out."

Walking to the men's room to inspect my wound, a pathway opened as folks cleared from my way while grimacing and looking at my face. At the mirror, a prominent slash ripped open the flesh upon the bridge of my nose. I hadn't realized that I failed to cover my injury with the tissues provided. The dressing was aligned just below, exposing a blood-filled hole for all to witness. Blood soaked my garments, and my lower face and neck were entirely crimson. Still not completely recovered from the trauma to my brain, I was not thinking clearly. Surmising that I had punctured bone exposing my airway to a new vent, I closed my mouth, grasped my nostrils, and tried to blow blood through my new blowhole. Fortunately, my diagnosis was inaccurate, and my mom was right, stitches would be required - but only fifteen.

The next day, we made our way home to finish off my Christmas furlough. I had a couple days left before heading back to Charleston. Some of my friends had returned early back to their schools as adventure and excitement lured them away from their childhood homes. As always, the common venue for assembly was the local bowling alley.

"Finn! What happened to your face?" Cathy Kiser wondered.

"Hey, Cathy. I was attacked by a bobcat while I was skiing," I quickly fabricated.

"No way!" She responded.

"Jumped me out of nowhere. I didn't even see it coming. It was a short fight, but obviously I lost."

"Y'all! Come here! Finn got attacked by a Bobcat!"

After a night of lies and libations with old friends, we said our goodbyes and returned to our homes. Most of us would be returning to school while a few had already entered the workforce and suffered the daily grind of regular employment. I was reminded that I almost declined college in favor of toiling on a drill rig. I paused in contemplation of my decision before acknowledging to myself that I was satisfied with my choices. I observed and cemented in me a long-lasting principle that reflecting on the past is worthwhile while dwelling on what might have been is pointless. Memories seem to me much more enjoyable when doubt is absent past decisions.

"Hey, Frankenstein," Ash directed at me.

"What?" I wondered.

"You look like Frankenstein. Your face is ugly. When did they stich on a new nose to your face?"

"Shut up, Ash. You're ugly, but you don't have an excuse," I joked as I lightly punched his shoulder. "Aren't we all going to brunch?"

"Dad said we are going to The Tortilla Factory, Finn." Leigh informed us as she entered the kitchen.

"Yes!" Ash shouted.

The Tortilla Factory offered cheap Mexican food that was a favorite of us all. It was Saturday and there was sure to be a crowd. Sunday, Levi and I would make our way back to our institutions. Today would offer no distractions as Mom and Dad insisted that we remain intact for one more day of family time. I didn't recognize it at the time, but reflecting back, I am certain my mother watched her children with mixed emotions as we joked and told stories. She smiled, proud of her offspring, while foreseeing a future and knowing that the gatherings of her children would dwindle. Next in line to leave her home was Leigh followed by Ash.

Chapter 26
Regimen Returns

Approaching Lesesne Gate, the unmistakable aroma from the nearby papermill filled the afternoon air. Activity surrounded the four front sally ports of barracks as cars paused curbside to empty returning cadets. Upper classmen lingered, greeting one another after nearly a month's long absence. Knobs rushed to their rooms to prepare their uniforms for the evening's return muster and accountability formation.

"Makinen! Wh...wh...what happen' t...to your face?" Gutierrez questioned.

"Sir, no excuse sir." By now I was smart enough not to engage longer than necessary in order to break contact.

"Get to your r...r...room."

I did not wait, linger, look, or comment back to my First Sergeant and swiftly headed to my quarters. John was in the room having returned an hour before me. He saw me and immediately noticed my wound. "What happened to your nose Finn?!"

"I was skiing and was attacked by a bobcat."

"Shut up, Finn. I've been around you too long to not know when you're bullshitting."

I shared the true story of my frozen calamity; the details of blood staining the slope, the crowd that surrounded me, and the helicopter that was called in to medivac the woman who broke my fall when I landed. John always knew when I was bullshitting - most times.

2100 muster formation was uneventful. All my classmates had returned to continue our progression through Knob Year. It was a quick accountability of all cadets and our company reported, "All present and accounted for." As when returning from our Thanksgiving break, there was aura of relaxed standards, seeming slightly more this time. The discipline remained rigid, and we were expected to maintain our lowly position as Knobs, although we seemed slightly more human to the upperclassmen. For the seniors, the achievement of graduation was tangible. As goes the head so goes the body, and the Senior class was the head of the body. They had less interest in "their Knobs" and more on their upcoming careers as

MILITARY BRAT   Pete Masalin

military officers or private business luminaries.

For the most part, my classmates and I navigated through the second semester with comparative ease when compared to our first. Partly, it may have been attributed to our acclimation and improved adherence to the Fourth-Class System. We were better cadets. Mostly, I believe it was because our chain of command tired of constantly being our masters. They had laid waste to whom we were when we matriculated. Since our arrival in August, they had beaten the lazy, undisciplined bodies of the individuals we were into functioning members of the Corps of Cadets. Rack sessions still occurred, demerits were issued upon inspections, and we still performed duties required of us as freshman privates but with far less frequency.

Occasionally, we would arrive in the dark morning hours to assemble for breakfast formation and our NCOs were not present. Confident we would assemble without their guidance, they would sleep in and arrive just prior to marching us to the mess hall. The lighting provided just enough light to know they weren't there, but not enough to recognize people from a distance.

One morning, I descended the staircase and noticed the absence of leadership. Stepping off the last riser, I slowed my pace and walked behind my classmates. I grabbed the arm of the man next to me in formation and pulled upon it extending it from his waist. We were always required to "brace" within the battalion. Bracing required that one stand rigid, pulling one's chin towards the back of the neck and clamping both arms to the side.

"You bracing?" I asked.

"Sir, no excuse sir," responded my classmate.

"Start running."

As he ran, I took my place next to him in formation. Soon Sgt. Banner arrived on the scene and moved directly to Jefferies' position. Banner scanned the surroundings and found no other upperclassmen present.

"Jefferies."

"Sir, yes sir," Jefferies panted.

"Who told you to start running?" Banner pressed.

"Sir, no excuse sir."

"Stop running."

Jeffries gathered himself and took his place in formation as Sgt. Banner tried to solve the mystery of Jefferies rack session. Some had witnessed what I had instigated but remained silent. Our task master evaluated the situation and thought foul play was the cause.

"Who did this?" the NCO asked us while walking the line. "I want to know who did this." Nobody responded or relented. Because of his tardiness, Banner had no more time to investigate further. "Get in formation. It's time to march to chow."

Certain that the morning trick on Jefferies was reported to other members of our charge, I sensed continued investigation would be required. If greater examination did occur, we never knew it. I expected increased scrutiny to expose my provocation. I was wrong. Apparently, their extended slumber was more important than our pranks. With great frequency we were left alone to assemble in the morning. Soon, we all recognized the opportunity, and other classmates joined in the fun. We racked each other. There was always the knowledge that it was probably a classmate; however, it was possible that an upperclassman stood in our presence. Many times, our supervisors arrived witnessing knobs either running in place or pumping out push-ups.

They never intervened. Why would they? We were doing their work for them. I'm certain they found humor by our mischief within our ranks. So did we. Within time, the adrenaline of getting caught while pulling pranks faded, and we all became wise to the game. It became boring practice and it stopped. We needed to find more inventive ways to trick one another.

Saturday Morning Inspections or SMIs were an intermittent formal inspection of our rooms and personal appearance. They involved intense preparation for which Knobs stayed in their rooms on Friday nights cleaning, shining shoes and polishing brass. Rifles needed to be well-cleaned and oiled. Rooms needed to be spotless and uniforms flawless.

MILITARY BRAT   Pete Masalin

    Prior to the room inspection, cadets would form on the quad at attention, ready for rifle and uniform inspections. On this day, we were assigned the Commandant of Cadets as our inspecting officer. The Chain of Command was nervous to draw the senior disciplinarian of the school's staff to perform this task. Colonel Crane was a retired Army Infantry officer and an alum of The Citadel. He was known to be a hard and intimidating man who delighted in his reputation.

    Col. Crane passed through the ranks scrutinizing each man. He handed out demerits freely. "Gross personal appearance, unsatisfactorily shined shoes, rusty barrel." Arriving in front of my classmate, Baker immediately performed the mandatory "inspection arms" drill maneuver with his rifle and presented it to the Colonel. He ripped the weapon from Baker and looked down the barrel. Slowly, the Commandant extracted a rolled piece of paper from the muzzle. Standing behind Baker, I could see the contents as Colonel Crane unfurled it.

    "Miss October!" stated the inspector.

    In front of my eyes and within the inspecting officer's hands, an image of a fair young maiden in all her glory was presented for inspection. Colonel Crane was a seasoned warrior who demonstrated poise and composure on the battlefield. From my position, I observed his every expression as he stood face to face with my peer. Crane's jaw tensed and his eyes widened as he examined the centerfold. He slowly raised his stare to affix his attention on Baker.

    "Sir, no excuse sir!" Baker fearfully and unprompted shouted out.

    Colonel Crane stood silent for a moment and continued his menacing glare into the eyes of the scrutinized cadet. He neatly folded up the picture and slipped it into his pocket before returning the M-1 Garand rifle to a trembling Knob. "Outstanding Personal Appearance!" the Colonel directed.

    During the inspection, our Company Commander, Cadet Captain Linville, trailed Colonel Crane through the ranks, taking notes and recording the results of each inspected cadet. He seemed confused.

    "Sir, did you say Outstanding Personal Appearance?"

MILITARY BRAT — Pete Masalin

"Yes. October is my favorite month."

We all were stunned by what had just transpired. Nobody questioned the decision, but it was clear that no one understood how Baker could escape such an event without added demerits at a minimum. Instead, he was awarded merits for his personal appearance. Colonel Crane was wise. Once a cadet himself, he knew the workings within the thick walls of Stephens Barracks. He recognized pranks for what they were. He knew that no cadet, especially a Knob, would intentionally stuff his own rifle barrel with pornography sure to be exposed at an inspection.

Our Company Commander and Company First Sergeant were less forgiving. Embarrassed in front of the Commandant, the playmate presentation failed to humor the leadership. Gutierrez's face signaled obvious markers of stress and fury although he remained silent. Despite Colonel Crane's dismissal of the prank, Baker knew he would face reprisal, and we all knew we were sure to join him. At the completion of an otherwise uneventful and successful SMI, our commander escorted the Commandant through the front gate, saluted his departure, and quickly returned his attention to his Knobs.

"Knobs! G...g...get your asses d...down here. Now!" our First Sergeant bellowed.

Roars of his supporting staff demanding our assembly broke within the barracks walls. Hastily we rushed to formation taking our positions at attention.

"Who p...p...put the picture in Baker's rifle!" Gutierrez demanded. "You w...will n...n...not see liberty t...today until someone s...steps forward."

"You want to play games? We can play games all day until the person who put Miss October in Baker's rifle owns it!" Corporal Hovis warned.

There were no rats in the ranks. None of us accepted responsibility. Jesse stood resolute in his befuddlement. It was apparent that he was unaware of who planted smut down the bore of his weapon. He had cleaned it well, but someone made one more adjustment ensuring he would present a "dirty" rifle.

Frustrated by the solidary of my classmates and their inability to

MILITARY BRAT   Pete Masalin

secure a confession, mass punishment ensued. "Start running!" At first, only a few started to run in place.

"Everyone. I mean everyone start running," commanded our staff.

"Hit it! Get back. Hit it. Get back." We were exercised relentlessly. The staff's hope was to break us, at least one of us to confession. Our inspection ready shoes and uniforms were ruined by perspiration from our bodies and scuff marks on the toes.

Twenty minutes of punishment continued until Colonel Crane, hearing the commotion, reentered the sally port of Stephens Barracks. Quietly a sentry was dispatched from the gate and our 1stSgt Gutierrez was summoned. He saw the Commandant in the shadows. Startled, he commanded our rack session to cease. His face was pale, and he left us to meet the Colonel. We witnessed a tense dressing down but could not hear the conversation. Gutierrez rejoined us and quickly released us for our well-earned liberty.

Scrambling to our rooms I was behind Jesse and said, "Maybe next time you won't show up with a "dirty' rifle."

Those who could hear my comment laughed except for Hovis. He eyed us with contempt but dared not implement any rebuke with our morning's inspecting officer overseeing our dismissal. Within minutes Knobs raced to rooms in preparation for our release from campus.

"That was crazy," John claimed as we changed uniforms in our room. "Did you do that to Jesse, Finn."

"No way, O'Malley. I wouldn't set Jesse up like that," I denied.

Having caused the punishment of our entire company of Knobs. I would never admit to the crime even if I had been the culprit. No one ever claimed the deed. Whatever counseling Colonel Crane had provided to Gutierrez it must have resonated because the indiscretion was never mentioned again, at least not by our staff. We Knobs, however, saw great humor in the feat even if we all paid an equal price for the sin of one. We held a bond borne of mutual suffering and support.

As Knob year accelerated to its conclusion, I marked days of importance as intermediate objective points until we could no longer

MILITARY BRAT   Pete Masalin

be considered plebes. Spring Break offered an extended visit home with friends and family. Returning to campus, Knobs were more an accessory of campus life than a focus of discipline requirement. Final exams would soon be upon the Corps of Cadets focusing attention to finishing the semester for underclassmen and graduation for Seniors.

Corps Day was the last major campus event before commencement. It recognized and celebrated the birthday and history of the school with full pomp and circumstance. Winter was behind us. New growth and flowers bloomed in the South Carolina spring. Announcing the warmth, young ladies adorned in sun dresses and sorority wear crowded the parade field and surrounding barracks searching for a glimpse of their dates in full dress uniform. It truly was a presentation of The Citadel's full splendor. Visitors witnessed the Corps with uncommon access. The barracks were opened for public viewing. Summerall Field swelled with the ranks of cadets in parade. Cannons rocked the air. The regimental band filled the atmosphere with the offerings of John Phillip Sousa as the cadets passed in review before enthusiastic guests. Being part of the pageantry and heritage of such an institution served to reaffirm my decision to endure its rigor.

Preparing for final exams was less of a milestone for me than it was simply a requirement. My attention was drawn to Recognition Day. Similar to Hell Night in its mention among upperclassmen, Recognition Day held mystery to all Knobs. Scheduled three days before graduation, we were told that we would earn the right to be called by our first name. We knew nothing more and were alert for clues of the ceremony's requirements. A week before the event, 55-gallon trashcans were placed strategically above the stairwell of each division. Returning from meals, the upperclassmen carried cartons of milk, jelly, condiments, and food ruminants sure to spoil if left unrefrigerated. These items were not destined to be added supplements for their time of study. No, they were deposited in trash containers and never emptied.

Back in Bibbs and Stanton's room we wondered what was being planned. "What's with the trashcans?" Pat questioned.

"That shit is beginning to stink," I said.

Jesse noticed that someone was pouring window cleaner into the mix. "Why would they be adding Windex?"

"Windex. I saw Hovis adding toilet paper and dishwashing soap," Art Bibbs added.

O'Malley entered the room and joined in. "What's up? Have you smelled the trash cans?"

"We were just talking about that, John," Pat replied. "What's your take?"

"I don't know, man. Knowing these bastards, they'll probably dump them out before field day so we can clean it up," John concluded.

"I was going to the latrine one night and I saw someone peeing in one," Art warned.

"No way?!" I challenged.

"I swear, Finn," Art said.

"All I know is those things are filling up fast and smell nasty." That was my final comment on the matter.

John O'Malley was right. They would dump them out; however, cleanup on field day was not their motive. After exams and the morning three days before graduation, Recognition Day was upon us. Dressed in our shorts, T-shirt and running shoes we were rallied to cram into the confines of the stairwell. The difference from Hell Night was that all upperclassmen participated, both rank holders and privates. All screamed encouragement in the form of profanities and general insults. Packed in the stairwell and bracing, the flow of liquid and solids crashed upon our skulls and shoulders.

The odor was rancid. I closed my eyes and sealed my lips to safeguard myself from ingesting the sour deluge. The torrent of fluid was heavy hitting us with full force from elevations as high as fifty feet. Minutes later, it stopped, and I felt safe enough to open my eyes. From my position in the back, I looked upon the cranium of Rich Dawson standing in front of me. It appeared that residues of toilet paper and what I hoped were rotten banana pieces clung to his head. Molded cheese rested on the shoulders

MILITARY BRAT — Pete Masalin

of others. None of us escaped the effects of our Recognition Day baptism. Some held back urges to vomit sure to aggravate an already bad situation.

Quickly the sophomores ushered us from the stairwell into formation and ran us around campus. Depleted, they returned us to the barracks and paused our formation. Before we could rest, the junior class would have their turn. They ran us a different route calling cadence and required our participation further draining our endurance. Again, we returned to the barracks to meet with the senior class. We were on the run again. The scene was replicated on the entire campus by each company as they recognized their Knobs.

Our seniors, led by Captain Linville, double-timed us to The Citadel Marina on the Ashley River. Low tide exposed the pungent pluff mud, and he decided it offered an excellent setting for push-ups. Directed into the gooey terrain, we struggled to maintain solid footing.

"Drop and give me 15," he commanded.

His classmates joined in. "Let's go, Knobs! Start pumping them out."

Achieving our commander's direction, we returned to formation and ran back to Stephens Barracks. Covered in mud, some of us suffered small lacerations from oyster shells hidden in the pluff. The wounds were not easily seen, masked by the drying marsh soil. We were given a moment to rest once situated in formation inside the battalion. The gates were covered with blankets to avoid detection by the spectators outside. Each Knob was assigned an individual upper classman for completion of the ceremony. Push-ups number those equal to our class year marked the end of the ritual. I drew Sergeant John Banner as my tormentor. It was fitting that I finished Knob Year with him as he represented my introduction to it.

"Well, well, well, Makinen. Here we are again. You know the drill."

"Sir, yes sir." I smiled and started knocking out push-ups.

I continued to execute push-ups until exhaustion. Fatigued, I was allowed to run in place for recovery until I could continue in the leaning rest. After completing my requirement, Sgt. Banner instructed me, "At ease."

MILITARY BRAT   Pete Masalin

Standing, bent over with my hands clenching my waist, Banner reached out his hand, smiled and cheered me on, "Good job Finn! From day one, I knew you would make it. You can call me John."

I stood erect, met his hand with mine, shook it, and replied, "You're a sonofabitch."

We both laughed at the moment, John patted me on the shoulder. "Welcome to the Corps." He then turned his attention to my classmates and his recognition of them.

Others, who earlier that morning had ridden me as they had done all year, greeted me with smiles, handshakes, and an exchange of first name.

The challenge had been met. I was no longer a Knob. It wasn't lost on me that some would never attempt such an indoctrination, but also, I remembered many who started with me and acquiesced. It was a triumph for me and those standing with me at the end.

Chapter 27

Recovery

  Immediately upon my release for Summer Furlough, I travelled to meet my family at a rented house overlooking the Severn River. The United States Naval Academy held position on the opposite bank standing in plain view. My brother Levi was to graduate and receive his commission as an Ensign, and no one could be prouder than my father. John Makinen offered no outward expression of his satisfaction with his first-born son's achievement. He knew the feeling all too well that Levi was enjoying, having attained the same stature of a Naval Officer a quarter of a century before. Dad didn't need to say anything. One could easily witness the pride he held in his eldest's advancement into a career from which he retired.

  Levi arrived at the house, greeted his family, and directed me to dress in proper civilian attire. "Finn. Let's go. Put on some decent civies and come with me."

  "What's up, Levi? Where we goin'?" I questioned.

  "I'm taking you to the Academy to link up with some of my buds for beers out in town," he said. "You need to wear civies like the rest of us so you can pass as a First Class Middie and join me in the barracks before we head out."

  "Excellent! Give me five minutes."

  I was eager to leave with Levi. The alternative was card games with Mom, Leigh, and Ash. I was ready in three minutes.

  "Bye!" I shouted.

  "Whoa. What time will you have Finn back, Levi?" Mom wondered.

  Levi laughed and taunted, "Don't wait up."

  "I'm serious. Tomorrow is graduation and we will be starting early. I need Finn back at a decent hour."

  "Take me, too," Ash begged.

  "Sorry, junior. Your hair's too long and you'd never get past the guards."

  Leigh attempted to plead her case to join us, but Levi ended it quickly.

At 16, a tall, attractive teenage blonde would be the attention of many a midshipman.

"Leigh, I love you sis, but there is no way in hell I'm bringing you with us. You definitely would not be allowed in the barracks. On the other hand, I am afraid you just might get in," Levi joked, prompting quiet laughter from my dad.

My mother quickly took control of the situation. "Ash, Leigh, let's play Hearts. Levi, I'm serious. Finn needs to be here at a decent hour. And he needs to be clear headed! You two hear me?"

Together, Levi and I responded, "Yes, Ma'am."

Traveling to campus, we drove through Annapolis. It was a historic, picturesque waterfront town much like Charleston. The charm of the architecture and town shops reminded me of the small city where I spent my last year. As a kid, my father took us through the town often; however, I didn't hold the same perspective as I now did. Just as with The Citadel, the Naval Academy was an important historic attribute to the municipality.

The campus was spotless and well prepared for the visitors that crowded the surroundings while touring the chapel, John Paul Jones's sarcophagus below it, the Herndon Monument, and other sites of interest. I was particularly interested in the Herndon Monument where the ritual of "Recognition" is required of plebes at the end of each year. The tall obelisk is lathered in Crisco and a plebe sailor cap is glued at its peak. The plebes team form a human ladder, crawl over one another to replace the sailor's cap or Dixie cup with a midshipman's cover. I remember watching Levi's class struggle to accomplish this feat when he finished his *Plebe Year*. While entertaining, it was not as physically taxing as what I had endured at The Citadel.

Arriving with Levi to Bancroft Hall, the barracks housing my brother's Company, we easily passed the sentry. Levi whispered, "They think you're a First Classman."

I smiled as we walked by the guard. Within the hallways, I passed by many plebes. They were relaxed as the end of their indoctrinating year was soon closing. The temptation was just too easy to not act.

MILITARY BRAT — Pete Masalin

"Get your eyes off me!" I commanded upon a passing plebe. "Start running!"

The plebe's eyes quickly looked away and an expression of confusion gripped his face. Start running? He stopped for a moment wondering what to do.

"Carry on," Levi quickly interceded.

"What the hell, Finn. Knock that shit off! This isn't The Citadel," Levi scolded.

"I know." I smirked at my own amusement.

"We need to link up with two of my roommates, Greg Milton and Geoff Hudson, before we head back into town," Levi said.

"Who are they?" I asked.

"You met them before. They came home with me a couple of times. They're going to be Jarheads tomorrow. Just like you someday."

"Cool. I…"

"Just don't be a fool," Levi interrupted. "I can take you home early if you act like an ass."

In Levi's room, I was reacquainted with Greg and Geoff. And of course, it wasn't without a fair amount of ribbing about my school versus theirs. We quickly directed our attention to what drinking establishment we would park for libations and lies. Two different institutions with very similar environments led to humorous storytelling and often empty pitchers. Our small group of four swiftly grew to more than a dozen of Levi's company mates. Mostly, I listened to the recanting of their journey from plebe to graduation, interjecting stories of my Knob Year when asked. It was an enjoyable evening with enthusiastic and capable young men who the next day would graduate and enter the ranks of warriors.

I was proud of my brother who had been my partner in many escapades of our youth. I was thankful that he thought enough of me to include me in the celebration of his passage from Midshipman to Officer with peers he held in high regard. According to our mother's wishes, Levi returned me to my family sober and at the early hour of 2200.

MILITARY BRAT   Pete Masalin

On a warm June day, the Makinen clan took their seats in the Navy-Marine Corps Memorial Stadium to witness Levi's graduation. The graduates were brilliantly illuminated as the bright summer sun reflected off their full-dress white uniform. Seated in rows aligned tangent to an elevated stage, hosting Admirals and dignitaries, they waited to individually walk across the platform when summoned to accept their diploma. With the final certificate issued, the last recipient returned to his seat with his class.

"Ladies and Gentlemen, it is my honor and privilege to present to you the newest graduating class of The United States Naval Academy!"

Cheers roared throughout the stadium at the announcement. Midshipmen covers filled the air flung by the entire class in revelry. Fresh Naval Officers turned to each other, shook hands, and exchanged hugs. Ceaselessly, clapping erupted from the stands. Levi was on his way. We all stood proud among the crowd of strangers equally as proud of their newest Navy Ensign or Marine Corps Second Lieutenant.

In my short summer, Levi's graduation was the highlight of my furlough from The Military College of the South. I joined a construction crew performing general labor jobs. I much preferred the demanding physical requirements of the construction environment than a closeted indoor occupation of a retail store or restaurant. Never was the following day the same as the previous one. One day I could be hauling scrap wood and brick in clean up and the next I would be raking the final grade on a finished lot. My days started at 0700 and typically ended by 1600. Plenty of time for me to carouse with friends or attack secreted fishing holes with my closest allies.

Formations were forgotten as were uniform and grooming standards. Haircuts were not required, and I wallowed in dirt and sweat each day. Sometimes it's good to not shy away from grime and grit and just be a pig. I kind of liked it. Years later, while deployed in the desert, I went as long as a month without a shower. I attribute my endurance and resilience in this environment to my days toiling under the sticky Virginia sky.

"Finn! Let's hit that pond in Great Falls tonight," Tommy Hanson suggested.

MILITARY BRAT   Pete Masalin

"I'm ready. I'll throw my john boat in my pickup after work. You come over with your truck and will add my canoe."

"Great! We can grab Jimmy and Rick, too," added Tommy. "It's been a while since we've been there. We should slay them this evening."

"Yeah. It's a great evening to be on the pond," I agreed. "Jimmy and Rick can have the canoe."

Tommy and I had been accomplices in many missions since we started high school. We often thought alike and provided cover for each other. We were an effective team. The canoe was heavier than it needed to be and the trip to the pond from where we parked was a long trek. It was a smart call to assign Jimmy and Rick the canoe for the evening's water operations. The four of us worked together as summer laborers at the same construction site. My furlough was soon to end, and it would be my last opportunity to fish with my friends.

After cleaning up, we all assembled at my home, loaded the trucks with the boats, and quickly headed out. On the way, we stopped at the 7 Eleven for provisions: beer and more beer. One can never be too hydrated while on the open water. Tommy in his truck carried the canoe, and I in mine hauled the aluminum john boat.

"Oh, hell no!" Rick yelled. "We're taking on water."

"Finn, Tommy, y'all got to get over here," Jimmy pleaded.

"We can't just yet. Tommy's got one hooked," I called out. "We'll get there as soon as we can."

"Finn, I'm not hooked on anything. Let's go help them," Tommy quietly informed me.

"I know, but the pond ain't that deep, and they're not going to drown," I laughed. "Let's watch them for a while they try to get back to shore."

Our hidden fishing hole offered exceptional fishing, and the best spots were known to all of us. While we were all friends, competition between us to catch the biggest or most fish gave us a cutthroat drive - above our bond. It was every man for themselves, or at least Team Finn and Tommy versus Team Rick and Jimmy. Rick and Jimmy, in their enthusiasm to beat us to the water, made a tragic miscalculation in their launch plan of the canoe. They loaded the paddles and fishing gear, jumped into the craft, and rode it as a sled downhill to the shore. Cheering and smiling as they passed us easily to launch on the water well before we reached the pond bank.

"Hurry! We are sinking!" one of them called again.

"C'mon, Finn. Don't you think we should go help?" asked my partner.

"They sure were in a HURRY to beat us to the pond. I think we should give them a little time," I said. We were across the lake and judging the situation from afar, I thought it was unlikely we would make it before they sank.

"Let's go anyway," Tommy argued to which I finally nodded. "We're on our way!" he yelled.

It was too late. We could not make it to our competitors before they were swamped. In chest high water, Rick and Jimmy walked the barely visible canoe towards where they had launched it. The sun set and the recovery of their equipment was completed under the dim light of a purple sky provided by evening twilight. Both teams arrived simultaneously to the beachhead. Ours was the much more successful amphibious landing than Rick and Jimmy who stood before us sopping wet and lifting empty tackleboxes filled with water.

"What the hell happened?" Tommy probed.

"I don't know. It just started taking on water," Rick said.

I pulled out my flashlight to inspect the canoe. "Shit! You dumbasses ruined my dad's canoe."

"No way!" Jimmy retorted.

"Yeah. Brilliant! Let's go sledding down a grass hill. My dad is going to be pissed. Look at this gash in the hull."

"Damn it, Finn. I'm sorry. I will repair it," Rick said.

"Damn straight you will," Jimmy added.

"Jimmy, it was your idea. You're going to help pay for this," Rick demanded.

MILITARY BRAT   Pete Masalin

"Are we still going to fish?" Tommy wondered.

The conversation went silent. We looked at each other's faces. Then everyone stared at me trying to gauge my disposition. I couldn't stay angry.

"Are will still going to fish?!" I repeated the question. "Didn't we come out here to fish? Don't we still have some beer? What else would we do?"

We started a campfire so that Jimmy and Rick could dry out. Each of us baited our hooks, cast out our lines, and enjoyed the transition of the sky from dusk to a starlit heaven. Rick, Tommy, and I reeled in a couple of fish as we sat on the bank. Jimmy's only catch was a buzz as his focus was primarily on beer and storytelling. Sitting with my friends, I said nothing of my return to The Citadel in a few days, bringing my summer to an end. The fire was slowly replaced by embers as the night expired. The final yarn spun, we doused the fire pit with water, and loaded the trucks.

"This was the best day fishing all summer y'all," Jimmy declared slightly intoxicated.

"Yes, yes it was, Jimmy."

Chapter 28
Upperclassmen Return

My apprehension of reporting to The Citadel was absent as I arrived in Charleston. This year I was afforded the privilege of owning an automobile on campus and the ability to drive. Walking through the lanes of the ancient city to reach distant destinations was no longer required. My summer employment afforded me the resources to purchase a used Ford and drive myself to school. It was a welcomed perk permissible to all upperclassmen.

Second year cadets have little authority in the hierarchy of the command structure. Still, it was great not to be a Knob. Sophomores are, most importantly, soldiers aligned in parades filling the ranks of the Corps. It is their primary purpose. Some were selected as corporals to assist squad leaders who direct and provide for the accountability of squad members. Some would consider the position an honor while others considered it an added burden not to be desired.

There were many cadets that prided themselves in their efforts to shun rank and remain a Private throughout their Citadel career. It was not looked upon unfavorably by cadets. We were brothers first and always. Our Knob year ensured this. First Classmen that successfully navigated their college years absent position were often admired for their achievement and freedom – Senior Private. After graduation, rank and position didn't matter. It was the common bond of the common achievement that mattered, The Citadel diploma and ring.

I was not that fortunate. I returned as a Corporal and Company Clerk. My reward was that I was able to spend extra time writing reports and reporting early for Cadre. As an added bonus, I carried a clipboard and served as principle notetaker during all inspections. What an honor.

Just as the previous years, Knobs reported to their assigned places of duty. As a member of Cadre, I was witnessing this year with a new perspective, much better than the viewpoint of last year.

"What are you looking at! Get your eyes off me! Get your hand off my desk!" Familiar phrases reverberated within the barracks. Mothers cried. New Freshmen gazed into the distance - lost and confused. I smiled and thought to myself, *some things never change except on which side you witness Knobs reporting to the Corps of Cadets.* This year I was on the better of the two sides.

"Hey, Finn. What's up?" Cadre was over and the balance of my classmates were reporting back to start the new year.

"How's it going? How was your summer, Tim?" I replied to Tim Gray as he passed through the gate.

"Great, man. Had a blast. I hated to come back," Tim said.

"Why did you? Start running." We both burst into laughter.

"Never again, Finn. Never again."

It was a scene repeated as we all welcomed and greeted the return of friends. Knobs no more, the year started with an expectation of greater ease and reduced pressure. We still had the rigors associated with an institution of discipline and military bearing, yet we entered the first semester of our second year absent harassment.

The regimen of The Citadel was easy to manage. Inspections at formations were no longer an every muster occurrence as it was when we were Freshman. No more bracing, no more Knob Knowledge, no more getting racked. We were low in status. Just not the lowest. The most that was required was that we needed to be at our appointed place of duty at all times, attend our classes, keep our uniforms relatively neat and prepare for inspections when necessary.

Most of us marched through the year without incident. Those that did suffer punishment earned their penalty because of their own stupidity. In some cases, the severity of the infraction caused dismissal or attrition. I had a new roommate for my second year. Thad Cohen arrived at The Citadel as a highly ranked tennis prospect. Given a scholarship, he proved himself worthy by winning many matches and was highly ranked in the conference. Thad was not only a player on the court, but he fancied himself a highly ranked ladies' man out in town. Weekends occupied his time with one of many female friends.

One Saturday night, after liberty ended, Thad visited classmates Jesse Baker and Graham Grayson's room. Graham was an offensive lineman and carried some bulk on his large frame.

"Jesse, Graham. I need your help," Thad said softly as he entered the third-floor room.

"Hey, what's up?" Jesse asked.

"Liz is waiting for me by the Alumni House," Thad said. "I need to go meet her."

"How can we help you? The gate is locked." Graham wondered.

"No problem. I brought some webbing. You can lower me out your window."

"Webbing?!" Jesse replied in shock. "The webbing we use connected by our breastplate?"

"Yeah. I tested it. It's strong enough." Thad said.

"I don't think so, Thad," Graham declined.

Thad tied a loop around his waist and started to unroll the webbing. "All you have to do is hold the other end and lower me to the ground."

Reluctantly, Graham and Jesse held tight to the opposite end of the white cotton fabric. Standing at the door, Thad extended the roll making his way to the window leaving Graham and Jesse as anchors to counter his weight as he descended.

Sitting on the windowsill Thad commanded the two accomplices to walk from the door to the window keeping the tension tight as he rappelled against the barracks wall to the ground. Halfway between the door and window the line went limp. Jesse and Graham faced each other in shock and ran to the window. The scene below was grim. The tether connecting the escapee and his men on belay snapped and dangled in the wind. Thad lay below, crumpled and writhing in pain.

"Thad! Thad!" Are you okay?" Jesse shouted.

No response.

"Thad! Thad!" Jesse again shouted.

"Quiet. Do you want to alert the guard?" Thad warned. "I'm fine. I'll see you in the morning." Dressed in sweats, Thad disappeared into the darkness.

MILITARY BRAT   Pete Masalin

We would later learn that Thad was not fine. The result of the fall was a broken ulna on his left arm and a broken ulna and radius on his right. In the morning, Thad returned in secrecy so as not to disclose his unauthorized absence. He avoided punishment by fabricating a story of how he "fell in the shower." Falling in the shower is a well-known claim in military culture when someone suffers injury, and the truth is to be avoided.

Seeing Thad in the morning after Sunday brunch, it was obvious that he would not finish with us. Both arms were adorned in casts starting just above each elbow extending to the palms. Supports were affixed to his waist keeping both arms slightly elevated.

"If you think I'm going to wipe your ass in the morning, you better think again," I cautioned Thad.

Thad looked at me and embarrassingly smiled knowing what he had done was incredibly reckless and consequential. I tried to cheer him up with comedy.

"It's fortunate that you didn't break your upper arm. That would have been humerus," I offered. Thad didn't laugh.

I had been forewarned of his condition before I saw him. He escaped being disciplined for going AWOL while attempting to maintain his scheduled rendezvous with his paramour. In the end, it didn't matter. He was going home. No more tennis matches. No more parades. Thad was incapable of carrying out the duties of an athlete or cadet. And he indeed needed someone to wipe his ass until he healed.

I partly attributed Thad's demise to his selection of Reserve Officers Training Corps. ROTC was required curricula for all cadets. Those not intending to enter service were able to choose an armed forces branch of their choice as a credited elective. The Air Force offered instructions of leisure. Physical activity requirements included rounds of golf and Friday afternoon tea parties at the Officer's Club. Had Thad selected the Army or Marines, he would have received instruction relating to basic wall scaling techniques.

Each branch of service was supported and represented at the institution by an assembly of officers and men from the Department of

MILITARY BRAT — Pete Masalin

Defense. Army, Navy, Air Force, Marine - their presence was prominent on the campus. One, a Marine Corps Major who reported aboard my Second-Class year, immediately caught the eye of faculty and cadets alike.

Major Henry Williams, USMC, arrived at The Citadel in the manner in which he was trained. "Swift, Silent, Deadly" is the motto of the Recon Marine. Nobody knew of or saw him coming. Sitting in a classroom in Jenkins Hall awaiting instruction, we were first introduced to our new Marine Officer Instructor or MOI.

"Good morning, ladies. My name is Major Henry Williams, and we are going to spend a lot of time together. Any questions?"

It was a rhetorical question, but midshipman Rob Clary misinterpreted Major Williams' disposition. "Sir, do you have a family?"

Somewhat taken aback the Marine leader paused, looked directly into the eyes of the cadet, his smile reminiscent of a perturbed police officer when asked by a any traffic violator or speeder why "they were pulled over" and rebutted. "What's your name?"

"Sir, Cadet Clary."

"Well, Mr. Clary, if I fucking wanted you to know my life history, I'd invite you over for dinner. Did I ask you to join me for dinner?"

The room was silent. We all immediately comprehended the seriousness of our new MOI and his dedication to molding us into Marines. He wasn't a big man. In fact, he was smaller than average. Nevertheless, we were certain he could kill us individually or together if he desired to take such action. He was intimidating in his delivery, his movements were precise, and his Marine uniform was tailored to fit a lean, but muscular frame.

"Since you asked Mr. Clary, I'll share this with you and everyone else," the Major said. "You idiots chose to come to a school that restricts you to campus during the week. You march everywhere. You wear a uniform reminiscent of the postal service. You have no women here nor do you have any liquor."

We sat motionless, stunned by the insult. All of us except Rob Clary.

He was taking notes, trying to redeem himself. No notes were needed.

Williams continued, "I, on the other hand, attended a school that had all the things that you don't. I chased women, I partied on campus, and pretty much raised hell for four years before accepting my commission as a hard charging, steely- eyed young United States Marine Corps Lieutenant."

He walked up to Clary who was still taking notes and stopped in front of him. Rob looked up and understood the moment, quickly putting his notepad away.

"Men, if you need to take notes for this, you might want to consider transferring to the Navy, Air Force or Army ROTC. Forget the Army. They can't write," Major Williams suggested, causing us to break the silence in an uproar. His sly smile returned.

"Seriously men, my job is to prepare you to lead men into combat. We have no room for men of soft and weak constitutions. Everyone on this campus will know you are future Marine Officers. That red badge with the Eagle, Globe and Anchor you wear on the chest of your uniform will mean excellence. Many will want it, but only a few can earn it."

Guttural grunts of "Ooo rah" and clapping erupted in the assembly and continued while our new MOI, Major Henry Williams stood quietly, satisfied that he had properly introduced himself to his candidates. Instruction was over. Major Williams ordered "Carry on", exiting the room leaving us to deliberate his arrival.

"He's so sharp that I'll bet his shit is creased when he takes a dump," Ken Washington joked, evoking laughter.

"Clary, notes? Really?" I asked Rob.

"Shut up, Finn. I didn't know what to expect."

"None of us did."

The result of our initial meeting with Major Williams secured our confidence in him and as time continued, he would prove his dedication to us. He wanted us to excel in our efforts while striving for exceptionalism in our performance. Affectionally, we assigned him the moniker of "Rojam." It was a simple call sign, Major spelled backwards, but the second syllable seemed to define his driven nature, "jam."

My second year as a cadet progressed with regularity as traditions and events repeated themselves. May came quickly. Another recognition day and a graduating class prepared to walk the stage. As I prepared for my second summer furlough, I looked back upon my Sophomore year. Monotony was the best description I could think of to define in one word what the year represented. Second year cadets most notably are not notable.

Mostly, we were cannon fodder to fill the ranks of the Corps of Cadets. In many ways, Knobs were a more important component of the school. Knobs received attention, lots of attention and not only from the implementation of the Fourth-Class System. Each Company assigned a Senior cadet to serve as the Academic Officer whose primary duty was to manage Knobs' academic progress. A professor of the academic staff was assigned to each company serving as the Academic Tac Officer and carefully monitored Knob grades. On Parents' Day, parents of Freshmen crowded the campus to finally see their Knob after many months' absence. Sophomores were bland and unexciting, and I was satisfied to be just that. Another year gone!

Chapter 29
Halfway Home

Again, Cadre. My summer was shortened, marking the halfway objective to a diploma. It was easier to reacclimate to Citadel life after a summer of leisure and construction work. My responsibilities as Supply Sergeant afforded me significant interaction in the onboarding process of Knob Recruits. My job was to account for their assignment of rifles, equipment, storage of personal gear and civies. It was not always an easy task with new matriculants in a state of confusion and uncertainty. Patience was necessary and discretion required when moving Knobs about the campus in front of parents delivering their children and trusted us with their safety.

Junior year offered more responsibility in leadership positions and direct interaction with the new class. Juniors were the squad leaders resulting in greater interaction during cadre. It was the Squad Leader who was the primary charge in educating and training Knobs in the traditions, military bearing, grooming, drill, and inspections required of a cadet. The Squad Leader, Cadet Sergeant, served as the critical link between converting a civilian slob to finely honed cadet. He wasn't always successful, but the school's history proves that he mostly was.

Following the indoctrination period of new arrivals, academics again started. My classmates and I enjoyed the elevated status of being a Junior. With each advancing year, we received more privileges. Extended liberty periods during the week and wearing a blazer instead of a uniform when out in town were highly regarded additions. For some Second-Classmen, missing morning formation and breakfast added additional sleep; however, this was not a freedom afforded Junior members of the USMC NROTC. Enter Rojam.

True to his mission, Rojam required all Juniors, members of his unit to greet the day at 0430 for calisthenics and a run. Tuesday and Thursday mornings, PT or Physical Training sessions were our appointed place of duty. The next summer, a couple dozen of us would be shipped to Quantico, Virginia, for assignment to Officer Candidate School. Rojam was to be assigned Temporary Orders as the OCS Executive Officer, coinciding with our orders. He would not be embarrassed, and we would be prepared.

MILITARY BRAT   Pete Masalin

"Candidate Makinen! You're leading calisthenics this morning," Gunnery Sergeant Hampton our Assistant MOI commanded, pulling me from the formation.

"Yes, Gunny."

"Good morning, ladies!" Rojam boomed as he approached.

"Good morning, sir!" everyone yelled back.

"It's a great day to be an American," Major Williams claimed.

In the darkness, we completed our stretches, push-ups, jumping jacks and burpees before heading out in a formation run. Rojam directed us as we ran though the campus shouting *jodies*.

"C-130 rolling down the strip. Recon daddy gonna' take a little trip..." It was not a secret that we didn't enjoy early morning PT. Likewise, it was no secret that we enjoyed trying to wake up everyone on campus.

Cadet life included its own stresses, but when compounded with 0400 wake up calls, followed by 0430 PT sessions, it added excited expectancy for weekend relief. In many ways, one could compare a Citadel cadet to a projectile cradled by a medieval catapult. Each Monday, we would start refreshed and relaxed from the previous weekend break. The oncoming days would twist tension on the cantilever spring of our conscience, pulling us back in anticipation of our weekend launch upon downtown. Friday, after parade, we were hurled over the barracks walls with great force with only a general direction of the target. Where we landed was usually uncertain and never precise.

Among the traditions of The Citadel was the well-known Senior Party. These were not formal affairs. To the contrary, these were events typically held at County Hall in town. The party was famous or infamous depending on the position from which you participated in the revelry. The coeds from the College of Charleston sororities eagerly waited for an invite and attendance. The Charleston Police Department added staff and elevated an alert.

MILITARY BRAT   Pete Masalin

"Oh baby love, early in the morning.
you come creapin' in my mind,
oh baby love,
oh baby love,
early in yearning,
Ready for your touch,
oh baby love,
Ready for your touch,
oh baby love.
Ready for your touch, oh baby love"

Mother's Finest belted their funk/rock styling from the stage. County Hall was packed with party goers participating in a raucous scene best described as one shot short of mayhem. The floors were sticky and damp from a cocktail of beer, liquor and quite possibly vomit. These were the best of times.

"Finn!" Jesse screamed at me while waiting in line outside the men's room. "This is crazy!"

"I know!" I shouted as loudly as I could. "Whoa! That's crazy, brother!"

While standing in line, two girls left the men's latrine propping each other up as they meandered by us and others making their way back to friends. One had forgotten her skirt, oblivious to her condition or the location of her wardrobe.

Grinning wildly, Jesse cheered, "I can't believe what I just saw!"

I just shook my head and hollered, "What a great party!"

Back with my friends, I surveyed the scene. Tables rocked and buckled under the weight of partiers bouncing atop them rocking to the tune of "Mickey's Monkey." Mother's Finest ended their last song and the lights brightened, illuminating the scene. As I prepared to leave, I conducted a battlefield assessment. Casualties lay throughout the venue, face down in the filth and remnants of the night's engagement. Comrades assisted in the collection of the wounded and made their way back to The Citadel. My classmates and I made a safe return. Less fortunate stragglers assembled at an impromptu rally point on Lockwood Drive offered by the Charleston Police. Recording rank, name, and serial number, The Citadel's Officer of the Day signed for their release and escorted them back to the ranks.

Calendars quickened towards the close of another year. Intermediary objects along the way were met with their usual fanfare. Each event marked advancement to the annual culmination of approaching commencement and another summer furlough. However, two weeks before graduation, an important board was to be held that would determine the senior leadership of our Corps of Cadets of the following year. It had been my goal to command the company of which I had been a member my entire cadet career. The competition was keen and the selection process careful. The administration recognized the importance of placing competent and thoughtful leaders in place to preserve the institution and its integrity. Why I was considered was a mystery. I never received any academic accolades placing me at the top of my class. Still, I was honored to be considered.

"Makinen," I answered the phone.

The voice on the other end was unmistakable. "Cadet Makinen, I need you to come to my office right now." Lieutenant Colonel Harvell required my presence.

"Yes, sir. Can you tell me what this is about?"

"You just get your butt over to my office right now."

"Yes, sir. I'm on the way. I'll be there in 10 minutes."

"Make it five, Makinen."

LtCol. Harvell was known as a firm man, but a decent one. He was always fair and highly regarded and revered by the cadets and alumni that knew him. As the Assistant Commandant, he was the chief disciplinarian and issuer of punishment. He thought highly of The Citadel, his Alma Mater. He was a Charleston native, former enlisted Marine Corps Sergeant, and retired Army Lieutenant Colonel. When he asked something of you, you

MILITARY BRAT — Pete Masalin

complied, both because he demanded it and because you respected him. He well represented what it was to be a Citadel Man.

Making my way across the campus, my mind raced to determine what was the purpose of this unscheduled meeting. My mind was blank as to the cause and my uncertainty caused mild anxiety, assuming I would be required to defend something unclear. It was always best to know the reason for meeting with LtCol. Harvell. Arriving to his office, I rapped upon his open door. He raised his head and met me with an expressionless face.

"Mr. Makinen, come in and grab a seat."

"Yes, sir." I made my way across his office and sat in the open chair in front of his desk.

"Do you know why I called you here?" he quizzed.

"Colonel, to be honest, I'm not certain."

"It is my privilege to inform you that the board has selected you to be the Company Commander of your Company next year. Congratulations."

Chapter 30
Lightning Strikes

I made my way home after finishing my Junior year for a quick visit. Three weeks later, I would report to OCS at Quantico, allowing for a short visit with family and friends. Levi was at submarine school as an Ensign in the Navy, choosing the path of his father. I would joke with both of them, holding one hand high in the air stating, "There are Marines..." then placing the other hand a foot below the other and claim, "...and there are sub-marines."

Leigh was excited to be graduating from high school and moving on to her own college years. Ash, halfway through his high school years, was thrilled to soon become an "only child" and rule the home absent sibling interference. Tommy and I reunited for a few trips to our favorite fishing holes. I shared pints of ale and swapped stories with many other friends during my short break. My abbreviated break was welcomed, but my mind was focused on what I had prepared for all year long – Officer Candidate School. I was ready and eager for my deployment to Quantico.

It was time. I drove to Quantico with my orders reporting to OCS. There was no chaos in the process. Marines, known for their attention to detail, had carefully planned for my and other candidates' arrival. In short order, we were assigned our platoons, issued rifles, and designated our squad bays. If I thought the living conditions were Spartan at The Citadel, I was introduced to a new condition of austerity that made my school's accommodations seem plush. The open squad bay furnishings consisted of cold steel tubular bunk beds or racks, footlockers and standing full presses to hang camouflage utility uniforms. All were aligned even distanced between racks positioned along the long axis bulkhead or wall on each side of the living quarters.

Staff Non-Commissioned Officers barked out commands directing our every move. In some ways, it was a repeat of my first day at The Citadel. The leadership howled orders as we received haircuts, were issued uniforms and equipment, and processed through the hospital for physicals and vaccinations. However, OCS was not a college. It was a training ground to prepare men for battle. The simple mission of the Marine Corps was to seek out and kill bad guys. It was not the purpose of training to make friends with the enemy. Everything we would be taught, every classroom instruction, every physical activity was to prepare us to lead men and destroy any foe.

"What are you smiling at candidate?!" A Gunnery Sergeant, only tall enough to reach my shoulder, planted himself in front of me and screamed in my face.

"Is there something you want to share with me?" My newly appointed Platoon Sergeant, GySgt. Nino formally introduced himself.

"Sir, no sir," I responded.

"Sir! Sir! I am not a sir. I work for a living. When you speak to me you will address me as Platoon Sergeant. Do I make myself clear?!"

"Yes, sir...I mean yes, Platoon Sergeant." I half smiled in response. I thought to myself, *I played this game before in Charleston.* It soon became apparent that I was not in Charleston.

Leaning in, the brim of Nino's drill instructor hat met my nose. "You need to understand something, Candidate. I will fucking kill you. I may get court martialed, but I will kill you. I will choke you until your eyes pop from your head and step on them with my boot. First, you will be blind, and then you will be dead. I will enjoy it, and it will be worth it if you ever smile at me again. I may get court martialed, but you'll be dead!"

"Yes, Platoon Sergeant." I reasoned that he couldn't kill me; however, my mind told me he would.

These were combat tested warriors assigned the task of shaping Marine Officers. Gunnery Sergeant Nino had most certainly witnessed leadership failures on the battlefield, and he recognized the importance of his tutelage. None of what the Candidates were asked to perform was for harassment or fun, and very quickly we all understood our purpose and objective.

Inventory fitness assessments were the first order of business. Rojam had prepared us well. Our Physical Fitness Test (PFT) scores were high. The Citadel had an official USMC obstacle course on campus that we incorporated into our preparation during our morning preparatory PT sessions. All total, the more than two dozen of us that reported to OCS performed in the top tier in our physical readiness. From 0400 until 2100, each day involved excessive exertion, testing our bodily limits by day's end. Sleep fell upon us easily.

Summer in Virginia had not changed since my youth. The air was stifled by dense humidity. Temperatures often spiked to 90 degrees or more on most days. Clouds massed from clear morning skies to billowing thunderclouds by mid-afternoon. There was great danger for anyone who lacked peak fitness. OCS was not only a leadership training camp, but it was also grueling corporal punishment designed to separate the weak from the strong.

The Endurance Course was a beast of a challenge. Dressed in combat gear and carrying a rifle, Candidates were required individually to run through the forested hills of Quantico. Along the trail, obstacles impeded progress requiring that we navigate over, under and through them unassisted. The final challenge was to wade through chest high water and race up hill to butt stoke dummies waiting for our attack.

The "Quigley" was a combination of a forced march with a series of water obstacles. It was the water that everyone remembers. Candidates low crawl through a long series of water filled trenches hiding waterlogged timber, sunken concrete pipes allowing just enough air for one's face to collect breath and proceed under a long, barbed wire covered obstacle hovering above a soup of muddy Virginia clay.

"Holy shit, Finn!" One of my platoon members had addressed me, pointing to an open field. "Check that out."

"Whoa! What the hell. That can't be good," I said.

The staff prepared for casualties and expected them. As we made our way back from field training to the base at Brown Field, I witnessed three Candidates being attended to by frantic Navy Corpsman. They seemed unconscious, naked, and soaking in blue plastic kiddie pools filled with water and ice. Their hearts were racing, and their core temperatures were dangerously high. Obviously, the oppressive climate broke them, and they laid motionless suffering from heat stroke. In a desperate attempt to restore their elevated temperatures to normal, they were stripped and submerged in public view.

"I'm glad that's not me," I said as we approached the scene.

"You got that right, Finn. They'll probably be doing the sea bag drag later today," my buddy offered. The "sea bag drag" was a euphemism for being expelled from OCS.

"If they don't die first."

Heat stroke was a killer. The staff were keenly aware of the danger and made every effort to prevent the condition by encouraging hydration and a buddy system to monitor one another. No matter how vigilant we all were in prevention, sometimes the torch of summer claims its victims. We didn't linger at the triage area instead continuing to our rally point. I learned later that evening that two Candidates succumbed to their condition and expired. They weren't from my OCS Company; however, such news is transmitted quickly throughout the training command. In the squad bay that evening. Gunnery Sergeant Nino held an impromptu class with our platoon imparting additional instruction about heat stroke prevention.

Sadly, heat stroke was not the only casualty causing occurrence I would witness. My company, Golf Company, set up a bivouac for a three-day exercise of small unit tactics. Squads trekked to different stations of combat scenarios to practice frontal attacks and envelopments. At the base camp, the officers monitored the training over the radio. Staff NCO's and tactics instructors observed us and provided critiques at the completion of each attack.

One afternoon, lightning cracked the sky, and the heavens opened upon us with a downpour. Heavy rain soaked our bodies and softened the ground. An alert was passed on the radio network to cease all operations and return to base camp. Training halted while thunder rattled the air, and the command staff evaluated the conditions.

"We're Marines. Ain't no little rain shower gonna stop us." Staff Sergeant Grimes, my Platoon Sergeant Instructor, informed us that we would likely continue our exercise.

MILITARY BRAT — Pete Masalin

SSgt Grimes was a hard charging hillbilly of Oklahoma origin whose chants during close order drill seemed fitting for the day. As we marched, he would shout; "Thunder, thunder. Drive those heels down. I wanna' hear some thunder."

On this day we heard thunder and lots of it. Soon after Grimes proclamation that Marines don't fear the rain, the order came from the command post to resume training. The conditions hadn't changed since we paused, but it was determined that we needed to finish our mission. We exited our tents, reassembled into our squads, and marched out.

In our route from one station to the next, we marched in single file along a narrow path. Candidates were expected to move along the trails on our own without staff directing us. Travelling to our first objective since the break in training, our rifles were slung over our shoulders and our metal helmets, commonly referred to as steel pots, sat atop our heads. Every sound was muted by the torrent of rain crashing to the ground. Visibility was limited by streams of water descending from black clouds.

"Boom!" A loud and bright explosion crashed into the midst of our patrol. I was confused. I thought someone had detonated an artillery simulator as we walked the wooded ridgeline. We were a squad of 13. Everyone in front of me lay sprawled out in mud. Only two people were upright behind me. Quickly, I realized that we had been attacked from above by an errant bolt of lightning. Exposed in the open high ground, wearing steel pots, and carrying rifles, we were an attractive target for electric energy seeking release. Most of those knocked down recovered to their feet except two: my good friend and Citadel classmate, Vick Toller, and a VMI cadet, Bill Simons. Vick and Bill were in bad shape. Their rifles had been ripped from their shoulders and rested several feet away. Both were unresponsive and seemingly dead.

"Bill, Vick!" Immediately, squad members called their names and did their best to attend to their conditions.

"Bill's breathing," someone confirmed.

"So is Vick, but I think he's hurt bad," said another.

Others remained dazed and unclear of the situation, uncertain of where they were, and what had just happened. We were a few miles from the CP, alone in the wilderness without any staff members in sight.

"I'm heading to the CP for help," I informed the squad. I was fortunate to be spared the effects of the blast.

"Hurry, Finn. These guys are in bad shape."

I was off and as I ran, I shouted, "Man hit by lightning!" repeatedly in attempt to alert nearby staff. After about two miles, GySgt Nino saw a crazed candidate rapidly approaching.

"Hey, Makinen! Calm your ass down. Why are you acting all crazy out here?" Nino asked.

Panting heavily, I tried to converse in a full sentence. "Man hit by lighting...up the...trail," I heaved.

The Gunnery Sergeant's eyelids broadened. He asked for confirmation.

"Man hit by lightning?" He doubted me at first.

"Yes! The whole squad," I confirmed.

"Shit! Where?"

By now, I had slightly regained my breath. "Platoon Sergeant, they're about two miles up the trail. Two are down hard."

"Okay, okay, calm down. I need to be sure. You're saying lightning hit your squad," he clarified.

"Yes, Gunny. I'm heading to the basecamp."

"Can you make it? he asked.

"Yes, Gunny."

I heard panic in his voice as he got on the radio. I didn't wait to hear his report as he called for aid. I turned from him, returning to my mission. As I left, the Gunny paused his transmission and offered me some final words of encouragement. "Go! Move your ass!"

As I approached the CP, I could see uneasy activity. Everyone was alert and commands bellowed in the air. I was certain they were on high alert. The Company Commander and Executive Officer were waiting for me, I could see them standing at the CP tent, watching me as I arrived.

"Candidate Makinen! Get over here!" It was a familiar face. Major Williams was assigned as the XO. "How many are down?"

"I think two, sir," I informed.

"Who?"

"Toller and Simons, sir."

"Toller, Citadel Toller?" he asked.

"Yes." I affirmed.

"Shit." He then turned to Major Dunford.

Major Dunford was the MOI at VMI, and like Rojam, he was assigned duty to OCS over the summer. He recognized that Simons was one of his Candidates. Earlier, they conferred and decided that training should continue. If they lost two Candidates to a lightning strike, and it was determined that the decision was material in the accident, their careers could be in jeopardy. It added weight to the matter that these were candidates they knew and knew well.

"Candidate Makinen, Come with us." Major Williams demanded that I join them as they jumped into a white passenger van.

"Down this road?" Major Dunford asked me.

"Yes, sir."

"Just tell us where to stop," the CO instructed.

"It's just up ahead. The trail to the right, around this next corner," I said.

The van stopped and was emptied of passengers. Rain continued to flood the terrain. Small footpaths became impromptu streams as rainwater fell from saturated clouds overladen with moisture.

"Candidate Makinen, can you drive?" Rojam asked.

"Yes, sir."

"Then you drive."

It's a strange thing about commands or orders. The one issuing such directives should be brief but as complete as possible to ensure the success of the mission. "Then you drive" was indeed brief; however, I certainly was left behind the steering wheel without an understanding of Commander's intent. Drive? Where, who, when were important elements absent my instruction. The rescue detachment left the vehicle to save the wounded. As they disappeared into the foliage, I acted upon my command, placed the van in drive and followed their route. What was a slippery route by foot was an impossible journey by vehicle. Deep in the forest, the wheels mired in mud, stopping my advance well short of the objective.

"Makinen! What the hell are you doing here?" Rojam approached with a team of Marines carrying two fallen men on makeshift stretchers.

"You said to drive, sir."

"I didn't mean into the fucking Amazon jungle. Look at this shit." It was obvious that Major Williams appreciated my initiative although he may have slightly questioned my judgement.

"You are relieved as driver. Gunnery Sergeant Nino, take the wheel." Rojam began redirecting the team in order to adjust the mission to include a vehicle recovery.

I rejoined my squad assigned as mules to push the clay sludge engulfed van. Toller and Simons were carefully loaded into their medivac. Both conscious yet obviously unaware of their condition. With relative efficiency, we steered the van to an unencumbered route and were instructed to return to the base camp. With Nino at the wheel, the CO, XO, and the casualties headed directly to the infirmary. Training ceased for the day as we remained in our tents wondering the fate of our fellow Marines.

Mission accomplishment is paramount. The loss of two men would not deter the progress of Office Candidate training. Our syllabus continued without delay. Fortunately, Toller and Simons suffered only minor injury with a period of irregular heartbeats requiring monitoring. Three days later, they returned to our ranks healthy and with appropriate new call signs. For the remainder of OCS and well into their Marine Corps careers Toller became "Flash" and Simons "Sparky."

MILITARY BRAT   Pete Masalin

    The hills of Quantico offered leadership training established by years of preparing men for conflict. It was tested and proven on battlefields around the world to be captured and imparted on new generations of Marines. Our instructors and staff were carefully screened and selected to demonstrate leadership by example more than by command. An important difference between OCS and The Citadel was that my time at OCS served as job training for the career I would enter. The Citadel provided an education within a military environment offering discipline. For me, both were required. Had I not attended a military institution and instead followed my high school friends to fraternity life, it was likely John Belushi's character of John Blutarsky in the movie *Animal House* would have been manifested in me. I could visualize myself, standing in front of Dean Vernon Wormer with pencils dangling from my nostrils as the dean disgustingly declares my mid-term grades, "Finn, zero point zero."

    As we assembled for our OCS graduation, I found myself sitting next to Vick Toller. "Finn, we made it brother," Flash said with a satisfied grin.

    "Yes, we did, Flash," I returned. "That was quite a summer."

    "Hell, a summer? It felt like a year."

    "What are you talking about? You spent half the time in sickbay," I laughed.

    "Shut up, Finn. I nearly died," Flash said wryly. He then paused before adding, "When are you headed back to school?"

    "School? I'm going to eat about three pizzas before I do anything. I'm starving."

    "Me too," he agreed.

    The graduation completed. We each joined our family, friends, and distinguished guests near the bleachers to greet them after the ceremony and thank them for attending. Following our farewells to departing guests, we returned to our barracks, returned our weapons and checked out of OCS. Vick Toller and I linked up with Prescott McDougle to embark on our journey back to The Citadel. The three of us were board selected as Company Commanders requiring our return without delay to Charleston in preparation of the incoming Knobs.

MILITARY BRAT   Pete Masalin

Cadre and their matriculation were now our responsibility.

Chapter 31
Gorilla in the Room

While familiarity was present in my return to Charleston, there was a most noticeable difference, I was in charge. The steamy August air containing wafts of sour papermill steam again polluted my nostrils. Sweat swiftly moistened my uniform during the day. Nights were rarely a relief from the unforgiving climate. Even so, I was excited to start the new and last year of my membership in the Corps. The first day, I gathered my Cadre and welcomed them back. Before discussing our duties, I allowed everyone to greet in comradery and fellowship. This was a team, and it needed to be cohesive to judiciously execute the mission of onboarding new cadets. Upperclassmen would follow, but the Knobs were the most immediate and highest priority.

"Welcome back, gentlemen," I opened. "It's great to see you. I am looking forward to working with you all. Know that you represent the finest of the Corps of Cadets as our new Fourth-Class reports to The Citadel. The first introduction these Knobs receive is from you and an intro for their parents too. I expect that the school will be well-represented."

"It's good to be here, Finn," said Chad Oswald, a Sophomore and Cadre Corporal.

"Yeah, Chad, I know. It's a little different then when you joined us last year isn't it?" I pointed out.

Everyone found amusement in my comment. "Yeah. Just a little," Chad replied.

"Tonight, I want you folks to get situated. Enjoy your time getting reunited. Tomorrow, we start full steam ahead," I said. "I am meeting with the XO and First Sergeant tonight, and we'll all get back at it in the morning."

My Executive Officer Josh Schmidt and First Sergeant David "Ziggy" Siegfried left with me to finalize our plans. In the morning, I held a company meeting to review the plan and give instruction. While we had all participated in matriculation at one time, this was a new year, and we all had new roles.

My instructions were clear: The Knobs would be Knobs, expected to adhere to the plebe system, but there would be no hazing, no malicious or unnecessary harassment, and no fraternization. The Cadre was expected to lead and lead by example.

I sensed some doubt in what I was communicating. "Let me be clear. We are here to lead, train, and foster growth in the Knobs. We will not be "easy" on them. I expect some attrition, but only attrition because a Knob realizes The Citadel is not for him, not because he was hazed or unfairly treated."

"Finn, does that mean they can't be racked?" a Cadre member asked.

"I didn't say that."

"What about Hell Night?" asked another.

"Guys. I didn't say anything about racking or Hell Night, and you know what I am talking about," I clarified.

"What the CO is saying is that you will not abuse your Knobs," Ziggy chimed in.

"Listen. Think about what it was like when you were a Knob. I lost 25 pounds in my first three weeks. I didn't have that weight to lose," I added. "If there was one thing I learned this past summer, is that you never deny food from your men. You don't harass anyone just because."

"Hey y'all, this isn't anything new," the XO stipulated.

"One final comment and I have to leave for a Commander's meeting. I witnessed my freshman year that you often learn more from bad leadership than you do from good leadership. Think about it. Be the good leaders you were chosen to be."

My team didn't disappoint. They managed Cadet Recruit registration with minimal disruption. I spent most of my time introducing myself and speaking with parents. The care of their sons was their principal concern. Some were worried, some were uncertain, and a few reminisced and shared their own stories of reporting as Knobs. Almost without exception, all were proud of the path their son had chosen. So was I.

Cadre complete, the remaining student body returned to campus. For tens of decades, the process repeated itself. The school had survived some of the most trying times by staying true to its purpose, creating disciplined citizens to serve in both the military and private industry. It had survived the most perilous time in our country's history, the Civil War. Certainly, it would survive the command of one Finn Makinen.

It was good to be back in Charleston. Possessing charm unequalled by other destinations, Charleston entraps visitors with magic reminiscent of the gentile allure of one's first love. For many tourists, the romance begins immediately. For Knobs reporting to the institution, the attraction takes patience. The city's charm was mostly disregarded, replaced by the hardship required of a plebe. There was little charming about one's first year at The Citadel, but by my senior year, I fell victim to the siren that is Charleston. While my responsibilities of command required attention beyond my studies, my membership in the First-Class afforded me greater liberty to enjoy time off campus.

"Can I get you another beer, Finn?" The soft, Southern voice of Ashley Long reached me.

"No thanks Ashley," I replied. "I think Jesse and Liz are just about ready to go."

This Wednesday evening, Jesse and I received a Charleston Pass, allowing us three hours out in town. As seniors, we were authorized liberty during the week and our blazers replaced our uniform of the day. Liz Anderson was Jesse's longtime flame residing at the Tri Delta House. He and I met our dates there before escorting our ladies to *Gaulart & Malicet*, known locally as "Fast and French" for dinner.

"Yeah, Liz should be here any moment. I'll take a beer, Ashley," Jesse requested, well aware of his date's usual tardiness.

"Me too," I chimed in.

"Okay. I'll grab a chardonnay and join you then," Ashley said with a smile.

Fifteen minutes later, Liz appeared on the front porch. "I'm ready."

"Just in time, Sweetie." Jesse rolled his eyes. "Let's get going before the restaurant closes."

Liz was not pleased with Jesse's comment and the two quietly conversed as we moved off the portico. Ashley and I quickly vacated in the direction of the café avoiding involvement in their discussion. All was resolved by the time we were seated, and the evening was a favorable recess from the usual fare offered at Coward Hall.

I saw Ashley often, adding another responsibility to my crowded agenda. However, my priorities were clear, and she did not top the list. I had no expectation that she was the future Mrs. Makinen or that the relationship would be long lasting. We appreciated our time together, but my mission was clear, and she sensed the same. My first obligation was my first assignment: graduation and commissioning. Second, there was the requirement to lead a company of cadets. And still ahead of Ashely were my classmates, brothers since day one.

My final Parents Day was the most memorable. With great expectation, Seniors anticipate the day of donning "The Ring." It is an easily recognized ring that alumni display on their fingers with appreciation of achievement and pride. The school hosts a ring hop with an enormous ring replica allowing arriving ring recipients to escort their girlfriends or fiancées in honor through the sculpture.

"Who are you escorting through the ring, Finn?" Pat Stanton wondered.

"I'm not sure," I replied. "What about you?"

"I met this chick from Columbia College," Stanton said.

"A girl from Columbia College? How long have you been seeing her?" I asked.

"I met her a couple of weeks ago. She's hot. I think she may be the one!"

"I hope she has all her teeth."

"Shut up, Finn. You'll see."

Pat was someone who met "The One" at least once a month. Most contemplated those they escorted with serious consideration. I was no different. As expected, Ashley and I ended our romance a month before

MILITARY BRAT Pete Masalin

Parent's Day. I had no date, yet my choice was a woman who, to this point, had most influenced my life and help shaped the man I had become. I extended my right arm and ushered my mother through the ring. I was uncertain who displayed the widest smile as we passed below the golden replica. It was meaningful for us both.

Prior to the pomp and circumstance of the Ring Hop, Summerall Chapel provided the venue for the presentation of rings on Thursday afternoon. The celebration continued at an evening soiree downtown. The Senior Class contracted a large tenth floor room atop the Francis Marion Hotel. Cigars and alcohol abounded in the large hall. As the night progressed, excitement and intemperance paired to create an unruly energy awaiting release. Overlooking the festivities, Vick Toller and I sat smoking cigars upon a large wood sculpted fireplace mantle.

"Flash! Check that out!" I directed his attention to the entrance way.

"Is that a monkey?" Eyes wide, Flash questioned his vision.

If a fuse was needed, it came disguised as a simian. A classmate's girlfriend offered a gift in honor of her cadet's achievement, a gorillagram carrying a bundle of helium filled balloons. As the hairy gift giver proceeded, celebrants extended cigars, bursting the mylar inflatables.

"Finn, this isn't going to end well," Flash said.

"You got that right. Let's get the hell out of here!" I remarked as I jumped from my perch.

By now, the individual inside the gorilla suit had reached his limit. Based upon what I witnessed as I exited, the strength of gorillas was overrated. He released the few remaining balloons, and as they floated to the ceiling, his black paws swung in anger. Immediately, cadets subdued the unfortunate guest to the floor. Ripped from the costume, pieces of hair burst from the melee. One last look back and I observed the beheading of the foe. The ape's head was tossed through the crowd like a beachball among fans in a raucous stadium at a sporting event. Peering down the hallway, a handful of new ring wearers were pulling the firehose from the wall.

"Oh shit! We have got to go, Finn!" Flash warned.

"Hell yeah!" And we quickened our pace.

Safe from the chaos, we landed on the first floor, racing to leave the building. "Evening Colonel." Flash and I addressed Colonel Crane in unison. Without delay we continued as the Commandant was met in the doorway by the Francis Marion Hotel's nighttime manager. Unsure of the damage being done above, Flash and I retreated from a certain confrontation.

We returned to campus and the security of the barracks awaiting the return of our classmates and reports of the battle. The accounts were not good. It was discovered that the assailed delivery ape was an off-duty police officer, and he had called for Tarzan. Tarzan immediately responded in squad cars and men dressed in blue. The makeshift fireman team reached the party goers with an activated firehose dousing all manner of men, furniture, and curtains. It has been rumored that, to this day, the Francis Marion Hotel maintains a long-standing prohibition of hosting Citadel functions.

That we created epic havoc and destruction is an understatement. Police cars and fire trucks with emergency lights illuminated the entire intersection of King and Calhoun Street.

Cadet Colonel Charles Willoughby acted swiftly and interceded on behalf of his classmates. Receiving a call from the Assistant Commandant, Lieutenant Colonel Harvell asked, "Charles, what the hell am I supposed to do about this anarchy caused by your class?"

"Sir, I will take care of it," Willoughby pleaded.

"Take care of it? Son, there's more than $20,000 worth of damage to a fine hotel downtown. You need to tell me how you expect to handle *it* and *the punishment* I should impose upon your class of marauding misfits," Harvell demanded.

"Sir..." Willoughby started.

"I saw more destruction to the Francis Marion Hotel than I did during some battles in Viet Nam," the Assistant Commandant said.

"Sir, I have a plan."

"This I got to hear. Bring it on."

MILITARY BRAT — Pete Masalin

"Colonel, I plan on restricting the entire Senior class to campus until we pay back every penny following Parent's Day Weekend," Charles pleaded.

"After Parent's Day, Charles? You have to be kidding me."

"Colonel, hundreds of parents are here to celebrate their sons' achievement in receiving their rings," Willoughby pressed. "If The Citadel restricts their sons from spending time with them after they have spent hundreds of dollars for travel and hotels, I think you may have another problem on your hands."

"Son, I don't like it, but you may have a point. Charles, I promise you, you and your class will stay on this campus until every last penny is recovered. No Charleston Passes, no Special Leave, no Emergency Leave, no nothing!"

"It will be done, sir," Willoughby said.

"Bunch of Delbert Dumbasses! It better be." Lieutenant Colonel Harvell hung up the phone.

It was a large sum of money; however, Charles had negotiated a deal better than we deserved. Restriction to campus relegated us to the same limitations of our Knobs. If it extended beyond the next weekend, the Knobs actually had more by virtue of regular liberty. It was the right thing to do. We embarrassed the school and ourselves. Miraculously, Charles collected more than the $25,000 needed to reimburse damages. And he did it in three days. Our restriction was lifted, and our class was now legendary in the eyes of some.

My last year was advancing swiftly. Seemingly, the year passed faster than my previous years at The Citadel. Knob year was easily the longest. Corps Day marked the beginning of the final stretch of my tenure as a cadet. In two months' time, those who joined me in this austere military venture four years ago would scatter to new challenges and journeys. We would remain as brothers over the years no matter the distance and time. Few institutions present an environment and rigor that builds such a bond of so many.

After saying goodbye to family and guests at the close of Corps Day festivities, my classmates and I lingered on the quad.

"We are almost done," Pat Stanton declared.

"Are you sure you are going to make it? I heard Freshman English is still giving you trouble," I joked.

"Shut up, Finn!" Pat shouted despite his laughter.

"Yeah, Pat was just smart enough to qualify for Army Infantry," Jesse Baker contributed.

"Actually, I was told he'll be on permanent KP," Art Bibbs said.

"Nah guys, I can't believe we've come this far. Knob year seems so long ago," I said, changing the subject.

Jesse Baker quickly jumped back in. "Do you remember when Gray reported in? I thought he was a girl with his hair below his shoulders."

"You were just jealous," Tim Gray said. "Your only 22, but your hairline is receding so far back you don't have a forehead. It's now a "five head!"

"I was sitting across from Gray freshman year when they shaved his head. He almost cried," Art Bibbs claimed. "It's a good thing he saved what they cut off. Maybe he can make a toupee for Baker."

The back and forth between friends continued for some time and more classmates joined in when returning to the barracks. I remember observing the same scenario when I was a Knob. I had anticipated one day being able to participate in such open camaraderie. Now, my day had come.

With only a few weeks before graduation, preparations for final exams were not the only items requiring attention of the soon-to-be diploma recipients. New car purchases were looming for our soon-awarded liberation into adulthood. As I was once fitted for the uniform of a cadet, new measurements were needed to ensure delivery of a Marine Officer uniform, *Dress Whites* in time for my commissioning. By now, my class load was light, having met most of my academic obligations. So was my grade point average. No matter, my employment was assured by achieving graduation. An investment by way of a USMC scholarship required I return payment in service to our country: four years active service as a minimum.

Rojam scheduled a tailor to arrive at Jenkins Hall to ensure his Candidates were properly fitted. We would be his first commissioned class from the ROTC unit he led, and he was proud of his leadership and our reward to join him in the ranks.

"Men, this is a glorious day!" Rojam professed. "Soon, you will adorn the uniform of steely eyed killers. No more will you wake up saddened having to walk the streets dressed in uniforms resembling that of a mail carrier."

A roar of "OOO-RAHs" filled the hall.

As we did the summer before, our orders would send us to Quantico, Virginia, as newly minted Second Lieutenants attending The Basic School. It would be our first stop in preparing us to lead men of war.

"With those glasses, I'm guessing you're not going to be a pilot, Flash," Major Williams taunted.

"No sir, but I know math, so I am sure I won't be Infantry," Flash tested back.

Rojam was a highly decorated Infantry Officer and Recon Marine. By now our status was elevated just enough that within reason and with respect, we could jest with the major.

"I'm not sure with eyes like yours the Corps can do anything with you," Rojam pointed out. "I'm going to give my highest recommendation that they make you a Hawk Missile pilot." A Hawk Missile has its own guidance system and needs no pilot - a one-way trip for Flash.

Chapter 32
The Stage is Set

The legacy has been long and new members add to it each year. This day was my entrance to its membership. It was the most festive celebration of all my days since entering the Corps of Cadets, and it would be my last. My final parade had been completed; an event when I passed my company command to my replacement and marched across the field to witness the Corps I was leaving pass in review. Those of us that reported together, endured together, and grew together would walk across the stage and receive that which we sought. Before the day was over, I would accomplish two achievements years in the making. I did not know I would attend The Citadel, but from the time I was a five-year old, sitting in a kindergarten class at Maunawili Elementary School in Hawaii, I knew I wanted to be a Military Man.

I thought two achievements were enough; however, my good friend and classmate, Pat Stanton was an overachiever. Not only would he receive his diploma and accept a commission in the Army, but he would marry his true love. To the surprise of many, Pat, a man who suffered infatuation of a new love nearly every weekend spoke the truth when he asserted his spontaneous ring hop date would be his wife just two months after his declaration.

"Pat, I never would have believed it. When you told me that Claire was "The One" just before this year's ring hop, I thought you were crazy," I confided.

"She really is special, Finn," Pat assured.

"I know and you two are great together," I said. "And you're getting married right after graduation. Why so soon?"

"Logistics. Both our families are here for graduation, the chapel was available, and we wanted to get married before I get shipped off to school with the Army."

"Well, you are going to be a logistics officer," I laughed. Pat was assigned the Military Occupational Specialty of Logistics Officer.

"You can't make the wedding?" Pat asked, knowing the answer.

"Man, I wish I could but, as you said, logistics. I am shipping out right away. I'm really sorry." I then smiled at my friend. "Either way, this is a great day for us both, brother."

"Yes, it is, Finn. Yes, it is."

I was lingering on the quadrangle of the barracks awaiting my last muster before graduating. Knobs no more, members of the freshman class approached me to offer congratulations. Just as I had a few years prior, they enjoyed their recognition and reveled in exchanging pleasantries absent the Knob moniker. Their surname was replaced by acknowledgement of their first name, and they addressed me by mine.

"Finn, congratulations! You're going to be a great Marine," Phil Bruce, one of my former Knobs greeted me.

"Start running!" I teased. Bruce delayed his response but joined me in laughter. "Bruce, I hope you have a great summer and good luck in your remaining years here."

Others joined us. "Good luck, Finn." Cam Seagal offered.

"You too, Cam. I think I enjoyed racking you the most. I'm going to miss that."

"Me too, sir...I mean, Finn."

"Wilson, it's Jeff, right?" I asked.

"Yup, Finn. That's the name my momma gave me."

"Finn, we all know your first name, but I'm not sure you can name us all," Scott Michaels challenged.

By now a large group of my former Knobs joined the gaggle. "You might be right, Scott. You men were the best knob class this year, and I really appreciated your efforts. Thanks."

I began to shake the hands of all who stopped by to wish me well. As I extended my hand, I grasped each one and reintroduced myself, "Finn, Finn Makinen." In return, they offered their first names.

"Good luck to you all. When you get where I am today, I can tell you, it will be well worth your decision to challenge yourself at this school. Best to each of you!" I left to join my classmates in preparation for the

MILITARY BRAT　　　　　　　　　　　　　　　　　Pete Masalin

graduation ceremony.

We marched single file, filling the outdoor seating fronting the stage on the steps of Bond Hall. It was a clear day and the sun shone brightly, roasting us in our grey, full-dress uniforms. The torment of the sun was slight when compared to the words of wisdom offered in the commencement speech directed upon uninterested ears. We were done. We wanted our diplomas and the opportunity to rejoin our families in celebration. Mark Mathews, who was hung over and sitting next to me, quickly succumbed to the heat and monotone encouragement of our honored guest. Finally, the order was commanded to award the diplomas. Magna Cum Laude, Summa Cum Laude and other honorees would receive their sheepskins first, followed by low academic achievers such as myself in alphabetic order.

"Distinguished guests, graduates, ladies and gentlemen, please hold your applause until all diplomas have been awarded."

Yeah, that was going to happen. Family members had gathered to witness and cheer the achievement of their cadet. Mothers and fathers, who once said goodbye to their boy on the first day he passed through the sally port, gathered to witness the result of an undisciplined and uncertain child transformed into the opposite – a Citadel Man. As each graduate shook the president's hand and received his award, small groups erupted, clapping, and shouting the name of their grad. Anthony "Tony" Carmen Zamboni held the last tube issued containing his diploma, he turned to the crowd and pumped his arms in the air. The crowd erupted, rejoining the triumph of my entire class while Tony took his seat. A final prayer was offered by the school's Chaplain.

"Ladies and Gentlemen, I present to you the graduating class of..." Before the statement was concluded, in unison we stood in place and launched our military covers into the air never to be retrieved. Children raced to gather the projectiles, and I raced to find my family.

"I am very proud of you, Finn." My father, standing next to my mother, welcomed me. Reaching them both, I embraced them collectively and thanked them.

"I love you, Finn. You did it," Mom gleamed with pride.

MILITARY BRAT — Pete Masalin

"I love you too, Mom."

Having graduated, I was filled with great satisfaction and personal reward. However, even when surrounded by joyous festivity and celebration, my graduation was not the highlight of my passage. The previous day, prior to the commencement ceremony I was privileged to participate in a private ceremony holding great honor in the award and how it was delivered. My family joined me at Jenkins Hall to swear an oath to country, and receive my commission into the Marine Corps. We met at the office of Colonel Pellingham, Professor of Naval Science and the head of the NROTC unit. He was to swear in his new lieutenants. The Colonel would not issue the oath to me.

Just before reporting to The Citadel, I attended my father's retirement ceremony from the Navy. On the day of my commissioning, I asked my father to don his dress white uniform and perform the task. It had been four years since he pulled from his wardrobe the uniform that he wore proudly for nearly three decades. He ensured he had a proper navy haircut and his uniform still fit him well. I stood before the Navy Captain in my Marine Corps dress whites, my mother on my right and her mother, Thyra Ofstad on my left.

"Attention to orders." On my father's command, I popped to attention. "Raise your right hand and repeat after me. I, Finn Charles Makinen, having been appointed a rank of Second Lieutenant in the United State Marine Corps..."

"So help me God." I finished my acceptance of oath and remained at attention as my mother and grandmother pinned gold bars to my shoulders completing the rite.

No words were offered as my father and I grabbed each other, I proud of him and he of me. It was a transformative moment.

I was no longer a Military Brat.

Acknowledgements

Lawrence Thackston and Rivers Turn Press: Thanks for your confidence in me and the opportunity to share this story: "The names have been changed to protect the guilty."

Mom and Dad: you were the captains on the voyage of misfits and chaos. Well done! "Here's to us. We can take it!"

My siblings: Steve, Kari, and Jeff, notable passengers on this journey. Thank you for the adventure.